There are so many to whom I would like to dedicate this book. Firstly, to all those who have supported me through the recent unusual, and difficult, days of lockdown and other restrictions. So, to family, friends and neighbours, for your many kindnesses, my appreciation and thanks.

To my readers. Many of you have followed the books over the thirty-plus years of their creation. I feel I have so many well-wishers and friends out there, watching on and encouraging me. Now, to join all the various characters who have tumbled out of my brain on to the page, here come another set. They have emerged from the keyboard on to the computer screen, and picked themselves up to ask, 'Well, what are you going to make all of us do?' So, here we go . . .

Deadly Company was written during the height of the pandemic in 2020–21. COVID restrictions on travel and contact with other people made it too difficult to set the story during a period of lockdown. So I have taken a step back in time, and the action takes place in February 2005.

Several years ago, I wrote a series of fifteen crime novels featuring Alan Markby and Meredith Mitchell. They appeared also in cameo roles in a couple of my later books featuring Campbell and Carter.

I have often been asked for another 'Mitchell and Markby' story. This book is the result and it narrates what is effectively Markby's last case before retirement. He and Meredith are married, settling into a new house together, and what on earth can go wrong? Well, the house they've chosen to make their first home together is the town's former vicarage. Some of the town's older residents are not aware of the vicarage's change of use. The property is surrounded by the Victorian churchyard; but not every visitor to that has come to place flowers . . .

I hope readers who remember and enjoyed the original stories are pleased to see Alan and Meredith again.

I would also like to take this opportunity of thanking Radmila May for her generosity in giving her time looking up points of law for me. My thanks, too, to my editor Clare Foss and my agent Isobel Dixon. And also thank you to my son, Chris, who patiently sorts out my computer glitches, time and time again.

Ann Granger has lived in cities all over the world, since for many years she worked for the Foreign Office and received postings to British embassies as far apart as Munich and Lusaka. She is now permanently based in Oxfordshire.

As well as writing the hugely popular Mitchell and Markby crime novels, Ann Granger is also the author of the Fran Varady mysteries, the Campbell and Carter crime series, and the Victorian mysteries featuring Scotland Yard's Inspector Ben Ross and his wife Lizzie. During her career as a novelist, Ann has penned many short mystery stories which are now available in a collection, *Mystery in the Making*.

Praise for Ann Granger's previous mysteries:

'Characterisation, as ever with Granger, is sharp and astringent' *The Times*

'Her usual impeccable plotting is fully in place' *Good Book Guide*

'There is nothing old-fashioned about the characters, who are drawn with a telling eye for their human foibles and frailties. Granger is bang up to date' *Oxford Times*

'Entertaining and lifelike characters . . . a satisfying and un-expected twist' *Mystery People*

'The book's main strength is the characterisation and the realistic portrayal of London in the mid-19th century' *Tangled Web*

For more information visit www.anngranger.net

DEADLY COMPANY

ANN GRANGER

HEADLINE

First published in 2022 by
HEADLINE PUBLISHING GROUP

First published in paperback in 2022 by
HEADLINE PUBLISHING GROUP

1

Cataloguing in Publication Data is available from the British Library

ISBN 978 1 4722 9011 3

Typeset in Plantin by Avon DataSet Ltd, Alcester, Warwickshire

Printed and bound in Great Britain by Clays Ltd, Elcograf S.p.A.

HEADLINE PUBLISHING GROUP
An Hachette UK Company
Carmelite House
50 Victoria Embankment
London EC4Y 0DZ

www.headline.co.uk
www.hachette.co.uk

Chapter One

February 2005

Alan Markby had long realised that strangers, even the most honest of citizens, seemed to sense he was a police officer of some sort. It usually took them about five minutes of innocuous chat; and then their demeanour changed, very slightly. Crooks of any sort twigged it from afar and kept away from him. You'd expect that. But the strange thing was that even the most innocent started to look a bit shifty after a while. It put a real damper on cheery chats at drinks parties. Perhaps people thought he was mentally reckoning up how much wine they'd knocked back. All the same, it was a bit of a shock to be taken for a clergyman.

It was late on a Saturday evening; the front doorbell jangled and he'd opened it to see a slightly built woman in a quilted showerproof coat and crocheted beanie hat. She was peering anxiously at him out of the early gloom of a February evening.

'Are you the vicar?' she asked hopefully.

'No,' said Markby. 'Sorry, but the vicar doesn't live here any longer.'

Her features crumpled in dismay. 'But I need to talk to him. Where's he gone? If Father Holland has left, then you must be his replacement.'

'No, as far as I know, the Reverend Holland is still the priest of this parish. But the church authorities have moved him out to a new house. I can give you a phone number, if it's urgent.'

She took a moment or two to process this information before rejecting it. 'But this is the vicarage.' Her tone was a mix of obstinacy and bewilderment.

'Well, it *was* the vicarage. The church decided to sell it. They thought the vicar would be better off in a newer area of the town, more residents. It's mostly commercial premises around here now and people don't live over the shop, as they used to.'

Why on earth was he explaining all this? A chill breeze was sweeping into the house displacing warmer air at an alarming rate. Behind his visitor, in the gloom of a winter evening, the trees rustled their branches in the old church-yard. It was no longer used for modern burials. Those took place in the so-called new cemetery. The creak and rustle of the trees seemed to Markby to be voices of those long departed, calling out plaintively to know why they were ignored by the modern world. But for some people the world did not move on, or moved at a slower rate. The visitor's attitude suggested she clung to a cherished belief;

and wouldn't move from his doorstep until he produced a clergyman. Her next words bore this out.

'You must be something to do with the church.' She was showing signs of distress now. 'Or you wouldn't be living in a vicarage, even if the parish priest has moved out.'

'Sorry, no. I'm not even a lay preacher. I'm a police officer.'

She clearly didn't believe that. 'I don't want a policeman. Anyway, you don't look like a policeman. You're too old,' she finished unkindly.

'It's the stress of the job,' said Markby. 'It's put years on me. But I am Superintendent Markby in charge of the local CID. I am due for retirement in a year's time but, in the meantime, here I stand. Like Martin Luther.'

'Martin Luther!' she exclaimed. 'What's he got to do with it?'

'Nothing, really,' he confessed.

'Then why—?'

Fortunately, at that moment, his wife Meredith arrived to see what was taking him so long; and to ask him if he was aware the cold air was filling the house to displace the cherished heat.

'This lady wants the vicar,' said Markby.

'Have you given her one of James's cards?'

'Not yet,' he confessed sheepishly.

'Why ever not? Here!' Meredith fished a small white card from a bowl on the hall table. She handed it to Alan who handed it to the caller. The woman peered at it suspiciously before taking it and squinting at it in the poor light.

'I haven't got my glasses,' she muttered resentfully. 'It's no good giving me anything to read. Not in this light, anyway.'

'It's the new address and phone number of the vicar. He left us a supply of cards when he moved out, in case anyone came asking for him.'

The caller used the card to point at the wooden plate fixed to the wall beside the front door. 'It still says there it's the vicarage.'

'No,' said Meredith. 'That's a new plate. It reads "The Old Vicarage". The new vicarage is where it says, on that card I've just given you.'

Their visitor was not placated. 'It shouldn't say it's the vicarage at all, if it's not.' For a moment, she appeared about to burst into tears. Then she turned and, without further ado, scurried away into the night.

'Don't call again!' muttered Markby as he closed the front door.

'Perhaps we shouldn't have bought a former vicarage.' Meredith was standing in the hall gazing at the door. 'At least, not one that's only just been decommissioned; and sold off. A lot of people probably still think it's the vicarage.'

'That's why James left those cards.'

Meredith still looked worried. 'Perhaps we should take down that nameplate if it's going to confuse people. Call the house something else. I hope she's all right,' she added.

'That woman? Why shouldn't she be? We don't have to rename the house because someone doesn't bother to read the plate properly.'

'Oh, come on! She was clearly upset about something. She's a respectable sort, and it's got to be nearly bedtime in her world.'

'Whatever it is,' said her husband, 'she's seeking spiritual advice. I am not equipped to give it. It's not police business.' He drew a deep breath and finished with, 'Nor is it ours.'

But in that he was wrong, and on both counts.

Callum Henderson would not have thought of himself as a superstitious man. He didn't worry about black cats in his path or crossed table knives or any such nonsense. His old granny had done, mind you. Full of such things, she'd been. For example, as a child he'd several times seen her toss a pinch of salt over her shoulder, after she'd spilled a tiny amount of the stuff.

He had questioned that, because it didn't fit in at all with her repeated instruction to avoid waste. So, just to get it right, he'd asked, 'Why'd you do that?'

Back came the reply: 'To blind the devil. He's standing behind me.'

'Why is he standing behind *you*?' had been his next question. Logical enough, but small children are generally pretty direct. So was Grandma, who'd never lost the ability to cut to the quick. Her thinking followed a straight line and never wavered.

'He stands behind every one of us. He's at my shoulder, your shoulder, everyone's shoulder.'

Callum already realised that adults liked to lay down

the law and didn't want any opposition, but this seemed to him so impossible that he had to argue it out. 'There's only *one* of him, so he can't be behind everybody. He'd have to keeping running from one person to the next.'

'Everybody!' said his grandmother firmly. 'The devil is everywhere!' In a hushed voice, she added, 'And he's able to appear in any form.'

His mother had entered the kitchen at that point and become indignant. 'For goodness' sake, Mum! You'll frighten the child out of his wits. He won't want to go to bed tonight.'

His mother and grandmother argued a lot and young Callum hadn't wanted another row to begin. So he piped up with, 'I'll be all right. There's a picture of Mary and Baby Jesus over *my* bed, so the devil will stay away!'

It was at that point his grandmother hugged him, burst into tears, and declared the child destined for the priesthood.

'Rubbish!' said his mother robustly. Guiltily, she'd added to her son, 'That's right, Callum. You won't come to any harm in your bed. Quite safe, there!'

'Callum not in trouble for once?' asked his father, who had arrived in time to catch her words. He ruffled his son's hair.

'Your mother says Callum will be a priest one day!' declared his wife.

Callum's father had thought this very funny and burst into laughter; at which his grandmother hit his father with the soup ladle she had in her hand at the moment. Callum had enjoyed that part of the exchange the most.

He still thought it unlikely the devil was hanging around in the kitchen in the hope of leading Grandma astray. She'd have chased him out brandishing the same ladle, as she had his father.

He had not, as it had turned out, ever considered the priesthood as a career. He'd become a landscape gardener. He wasn't even religious in any way his grandmother would have recognised. As an adult, he'd come to believe, if in anything, in Nature. 'Nearer God's heart in a garden . . .' That sort of thing. He found any kind of gardening a calming business. It put things in perspective. Therefore, on his way home from the pub that night, he didn't give it a second thought before deciding to make a short cut through the churchyard.

The pub was called the Black Dog and stood on the very edge of the town on a narrow road still called Black Dog Lane; and Black Dog Lane ran along the back of the old churchyard. Although no one wondered about the name now, Callum, thanks to his grandmother, knew about black dogs. Like black cats, they'd once had supernatural links. But that was nonsense, in Callum's view, on a par with the salt and the devil at your shoulder.

The churchyard gates were locked at night, so Callum scrambled over the wall, and dropped down into the frozen grass on the other side. It was a moonlit night and visibility uncannily good. The surrounding walls protected the area from the worst of the wind. Last week had seen several hard frosts, and traces remained in sheltered spots, such as against the drystone wall or under the churchyard yews.

In some places the frost lingered as small clumps of ice, like the coconut pyramids his grandmother used to bake. But if the temperature rose a degree or so, dispelling the frosts, they might see a little snow. Other parts of the country, further north, had seen some heavy snowfalls. Callum doubted they'd see snow tonight but before the winter months were out, some snow was certainly on the cards.

The moon's silver light threw a pale blanket across the ground, against which tombs and gravestones stood in sharp relief. Their black shadows patterned the ground like a spilled box of dominoes. There were trees, too, dotted around among the graves, singly and in clumps. Many were of venerable age and had seen several generations come and go. The wind did no more than cause a faint rustle in their branches. Beneath them, the shadows trembled and shifted when the breeze blew, but the gravestones stood as unmoving as the sentries outside Buckingham Palace.

Callum trod his way carefully between them, his footsteps crunching on the icy ground. It was disrespectful to walk on graves (thank you, Grandma!). Besides, as he'd had a few pints, he wasn't as steady on his feet as he would normally be, so was wary of hummocks and unexpected dips in the ground. Some of the very old graves had sunk. Callum was familiar with the varying odours of composting vegetation; but what was composting down there wasn't vegetable. Several plots had stone edging to trip you up. What a lot of money people used to spend on burials, thought Callum. Urns, carved angels and, dotted about the place, some proper tombs constructed as stone boxes.

Must've cost a fortune. But those who'd footed the bill at the time had taken pride in such things. They'd been important people in life, local gentry, and their heirs had thought it natural that their departed relatives, or their remains, should dwell in death as grandly as they had in life.

Those were the days, Callum had occasionally thought wistfully, when a landscape gardener could really let his imagination rip.

'*I could create a magnificent vista for you, m'lord, were that village not in the way.*'

'*No trouble at all, Henderson. I'll order it moved to another location. Change the course of the river? Yes, yes, we can do that, too.*'

It beat modern clients' requests for play or barbecue areas, hot tubs and low-maintenance borders.

Grandma was buried further away in the adjacent new cemetery, land purchased by the council a few years earlier to accommodate modern burials. Around where Callum stood in the lee of the rear wall lay mostly Victorian dead. But there were living things here, too, other than Callum, and he was aware of those. Mice, for example, rats, and a piebald cat that had been hunting them; it fled as Callum approached. He watched it leap across the graves and scurry up the nearest tree.

'Whoo!' called the ever-so-slightly tipsy Callum in its direction. He raised his arms and flapped them up and down. 'Watch out for foxes, Puss!' He was still chuckling when he saw the man.

There he sat, actually on a grave, with his back propped

against the upright stone behind it. Cheeky blighter. Grandma would have been over there in a second to tell him off about that. He wasn't a young man but neither was he old. He seemed, in the silvery sheen that coated his face, to be ageless, like the carved stone cherub that peered over his shoulder, looking down on him and enjoying his predicament. Like the cherub, he had a round face and snub nose, but lacked the curly hair. His eyes were open, so he hadn't collapsed there, drunk, to sleep it off.

'You can't stay there all night, mate,' advised Callum, stopping in front of him. 'Cold and damp, see? It'll get even colder before dawn. Your joints will set solid and you won't be able to get up!'

The other didn't reply, and showed no sign of being aware of Callum's presence. He just sat there, staring. Callum bent down and tapped the seated figure on the shoulder. At Callum's touch, the man moved, sideways, all of a piece, and collapsed in a huddle beside the grave. He wouldn't get up, nor would his joints ever bother him.

'You're dead!' Callum told him. 'Oh, hell . . .' he added.

Markby and his wife had retired to bed. He had put the woman caller out of his mind, more or less. A slight niggling memory had remained for the rest of the evening. Meredith, he knew, was still worrying about her. But that was because she had formerly been a consular officer, attached to various British embassies, and any Brit in distress kick-started her instinct to rush in there and sort things out. He had managed to go to sleep, but it wasn't for long. Distantly, somewhere at the far ends of some jumbled dreamscape, there was a thudding noise, and he was under attack. He was about to fight off his assailant when he realised his wife was shaking his shoulder.

'Wazzamatter?' he demanded, sitting up.

'There's someone at the front door!'

'No, she's gone . . .' he mumbled.

'Alan! Wake up, properly! Listen!'

Yes, someone was hammering at the front door and, in addition, whoever it was now rang the doorbell, three times.

'Oh, merry hell!' he muttered. 'She's not come back, has she? She must be barmy.' He flung back the duvet and started to get out of bed.

'Don't open the door without finding out who it is!' ordered Meredith. 'Look out of the landing window.'

Markby tramped resentfully out of the room, down the hall to the window in question, which overlooked the front of the house, with Meredith at his heels. She wasn't one to be left out.

Below, in the gloom, a shape moved. 'Oy!' yelled a voice.

'I'll "oy!" you!' Markby promised the visitor. He opened the window and leaned out. 'Do you know what time it is?' A blast of icy wind struck him. He should have taken a moment to pull on his dressing gown before investigating this new caller.

'Is that you, Vicar?' yelled the visitor.

Oh, no, not another one . . .

'No! This isn't the vicarage any longer—' He didn't get time to finish.

'There's a dead guy in the churchyard!'

Oh, wonderful! A witty drunk.

'Go home and sleep it off,' advised Markby. 'Don't wake me up and talk rubbish. You're too old for practical jokes.'

It was a burly chap down there, not a teenager.

'It's not a joke. I tell you, there's a fresh body in the churchyard, not a buried one. This one is sitting on a grave and he hasn't been dead very long, I'd guess.'

Meredith whispered, 'I think he's serious, Alan.'

'He might be serious. But he's still drunk. His imagination has been working overtime.'

'What if it isn't and he has found a body? You can't just dismiss it, Alan.'

Meredith, he realised, had sensibly pulled on a dressing gown. Bully for her! She might want to linger here but he just wanted to get back to his warm bed.

His wife poked him the ribs with a very sharp finger.

'Oy!' he protested.

'Go on, find out who it is!'

'Who are you?' Markby shouted down. 'And what were you doing in the churchyard? It's locked at night.'

Yes, it was, so why and how had this idiot been wandering about in there? Trespass, thought Markby, is a civil offence. He couldn't go down and arrest this midnight visitor, much as he'd like to. On the other hand, if the fellow really had found a body . . .

'My name is Callum Henderson,' yelled the caller.

Markby's brain had cleared. 'You're the landscape gardener!'

The visitor paused. His occupation being identified had given him a surprise. But he soon rallied and replied in kind. 'That's right – and you're the CID bloke, Markby. What are you doing in the vicarage?'

'I live here, dammit! But I remember you. We met at last year's Open Gardens event in the town.'

'That's right. Well, I climbed over the wall to take a short cut through the churchyard. I'm on my way – *was* on my way home from the pub, the Black Dog.'

'Stay there!' interrupted Markby. 'I'll come down and let you in.'

Minutes later, Callum sat in the kitchen with Meredith, drinking hot sweet tea. 'For shock,' she'd explained to him. Markby had gone to get dressed and could now be heard clumping rapidly down the staircase.

'It *was* a bloody shock,' said Callum gloomily. 'Oh, sorry, Mrs Markby, for the language.'

'Don't worry. Quite mild, in the circumstances.'

Markby appeared in a well-worn Barbour and wearing gumboots. 'Right, Callum, show me this body.'

'You'll have to climb over the wall, like I did,' Callum warned him.

'No, we won't. There's a gate in the back wall of my garden, leading straight into the churchyard. This way!'

Markby had brought a powerful torch and played its

beam along the path as they walked to the rear of the garden.

Callum's professional instincts distracted him from the fact that they were on their way to view a corpse, and he turned his attention to his immediate surroundings. 'Big old piece of ground you've got here,' he said, peering into the darkness. 'What are you planning to do with it?'

'I haven't got round to actually planning anything. I've got a few ideas. It was the garden that attracted me to the property. As soon as we heard it was on the market, I moved to buy it. We know the vicar personally, so we had advance warning that the Church Commissioners were about to sell the place off; and we got in ahead of anyone else.' After a moment, he added, 'This isn't the time to discuss it, but I might need some help. Would you be free?'

'Sure! I'd love to take it in hand,' said Callum cheerfully. 'Oh, we'd discuss any particular ideas you might have, of course.'

'Then we'll talk business at some other time. Here's the door.'

Markby produced a key and opened a wooden door in the wall. Victorian, thought Callum, running a hand down the sturdy wood panels as they walked through.

'Which way?' asked Markby.

Callum dragged his attention back to the present. 'Oh, over there, it's right by the back wall, well, nearly . . .'

The body was where Callum had left it. He was relieved to see it, huddled on the grass beside the gravestone. Crossing the churchyard, he'd been worried that the dead man might have disappeared somehow, and Markby would never believe his story. Markby crouched beside the body feeling for a pulse. Guiltily, Callum realised he hadn't bothered to do that. He'd assumed the chap was a stiff. Serve him right if the fellow had come to while Callum was hammering on the vicarage door. He imagined the man getting to his feet, and shambling off into the shadows before Callum got back with a senior police officer, whom he'd roused from blameless sleep to come out here at dead of night. He glanced across. That senior bloke now seemed to be looking closely at the dead man's hands.

'And this was how you found him?'

'Not exactly. He was seated on that grave propped up, his back against the gravestone. I spoke to him, he didn't answer, I shook, well only touched really, his shoulder – and he toppled over. I didn't touch him again. I panicked; I suppose. I ran away. I didn't go far. I knew I had to let someone in authority know. And I thought of the vicarage – I'd forgotten it had been sold off and it wasn't the vicarage any longer.'

'You've got a business; travel round from place to place. I suppose, like everyone now, you've got a mobile phone?'

Guiltily Callum confessed, 'Yes, but I leave it in the van. It's a bit bulky stuck in my pocket. Anyway, I don't suppose I'd have used it, if I'd had it on me. I wanted to see another human being, a live one.' He pulled himself together. 'What do you think? Perhaps he had a heart attack, sat down there and, well, kicked the bucket.'

Markby was listening, but had still been running the

torch beam over the body and their surroundings. He stood up.

'Listen, Callum, I'm going to call in the discovery of a body. There will be a team of officers coming out here, including a doctor.'

'I don't think a doc is going to be much use to him,' muttered Callum.

'A doctor is required to certify death. Not to resurrect this poor fellow. I can see he's dead. So can you. But investigations rest on a foundation of paperwork, like so much else.'

Callum mumbled, 'Oh, right.' It was dawning on him that he was going to be stuck here in the cold and dark for some time. He should have just left the corpse where it was and made his way home at top speed. That's what happens when you try and do the right thing. You get dragged in.

'We mustn't disturb the area any more than we have and we must stay here until they arrive. We have to make sure no one else climbs over that wall as you did, and blunders through, confusing the evidence. You must prepare yourself to make a statement. This has all the hallmarks of a murder scene.'

'What?' gasped Callum in dismay. 'It can't be.'

'Well, I might be wrong. Torchlight isn't the best way to view the area, and proper examination of the body is called for.'

The information had crystallised in Callum's brain together with the growing awareness of the implications of what had happened to him. If he'd been a little befuddled from drink before, his thinking was now as clear as a bell. He stared wildly into the darkness. 'The killer . . .' he gasped.

'He's unlikely still to be hanging about out there,' soothed Markby.

'Not now!' snapped Callum. 'But he might still have been out there watching when I was here earlier.'

'Oh, yes,' Markby agreed, 'quite possibly. You're sure you didn't see any movement out there in the gloom?'

Callum felt physically sick. There he'd stood, like a drunken idiot, attempting to make conversation with the victim. All the while, perhaps only a few metres away, the killer had been watching and listening.

'I only saw a cat,' he mumbled.

As he spoke, he supposed it was the realisation that he'd nearly tangled with a murderer which had made him say something that sounded so daft.

But Markby took his feeble observation seriously. 'What was it doing?'

'The cat? Hunting mice, I suppose. I disturbed it and it ran off and up that tree over there.'

'If you disturbed the cat mid-hunt, then the killer probably left the scene, at least some ten to fifteen minutes earlier. If he'd still been nearby, the cat wouldn't have been hunting here when you arrived.'

'Oh, I see. Even a cat can be a witness, then.'

But Markby had taken a mobile phone from his Barbour pocket and was busy setting the wheels of investigation into action.

'You don't recognise him, I suppose?' he asked, putting away the phone.

'No!'

'Mind taking another look?' Markby shone the beam of light down on the dead face again.

Yes, I do mind! thought Callum. He peered reluctantly at the pallid features. 'He looks deader.'

'Rigor setting in,' said Markby. 'Well? Recognise him?'

'What? Oh, no, never seen him before.'

'He wasn't perhaps in the pub earlier, the Black Dog?'

'If he was, I didn't notice him.'

'Busy night in there?'

'Fairly busy. But you don't study all the faces, do you?'

'Saw no one you recognised to speak to?'

'A couple of people, the girl behind the bar, the land-lord.' With a return of horror, Callum gasped, 'You're asking me for an alibi!'

'Any investigation involves asking everyone a lot of questions,' Markby assured him. 'Don't feel singled out.'

Yeah, right! thought Callum. He was beginning to feel resentment. It wasn't targeted at Markby, but towards the dead guy who was the cause of all this. Callum peered down at the body again. 'What's wrong with his hands?' he asked suddenly.

Chapter Two

Markby had reached that rank where he was no longer required to attend postmortem examinations of potential murder victims, either during or immediately after the grisly business. But this corpse had turned up very nearly on his doorstep. It gave him a personal interest. He felt quite possessive about it, so he'd decided to come along to this one on a very cold morning. With him were Detective Inspector Steve Kendal, whom he'd assigned to this case, and Detective Sergeant Beth Santos, a younger member of the team. The photographer had arrived before them. They recognised his parked car outside.

'I hate these things,' said Kendal, as they quit the car park and converged on the square, pale-grey building. 'You OK, Beth?' He rubbed his hands together briskly.

'I'll be all right,' said Santos. She'd taken the precaution of bringing along some woollen gloves, and was pulling them on as she spoke.

'I had a bacon butty in the canteen before we set out.

I'm beginning to wish I hadn't.' Kendal was keeping a wary eye on his superior, walking ahead of them at a brisk pace. 'Don't know why he's so keen to get started.'

'Cornflakes,' said Santos.

'What?' asked Kendal, startled.

'I had cornflakes for breakfast.'

'Blimey. You can't do a day's work on cornflakes!'

Her expression clearly said, 'Better cornflakes that stay down than bacon butties you throw up!' But she kept her silence. She thought she knew what worried Kendal. He didn't want to disgrace himself in front of the boss.

'They always make the things so damn greasy,' grumbled Kendal, his mind returning to the shortcomings of the canteen's bill of fare.

'If you keep talking about it,' Santos said as mildly as she could, 'it'll make things worse.'

Markby had clearly overheard this exchange, and spoke over his shoulder. 'It won't be a problem, Steve! Just think of it as work.'

The old man must have the hearing of a bat, thought Kendal crossly.

'Goodness, a deputation!' exclaimed Carla Hutton, the forensic pathologist. 'We aren't usually honoured with a visit from you, Superintendent.'

She was a pale, fair-haired woman with freckles. It was unsettling the way everyone looked so young these days, Markby thought. What is Carla's age? Mid-thirties? Could it be she's forty? Hard to believe. How had it come about that she'd chosen to spend her life among cadavers?

It didn't appear to get her down. She always seemed to him to be unnaturally cheerful, on the rare occasions he met her. She was waiting for him to speak.

'Well, I live in what used to be the vicarage,' he said so briskly that he fancied Santos gave him a startled look. 'It backs on to the churchyard, where the body was found. I was the first police officer to see it, admittedly in very poor light. But I suspected murder, for several reasons that will be clear to you.'

'Oh, yes,' Carla agreed, 'he was murdered all right. Stabbed. The weapon may have been some kind of kitchen knife, or something very similar. You can buy that sort of thing in any hardware shop or department store that sells kitchenware. Whatever it was, it was very sharp and probably pointed. Want to take a look?'

She drew back the sheet over the body in the same no-nonsense way she spoke. She might have been demonstrating anything from a completed piece of artwork to the latest in kitchen gadgetry. But it was a human form that was revealed, pallid and marked with lines of neat stitches where the incisions had been made and tidied up before they came. Carla looked down on him with professional satisfaction.

'It was a neat sort of killing,' she said, with what Markby could only think of as approval. But then, she had dealt with far worse scenes than this: the victims of road accidents, fires, industrial disasters. This stabbing was, as she'd remarked, at least a neat job. 'He was struck from behind. The blade entered between the ribs, and went up,

21

clean as a whistle into the heart,' she added.

There was a soft click as the photographer made another record to add to the many he'd already taken. He was a small, dark man who drifted silently around the area, his location only marked by the sound of the camera. Otherwise, he was like a professional mourner, present for necessity and form, but distant.

'The killer either knew what he was doing, then,' murmured Markby thoughtfully, 'or he got lucky.' He moved to the top of the slab to take a better look at the face.

Click, click from the camera and the shade that was the photographer melted away again. Then they all stood round and studied the dead man's features. It was a coarse face, as if roughly moulded out of some unresponsive clay, and there was a scar running from the left cheekbone to the jaw. The fatal attack had not been the first violent encounter in his life.

'He looks a tough character,' mused Markby.

'He looks a wrong 'un!' muttered Kendal.

'Oh, that too, Steve, certainly.' Markby nodded and glanced at Santos, to see if she had any comment. But she only pursed her mouth disapprovingly.

'Actually, he's very interesting,' said Carla cheerfully. 'Know what happened to the Empress Elizabeth of Austria?'

'Yes!' Santos spoke now unexpectedly. The other three looked at her. Her cheeks flushed. 'Well,' she said, 'I think I do. I mean, when I was about twelve, I was stuck indoors with my ankle in plaster. The old lady next door thought I might like something to read. She passed some old paperback whodunits over the fence for me. One of them was by Georgette Heyer.'

'I thought she wrote about Regency bucks and strong-minded girls, finding true love?' said Markby. 'My mother used to read them.'

Kendall looked bewildered.

'This book was definitely a detective story. There was a reference to the assassination of the Empress in it. She was on holiday in Switzerland and went for a walk along the shore of Lake Geneva, with a lady-in-waiting. A revolutionary fanatic stabbed her; the Empress I mean. No one, not even the victim, realised how badly she'd been injured. She got back to the hotel before she collapsed and died.'

'Well done!' said Markby. He didn't know this officer well. It was another reason he'd accompanied the other two today. He wanted to see how Beth Santos worked as part of a team. She had been with them four months now. She'd previously been with CID elsewhere in the country, but had asked for a transfer following divorce. Her old outfit had been reluctant to let her go. But Markby, whose first marriage had ended in divorce, understood the wish to start afresh in a new place, where no one knew about you. Beth Santos had caused a certain stir when she'd arrived, or so he'd been informed. She was undeniably good looking with thick dark hair and expressive brown eyes. She turned heads. There would be at least a couple of her male colleagues who might fancy their chances. However, perhaps she was now set on making the success of her career she'd failed to make of her marriage. He was pretty sure she could look after herself.

He turned back to Carla Hutton. 'Is that what happened in this case?'

Carla grinned. 'Something like that, perhaps. The victim may not have dropped dead on the spot. He may have staggered off under his own steam a little way, before collapsing.'

'So, the poor blighter didn't at first realise how badly injured he was?' asked Kendal. He had been feeling a bit left out of all this. Markby had been the first officer to see the body. Santos had read some ancient whodunit or other when she was twelve. Steve felt he had to contribute something to the discussion, and quickly. 'Did his killer arrange him in that ghoulish fashion, propped against the gravestone? Or was he just unable to go any further and sank down, propping himself against it for support?' Another thought struck him. 'So when did the murderer attempt to destroy the palms and fingertips?'

'When, indeed?' murmured Markby. 'Let's have another look at the hands.'

'They're in a mess!' warned Carla.

When Markby had noticed that the palms were mutilated, that night in the churchyard and by torchlight, they had been slippery with blood. Now they were dry, the flesh the waxy white of death; and he could see the palms, fingers and both thumbs had been methodically slashed in parallel wounds.

Carla Hutton said, 'Those aren't defensive wounds, in my opinion. If they were, the result would be untidier, slashes and stabs all over the place. I'd say all the cuts were made by the same knife, and inflicted perimortem. That's to say, so near death or the moment of death he couldn't fend off his attacker, or immediately after death occurred. Death may even have occurred during the attack on the hands. For my money, these were made immediately after death. There is no sign that the victim tried to fight off his attacker while the cuts were being made.'

Markby nodded. 'Steve?' he asked. 'Your opinion?'

Luckily, Kendal seemed to have forgotten his unsatisfactory breakfast. He brightened up at being consulted, and spoke up with something near satisfaction. 'Chummy thought he could mutilate the hands sufficiently to prevent us taking any prints. Well, he may find he was wrong!'

'Oh, yes, the pattern of loops and whorls isn't just superficial.' Carla nodded her agreement. 'Despite the damage, your experts may get some kind of prints, enough to identify him if he's on record.'

'Scene of the crime search turn up anything yet, Steve?' Markby asked.

'Nothing significant so far, sir,' Kendal admitted. 'It's a tricky area to search. So far, we've found plenty of bits of rubbish, cigarette packets and stubs, sweet wrappers, and so on. We've collected up all the cigarette stubs in the area of the body and sent them off to forensics. I reckon the victim and his killer might have met up there by arrangement. He wasn't just some guy on his way home after an evening in the pub, like the guy who found him. The nearest one is the Black Dog. It's not a big place. Henderson was in there all evening; but didn't recognise the victim when he stumbled over him after he'd climbed over that wall. I reckon it was a meet between the victim and his killer.'

'Good thinking.' Markby nodded his appreciation and Kendal looked relieved. 'If one of them got there first, he might have smoked while waiting,' the superintendent went on. 'We might get some DNA from the stubs. What about the rubbish bins provided for visitors to discard dead flowers and so on? There are a couple of those in the churchyard, I recall.'

'Sure, we checked those out. They contained lots of paper that'd been wrapped round flowers. Dried-out wreaths. Several foil boxes that smelled strongly of Chinese takeaway food. But there's nothing to indicate any of it is connected with the murder.'

'How long had he been dead before he was found, do you think?' Markby asked Carla Hutton.

'Not less than, say, twenty minutes? Definitely not as long an hour, as far as I can tell. Night-time temperatures are pretty low at this time of year and he was in a damp environment, sitting on cold ground, I believe. That has to be taken into account. As with regard to what the inspector was saying, yes, the deceased had had a few pints but not enough for him to be intoxicated.'

You were lucky, Callum, thought Markby. If you had dropped over that wall even ten minutes earlier, you might easily have come upon the killer about his grisly work.

Aloud, he said to Kendal, 'If the search team think they've nearly finished, tell them they haven't. There appears to have been a brief period of intense activity just before, during and after the murder. We now know our "body" may have walked. There has to be something! Get that team back in there. Widen the search area. Take a look in the new cemetery, if you haven't already done so.'

'Yessir!' Kendal was privately cursing the search team. The old man was right. There ought to be something to indicate the movements of the stricken man. 'We'll interview the witness who raised the alarm again, Henderson. He has made a statement, but he was still pretty shaken up at the time. He might have remembered something since. Sometimes happens when a witness has had time to calm down and stops running about in a blind panic. All sorts of odd scraps of information pop back into his head.'

'He raised the alarm, all right,' said Markby crisply. 'He hammered on my front door after my wife and I had retired for the night. But you concentrate on the new cemetery; and chase up the fingerprint boys. I'll speak to Callum Henderson. Santos, you can come with me. Either of you bring any mugshots of the victim?'

'I've got them, sir,' Kendall said.

'Then let me have one. Let's see if it jogs our landscaper's memory.'

'I should tell you, I'd come across Henderson before Saturday night, albeit briefly,' Markby warned Beth as they set off. 'He lives in one of the small villages, although

27

calling it that is stretching the description. It goes by the name of Abbotsfield.'

Santos was frowning. 'I haven't come across it yet.'

'No reason that you should have. It's the sort of place you drive straight through without realising it is a separate place with a name of its own. That suggests it was always a rural community. Now there's nothing much there at all, apart from some quite nice old cottages, some rundown bungalows, and a couple of large barns converted into desirable residences. If you like a quiet life, it'd be the sort of place for you.'

'One thing struck me as a bit odd, sir,' said Santos, as she followed Markby back to his car. She paused while Kendal drove off ahead of them. She'd come with the inspector in his car; and she was leaving with the senior officer. She already knew Kendal well enough to realise his feathers were ruffled. He was looking like a loser who'd taken a girl to a party, only to have her leave with someone else. If she had a question for the superintendent, now was the moment for her to ask it.

'Go on!' encouraged Markby.

'It's only that Henderson claims he was on his way home from the pub when he decided to cut through the churchyard. He says he always walks to the pub and back to his home, across the fields. Pretty long walk. I just thought it a bit odd.'

'Perhaps not so unreasonable,' said Markby. 'Not if you know all the short cuts across country and ignore the roads. Callum Henderson is an active, outdoor sort of chap.

There are people who run a couple of miles a day and think nothing of it. He walks. I understand, from what he said to me, that one of his short cuts has always been across the churchyard, even though it's locked at night.' He took out his phone. 'I'll have to call him first. He could be working anywhere.'

'Henderson. Landscapes and Gardens!' said a brusque voice in Markby's ear.

'Good morning, Mr Hen—' He was interrupted by the crash of something heavy falling in the background.

Then came Callum's voice again, more distant, as if he'd turned his head aside to address someone else. '*Hang on, Gus! I'll give you a hand. Give me a moment!*' The voice in Markby's ear grew louder again. 'Sorry about that! Yes?'

'This is Superintendent Markby, Callum. We'd like to speak to you again. If you have time, could you call in today? Or I could—'

'I've got a sixty-mile round trip to make today, to view a new site. I have to pick up some paving slabs on the way . . . Listen, can you come to me, straight away? I'm at home. We're just loading— *Gus! Leave room for those pavers!*' Another voice, a sort of growl, sounded in the background. '*Yes, well, just hang on. I'll be there in a sec. It's the cops!*' Back to Markby. 'Sorry, I have to supervise Gus or he gets over-enthusiastic. Can you come now to Abbotsfield? It's only a small place and you'll find me easily. I've a sign outside— *No, Gus!*' He rang off.

It takes time to learn a new area and Beth Santos had tried to familiarise herself with the pattern of minor roads around Bamford and the smaller residential areas. She was not surprised she hadn't yet found Abbotsfield and relieved Markby had elected to drive them. She was lucky to spot the signpost for it now; it was so small it hardly qualified as such and bore only the name of the place, no indication of how far away it lay. They found themselves on a single-track road with hedges to either side and what looked like pretty deep ditches. Ahead on the left, a break in the hedgerows indicated a gate into a field. It seemed to be the only place a car could pull off the road to allow any oncoming traffic to pass. She had just stored its location in her memory when something did come towards them.

A motorcycle rounded the bend ahead and made straight towards them at speed, the rider crouched over his steed. Markby wrenched the wheel and drove the car in the direction of the gate, lurching across the stony entry, clipping the hedge and coming to rest with the car's nose against the gate itself. The motorcyclist roared on regardless.

'Suzuki,' gasped Santos. 'Didn't get any of the number plate, sorry!'

'Young idiot!' growled Markby. 'He probably came from Abbotsfield and assumed he wasn't going to meet other traffic. He'll need to be more careful or he'll end up in the ditch or smeared across the road.'

They jolted back down on to the road and drove on another quarter-mile.

'Here we are,' said Markby.

Santos saw immediately why the place didn't warrant a bigger road sign. To the right straggled a row of modest cottages and a couple of thirties-built bungalows. Why anyone had ever thought of building bungalows out here, she couldn't imagine. Unlike the cottages, they were in a poor state of upkeep but inhabited, as indicated by front gardens filled with junk. This was where Abbotsfield's less well-off lived. The more prosperous residents clearly resided in the pair of converted barn dwellings to the left. Further on was another cottage building with signs of activity around it. When they reached it, Markby pulled up and opened his door.

'Henderson's place of business,' he said.

They both left the car and Santos followed the superintendent through opened wooden gates, tall and solid, leading into a yard. A sign nailed to one of the gates read C. HENDERSON LANDSCAPE GARDENING. Inside the yard two men were working, or had been working, loading a van. They'd apparently finished this task and were drinking from large pottery coffee mugs while waiting for Markby's arrival. On seeing the two officers approach, the younger, more prepossessing, of the two men put down his mug on a nearby birdbath and came towards them. Santos judged him in his mid-thirties with a shock of fair hair and sunburned face. This, she supposed, was C. Henderson, Gardens-as-you-like-'em. He was looking at her in a startled way. Markby he already knew, of course. But even if he'd never seen Santos before, he must have seen any number of women police officers. She stared back at him and won the competition, if competition it had been. He looked away, signalling to the other worker to come forward.

Closer study of the other man was quite a shock. He was a giant of a man with long, muscular arms, shaven head, broken nose and sphinx-like expression. His face might not show any reaction to their arrival, but his body language was wary. He'd recognised the law, even in plain clothes, and she had the sense that officialdom in any form was alien to his lifestyle. Despite Henderson's not-so-subtle beckoning to him, he still hung back.

Markby shook Henderson's hand and introduced his sergeant. 'This is DS Santos, by the way.'

Callum, in return, indicated the giant and said, 'Gus Toomey. He works for me.'

Toomey still came no nearer, but nodded his bullet head in acknowledgement.

'Sorry to hold you up, Callum,' said Markby, 'thanks for waiting for us. By the way, does anyone own a motorbike round here?'

Callum hesitated and his gaze slid sideways towards his workman.

'I do,' Toomey said hoarsely. 'Waddaboutit?'

'One came hurtling towards us five minutes ago. Narrow miss.'

The body builder gestured towards the far side of the van. 'Mine's over there.'

'Anyone else living around here got a bike, a Suzuki?' asked Markby.

Callum had been meeting their eyes frankly but now his gaze slid away into the middle distance. 'Not me. Drivers who know the area sometimes cut across country through here. We get the odd car, bike . . .'

He knows who the motorcyclist is, thought Santos, but he doesn't want to grass in front of the incredible hulk over there. Toomey isn't going to say, either.

'If you should find out,' said Markby calmly, 'tell him to take more care, would you?'

The gardener mumbled something. Then he spoke up more clearly. 'What can I do for you? I made a statement. Do you know yet who he is?'

'Not yet, but we'll find out. He was the victim of a knife attack.'

Toomey was doing an unconvincing impression of a man not listening. Callum glanced across at him. 'Want a cuppa or something?' he asked his visitors. 'Come into the kitchen. I apologise in advance for the mess.'

As well he might! Santos thought wryly, as they followed Henderson into the cottage. The place was an absolute tip. The original cottage had been extended and, in addition, she guessed an internal wall had been knocked down. This resulted in a pretty large area and made it easy for Callum to move around without the trouble of negotiating low doorways; or bothering with doors at all. The kitchen part of the space was over to the left. What remained had been turned by Callum into his office. An old-fashioned square wooden table was covered with catalogues, paperwork and general debris. By the window Callum's computer rested on a homemade desk-cum-table, chiefly remarkable for having odd legs. They were the same length, but varied in style. One was a barley twist leg from a much earlier piece of furniture, one was a length of post and the other two might have originated as supports for a piece of bedroom furniture. I don't know what his gardens are like, thought Santos, but he's no craftsman when it comes to indoor fixtures and fittings.

'I've been busy,' said Henderson suddenly and quite loudly. Even Markby looked startled. 'I haven't had time to tidy up.'

The words were addressed to the superintendent but Santos had the feeling they were directed at her. He must have noted the critical look she'd cast over their surroundings.

Hung on the wall behind the desk was a framed photograph of a, presumably family, wedding. It appeared to have been taken in the 1970s. In a reversal of traditional colours, the bridegroom wore white: a suit with flared trousers. The bride wore a peasant-style dress with balloon sleeves, together with a picture hat. The dominating figure in the group, however, was an older woman of formidable aspect, wearing a sensible two-piece costume, and a felt crash helmet of a hat. She didn't look pleased. Clearly, she was the mother either of the bride or of the groom. The reason for her manifest lack of enthusiasm might be because she thought the marriage or the bridal couple's fashion sense ill advised, or because this was not a church wedding. The building outside which they were all posed was obviously a register office. Also, thought Santos, studying the bride's voluminous dress again, this was a shotgun affair.

'No reason why you should,' said Markby. 'You weren't expecting us.'

If he wasn't, he should have been, thought Santos. Either us or another couple of officers.

'Coffee?' asked Henderson, going over the kitchen area and picking up a kettle.

'Thanks, Callum, but we'll only be here a few minutes, so don't bother,' Markby said to Beth's relief. There were mugs on the draining board of the sink unit, but they looked as though they had been perfunctorily washed up. There were dried coffee stains around the rims.

The landscaper mumbled something. Then he turned and leaned against the sink unit, arms folded, waiting for them to ask their questions.

'The mugshot, Santos!' Markby ordered.

Beth produced the necessary photo. Henderson detached himself from the sink unit and came across to study the print. He didn't walk in a straight line but took an awkward semi-circular route, as if to stay as far away from her as possible.

'Still don't recognise him,' he said when he was near enough to take the photo and peer at it. 'That's what you want to know, I suppose?' He handed the photo back to the superintendent.

'There was always a chance,' said Markby. 'Thanks for taking a look. Thinking it all over, has anything else come

35

to mind? I know when you called me to the churchyard, you were in a bit of a panic.'

'Wouldn't you be?' the landscaper demanded. Then he shook his mop of fair hair. 'I'll be honest. I've been trying not to think about it. But I have, can't get it out of my head.'

'You might have seen him around town, perhaps? In a pub? In a car park? Anywhere people come across others and might remember them?'

'I mostly drink in the Black Dog because it's the first decent pub I get to when I walk across the fields to town, right? I haven't seen him there. Or I haven't noticed him there, even if he was in the place. You could show that to Gus. He drinks in other pubs.'

With just the three of them in the kitchen/office, the room had been fairly full. Once Gus's substantial frame had loomed into view to join them, the room appeared packed, and the light that had fallen through the open doorway was blocked. He was handed the photo.

If asked, neither Markby nor Beth would have put much hope in Gus's cooperation. In his massive hand, the police photographer's print looked like a visiting card. His knuckles bore a cat's-cradle of scars that showed up startlingly white against his tanned skin. Bare-knuckle fighter, decided Markby. Unregulated set-ups, much beloved of the gypsy and traveller communities, but with plenty of supporters elsewhere. Toomey stared at the photo expressionlessly for a good minute in silence.

'Take it across to the window, if you want,' said Markby.

'Can see 'im OK.'

'Do you know him?' Markby prompted.

'Nah,' said Gus. 'Don't know him.'

Markby glanced at Santos. 'Have you perhaps *seen* him in town, Mr Toomey?'

Gus continued to stare at the photo. 'Might've,' he said eventually.

'In one or other of the pubs you drink in?'

Gus considered his answer. 'Never saw him drinking.'

'If you don't remember seeing him in a pub, can you recall where you did see him?'

Gus dragged his gaze from the photo and fixed it on Markby. 'Never said I didn't see him in a pub. I said I never saw him drinking.'

'Ah . . .' said Markby softly. 'What was he doing, Mr Toomey?'

'Just talking to different people or on his phone.' He frowned. 'I didn't take much notice.'

'And this was in more than one pub?'

Gus thought that through. 'Yeah.' He handed back the print.

'Thank you very much, Mr Toomey.'

'All right?' Gus sounded relieved that he wasn't going to be asked anything further.

'Yes, all right. That's all.'

Toomey left the kitchen silently. For such a big man, he had a surprisingly light tread. Markby thought, he'd be quick around the ring and it'd be hard to land a good punch on him. Both Markby and Santos watched him as

Gus withdrew to the far side of the yard, where he sat down, and lit a cigarette.

'Gus is OK!' Callum spoke up firmly. 'I know he looks scary to some people, and he doesn't say much, but he's OK.'

'Have you got an address for him? Should we need to show him any more photographs?'

'He's got a caravan,' said Callum. 'It's in a field, behind the cottages on the other side of the road. He comes from a family of fairground people. Gus travelled with the show until it folded. He still doesn't like the idea of living in a house of any sort.'

'Fair enough,' said Markby aloud, thinking, I doubt Toomey has any kind of permission for a long stay there, but I don't come from the council. 'One more thing. If I could check with you about the churchyard. Is that the way you always get into it at night, over the wall across the road from the pub?'

Callum reddened. 'It's the quickest route. Otherwise, I'd have to walk right down to the main road and enter through the new cemetery, the additional burial space the council added on years ago.'

'The new cemetery, as you call it, isn't locked at night?' Markby asked quickly.

'Well, yes, the gates are locked. But there's a gap in the hedge.'

'Callum,' Markby told him, 'I'm very much obliged to you. We won't keep you any longer for now.'

Henderson looked relieved. 'Then Gus and I can get going!'

Back in his car, Markby glanced across at Beth.

'Think what I'm thinking, Santos? About the activities of our mystery man in the local pubs? Goes in, chats to a number of different people, doesn't drink, moves on . . .'

'Drug dealer,' said Beth decisively. 'Gus probably knows it.'

'Yes, and he doesn't approve. Travelling families, like Gus's fairground people, are very old fashioned about that sort of thing. That's why Gus was prepared to tell us as much as he did.'

'Think he comes from a long line of professional strong men, you know, bending iron bars and that sort of thing?' she asked Markby now.

Startled, he stared at her and then nodded. 'Could well be. Or a roustabout, setting up and dismantling the heavy machinery of the rides. Now then, our dead dealer will have been part of a chain of supply. I doubt he was new to the game or the area. He'd been around long enough for Gus to notice him, so there's a very good chance he has form, and is somewhere in the system. However, we have not so far found any mobile phone belonging to the deceased. Gus saw him a few times in pubs on a phone. So, is it in that churchyard and we just haven't found it? Or did the killer retrieve it from the body and make good his escape with it, moments before Henderson climbed over that wall?'

'It's a very tight schedule,' Santos said thoughtfully. 'Henderson could have missed seeing the killer by less than a minute.'

'He wasn't looking for anyone else,' said Markby simply. 'He'd noticed a man collapsed on a grave, propped up on the headstone, and that was all he was looking at. Right, let's go and find this gap in the hedge into the new cemetery. For my money, that's the way the victim came into the churchyard to meet up with his killer. "The grave's a fine and private place." Do you know that quotation, Santos?'

'Sorry, no, sir.'

'There's me thinking you're of a literary turn of mind!' He smiled at her. 'And not just interested in body builders.'

'I do read books!' she said fiercely. 'But modern paperbacks mostly. I'm not into the classics or poetry. And I'm not interested in body builders, either.' She drew a deep breath and added stiffly, 'Sir!'

'Fair enough, point taken, Sergeant,' said Markby meekly. 'Well, the quotation is from a poem by Andrew Marvell. Let's say you want to discuss business without anyone observing you? Or, perhaps more importantly, the person you are talking to? What more private place than an old churchyard at night?'

'Pretty good choice of meeting place,' agreed Santos. 'If you don't mind it being creepy.'

'So, let's go and see how Steve is getting along.'

They found Kendal in the new cemetery. Coat collar turned up against the stiff chill wind and hands thrust into his coat pockets, he stood atop a mound of frozen mud, surveying the view.

'"Like stout Cortez, silent upon a peak in Darien . . ."'

murmured Markby. This gained him a sharp look from Santos. I've got to stop quoting poetry, he thought.

Compared with the Victorian churchyard, the new cemetery was almost clinical in aspect. There were gravel paths, and grass seemed to have been banned. The graves were in neat rows, the headstones small and functional in design. There were plenty of floral tributes in a variety of vases and pots; but Santos didn't see any hovering stone angels or elaborate carved or moulded edging around the plots. The whole area, old graves and new ones, was cordoned off by fluttering blue-and-white police tape, underlining its considerable size. Notices warned the public to stay away. Quite contradictorily, a board was in the process of being erected, asking the public to get in touch with the police if they had seen anything strange or any unusual activity. She supposed that any activity in a cemetery, other than that surrounding a burial, was unusual. It struck her that Kendal, despite his sombre surroundings, looked quite cheerful, considerably more so than earlier that day at the morgue.

The inspector had belatedly become aware of their arrival. He slithered down the pile of mud to greet them. 'Might be on to something, sir!' He spoke with enthusiasm, and led them to a spot near the boundary.

Here the neat aspect of the area, with its regimented rows of graves, was destroyed by two shattered ceramic pots. Their flower contents spilled across the gravel path. A headstone had been knocked askew; and the gravel of the path was scuffed and kicked into ruts.

'Looks like a struggle took place here, sir. If the victim was involved, he managed to get away and head off towards the old churchyard. Most likely he followed the wall, perhaps put a hand on it to support himself. And over here . . .'

Kendal set off and the other two followed. A few feet further on, they came across another recent floral tribute that had been displaced and lay in the path, crushed. Kendal gestured towards this but didn't slow his pace. They followed him onward until he crossed the boundary into the old churchyard where they all came to a halt, slightly breathless, before the gravestone where Callum had found the dead man.

'I reckon,' said Kendal, 'the victim was attacked, or got into a fight, back there in the new area. He may have received the fatal stab wound there, if the pathologist has got it right. At any rate, the victim got away. He stumbled along here in the dark, trying to reach the old churchyard. Look at it!' Kendal swept a hand across the immediate view. 'It's not like back there, is it?'

'You mean back in the newer area, where the smashed urns are?' Markby asked mildly. 'No, it certainly isn't.'

Kendal continued: 'It's a bit of a jungle here, isn't it?' He waved an arm to indicate the area around them. 'You'd think the church would make more of an effort to keep it tidy. I mean, even if they're not still burying people here, they must still be responsible for it. But if the bloke was trying to find a place to hide, this would look likely.'

Santos stared around her. She wouldn't have called the

old churchyard a jungle, not quite. But it was certainly an untidy sort of place with trees, bushes, headstones at all angles, and the occasional taller monument. Ivy clambered its way unhindered over the older memorials. In its own way, it was picturesque. She thought the new cemetery with its manicured rows of regular headstones more depressing than here. This was a place of sorrow but also one of peace.

Kendal was pursuing his theory with enthusiasm. 'Chummy thought he might be able to hide in here, but he only got as far as where Henderson found him before he sank down, propped against a tombstone, and died. His assailant had followed him; realised he was dead and decided to mutilate the hands to delay identification.'

'Right . . .' said Markby. 'Yes, Steve, probably that's what happened.'

Kendal beamed, happy at last.

Santos had been studying the surrounds and spoke, more to herself than to the others. 'They keep the new area so neat, I'm surprised they've let this one go like they have.'

'Wildlife,' said Markby absently.

Kendal looked startled. He appeared to think the superintendent was making some kind of tasteless joke.

Santos had already realised that Markby was one of those people who don't appear to be listening or making much close observation, but who actually missed very little.

'It's protected, I believe,' the superintendent added. 'It's home to all sorts of creatures and plants.'

'Tell me about it,' growled Kendal. 'There's a bloke called Finch who's already been down here bending my ear about it. He reckons we ought not to disturb anything. "It's a valued natural habitat!" That's what he told me. "It's a crime scene," I told him. "We're going to disturb the lot." So, then he threw a fit. Fortunately he had to leave because he had to get to some school where he teaches. But I'd have known him for a schoolmaster, even if he hadn't told me he was. He went off making all kinds of warnings about informing goodness knows what sort of organisation that worries about these things.'

Kendal paused; and Santos reflected that 'Finch' was a good name for a naturalist.

'Oh, and the vicar came to see what we were doing. He's worried about the bishop. That'll be his boss, I suppose,' concluded Kendal.

Markby said, 'I understand James Holland being upset. But he'll understand we need to be here. As regards the other chap, I want no distracting battles with local enthusiasts. If Finch continues to make a fuss, let me know. I'll handle it, Steve. Got to keep the general public on our side. He'll probably be quite reasonable when it's explained to him.'

Kendal looked as though he didn't agree. But Markby turned to make himself the leader of their little crocodile, and led the other two back to the new cemetery and the smashed pots. Kendal waited for him to speak again but Markby remained silent in thought.

The fact was that just as the fellow, Finch, had felt a

personal interest in the site, so did Markby himself feel possessive about it. From where the seated man had been found, the roof of what was now Markby's home, and the high back wall of his own back garden, were just about visible through the tangle of bushes, statuary and trees. He had felt that as an intrusion, almost as if a challenge had been thrown down on his own turf. But here, in the new area, with its rows of regimented headstones, he had no such sense of trespass on his personal space. He realised that both Kendal and Santos were staring at him, waiting for some comment.

'Yes, Steve,' he repeated. 'It does look as if the attack took place here, and the injured man staggered away, perhaps hoping to hide, as you say. Well done!' he added, to cheer Kendal up.

It is time I retired! he thought suddenly. Why on earth do I have to worry about Kendal's feelings? He's never struck me as a sensitive sort before. But he's been sulking since I took Santos off to Abbotsfield. He looked down at the crushed flowers and broken pots. Why here? Why had victim and killer chosen to meet on this spot? All the main gates, to this new cemetery and to the old churchyard, are locked from early evening until morning. That could be one reason. The fatal meeting would be unlikely to be disturbed by a wandering member of the public. Yet, within a short time, it had been.

Aloud, he said: 'According to Henderson, there's informal access to this new cemetery through a gap in the surrounding hedge.'

'Yes, sir, we've found it already. It's back here.' Kendal set off again. 'If all gates to the area were locked at night, victim and killer could have come through here.'

The gap in the hedge was narrow but clearly visible, and the bare earth between the two walls of trimmed yew was stamped into mud by the regular passage of feet. 'It was like that before we got here,' said Kendal, pointing down at the path. 'It must be in regular use as quick access to the place, if you don't want to walk round to the gates. We can try for some clear impressions of footprints, but it's all of a mess and muddle, as you can see.'

Markby pushed his hand into the hedge to the right and then did the same to the hedge on the left. 'There are a couple of old wooden posts in there,' he said.

Steve Kendal pushed aside the hedging. 'So there are! Must have been a gate here once.' He sounded more cross about the discovery than surprised. That, thought Santos, is because he didn't find the posts himself.

'More likely,' Markby suggested, 'there was a stile. Before the council acquired this land for new burials, it was a field. I remember it. There were sometimes a few sheep in it. There was probably an old right of way across it. The main part of the stile was removed when the cemetery was laid out; but people continued to use the gap to cut across the area. The council didn't block it off, to avoid any legal dispute. They trusted people would forget about the right of way in time. They haven't, not entirely. Old rights of way have many defenders.'

He stepped back and pushed each hand into a coat

pocket. 'The question is, did the killer and the victim meet here in the new cemetery by arrangement, just on this side of the hedge, trusting that their meeting would be undisturbed? Or did the victim intend to cut across the cemetery, and the killer saw and followed him?'

'He couldn't get out on the far side of the old churchyard,' said Kendal, 'unless he climbed over the wall, like our chum Henderson. There's that handy gap on this side where the old stile was, but the main gates giving access to both burial areas are locked at night.'

'Yes, yes,' said Markby absently. He stared down at the shards of broken flower vase. 'Oh, well, there's an answer to that somewhere and we'll find it. But first we need to find the weapon and the victim's phone. He must have been carrying one. He was seen in town using it, according to Toomey.'

'Who is Toomey?' asked Kendal suspiciously.

'Henderson's employee, lives at Abbotsfield. Carry on, Steve.'

Kendal took himself off, frowning, but Beth lingered a few feet away, looking curiously at the superintendent. Though he remained staring down at the broken vase, he did not really seem to be looking at it. She had thought he hadn't realised she was still there; but he did, because he suddenly spoke, addressing her.

'We need to find the murder weapon and the missing mobile phone urgently. Did the murderer take them away to hinder us? Yes, he probably did. Do you know what puzzles me, Santos?'

'No, sir.'

'Those slashed palms of the hands. It was so evenly, neatly done. I wonder if the killer's purpose was something other than delaying identification.'

'Why else would he do it?' she asked.

'I don't know. But it was so precisely done, the wounds parallel, a careful job. It was almost ritualistic in appearance.'

'A message?' Beth asked.

'Possibly. But intended for whom? Were the police meant to read it, or someone else?'

Chapter Three

It was early Monday evening and Meredith was on a train, on her way home. Alan might have spent his day viewing a corpse and trudging round a murder scene. She'd spent hers blamelessly, if less interestingly, at an office desk. These last few years Alan, too, had spent much more time at a desk. She knew he hated it. He wanted to be out there where the action was. She understood and sympathised. But it was the price of promotion. She felt the same way. The train rocked slightly. Nearly half of the men in the crowded compartment had their eyes closed. The women were somehow managing to resist dozing off. The early winter evening had set in and it was already dark outside.

I'm not going to be doing this for much longer, she comforted herself. Alan will be retiring at the end of this year. It could be a good time for me to retire, too. I've already had enough and I've dropped enough hints around the office. Perhaps Alan could retire earlier, and we'll get to spend some quality time together. It will mean a new life for both of us. Alan will devote himself to his garden in retirement and I know exactly what I'm going to do. I'm going to write a whodunit.

'You need to write a series,' a friend to whom she'd confided her ambition told her. 'Readers love a series.'

The longest journey starts with a single step, thought Meredith. Let me write one book first. Of course, planning this new career and actually making a success of it, when the time comes, well, that's the tricky bit.

Yet, ironically, she had no need to imagine murders. One had taken place on Saturday night, and a body found in the churchyard behind her house: a salutary reminder, if any were needed, that in real life murder is unparalleled in its sheer nastiness. But, although shocked, like her husband she also felt angry. How dare someone carry out such a dreadful crime not far from her own back garden? Almost *in* her back garden. Because that was what the churchyard adjoined.

From this to thinking about the woman who'd called demanding to see the vicar seemed a logical enough mental progression. It was a mystery and Meredith wondered what lay behind the curious visit. The woman hadn't just been worried about something. She'd been frightened and had screwed up enough courage to seek advice. Unfortunately, she'd run into a brick wall. I don't mean Alan was unkind to her, thought Meredith, but he did dismiss her pretty briskly. Perhaps I should have asked her in. I wonder if she went to see James Holland at his new address in his smart new-build vicarage in the middle of an estate of new-build houses. The woman in the beanie hat rang the doorbell of what she believed was still the vicarage. She'd done so because the house had been an emblem of stability and principled guidance in the town for nearly two hundred years. That made it considerably younger than the church itself, but church and vicarage together still gave the appearance of authority. It had therefore seemed to their visitor to be the place to take her troubles, to ask what she should do about whatever worried her. Somehow, thought Meredith wryly, I don't see her wandering round a brand-new estate of identical properties, trying to find the vicarage there.

Further back down the carriage, solicitor Jeremy Hawkins was more than alert. He had been travelling up and down this line for nearly twenty years. Yes, the commuting was repetitive and stifling and sapped the soul. But tonight there was no need to fight the urge to doze off. Tonight, his brain was churning.

The seats were arranged in groups of facing double banquettes, either side of a central aisle, so travellers were perforce arranged as cosy foursomes, whether they liked it or not. Jeremy had a window seat. He could at least look out, even if it was already too dark to distinguish much. A string of stationary lights indicated a street; moving lights a roadway. That would be filled with cars now, driven by people making their way home after a day that had been either boring, or interesting, or a bit of both. Whichever it had been, the chances were strong that it had been exactly like the week before. Tomorrow, they'd do it all again. Only for Jeremy, probably, was this evening's homeward trek different.

He shifted in his seat, as much as he could, and sighed. It helped to pretend his travelling companions weren't there. He was all too aware of them, of course. He could smell the stout, sweaty chap beside him, in the aisle seat, who had nodded off. The passenger in the window seat opposite was working on his laptop. The aisle-seat occupier by him was also a busy bee. He was doing the crossword. Jeremy wanted to tell them that they needed to relax; disengage from a long day tackling problems. But they couldn't and he couldn't. Even those who were staring fixedly at their mobile phones had a dreadful intensity in their body language as their thumbs tapped out text messages.

Jeremy wasn't thinking about problems at work. His mind was dwelling relentlessly on problems at home. Tonight, the worry was worse because this journey was different. Jeremy had spent a rare weekend away from home, without his wife, Laura, and he was haunted by the fear that he'd get back to find the already unsatisfactory situation had deteriorated further.

What if it had? He had no idea what he was going to do. Rob, their son, was depressed. Jeremy didn't have any medical training but didn't need it to diagnose that his son had some sort of mental health issue. Laura stubbornly refused to agree. She wouldn't even talk about taking their son to see a psychiatrist or the family doctor, even if the boy agreed to go. The problem was, he wasn't a boy. He was twenty.

Laura was afraid, that was the reason. She knew that there was a problem but couldn't face it. Robert was perfect in her eyes. He'd been the perfect baby, and a perfect pupil getting top grades. Then it had all gone wrong. He'd refused to try for any university. He'd gone travelling abroad for a few months but then turned up on the doorstep, having run out of money. He tried a couple of dead-end jobs and hadn't stuck with either of them for more than a few weeks. Nowadays, Rob either slept late, got up and hung round the house doing nothing, except stare at his computer, or rode off on his motorcycle to a mysterious meet-up with people his parents knew nothing about, and came home long after they'd gone to bed. Asked how he'd afforded the motorcycle, given his patchy employment history, he'd claimed to have bought it at a knock-down price from a friend who'd wanted rid of it.

Laura insisted all this was 'only a phase'. Rob would settle down when he'd decided what he 'really wanted to do'. In the meantime, this was Rob's 'gap year'. That's what she told anyone who asked what their son was doing.

Gap years were meant to be enjoyable. Their son was monosyllabic, sulky and looked like a ghost. The worst part of it, for Jeremy, was that he sensed that, deep down, Rob was deeply unhappy, perhaps even frightened. Knowing this made Jeremy afraid, too, and also made him feel inadequate. He couldn't talk to his son. Rob couldn't talk to his father. If ever Rob did confide . . . Jeremy felt panic rising in his chest. What would he, Rob's father, do? Ask Jeremy a question regarding the law, he'd know the answer, or he'd look it up. This fell outside his professional ken. Whatever it was, he wouldn't be able to handle it, Laura wouldn't, and most importantly of all, Rob would continue to drift away from them.

As if problems in his own home life were not sufficient, another branch of the family was doing its very best to drag him into theirs. Jeremy's trip north had been to visit his aged uncle, who was also his godfather. In addition to these ties, he was a client of the firm. The firm itself was an old and prestigious one in the City.

Old Uncle Philip Liddell had just turned ninety and had been, until now, a remarkably hale and hearty old fellow. But recently he'd suffered a minor heart attack during which he'd taken a bad tumble down some steps. He was now at home, taking prescribed pills, and supposed to be resting. But his son, Marcus, who handled most of the old fellow's business, had contacted Jeremy last Thursday in a panic. Marcus was not a chap who panicked easily and so Jeremy knew this was a genuine emergency.

'The old man wants you to draw up an entirely new will. He asks, will you come up and see him pronto? Stay over the weekend.'

'Entirely new will? Or insert new clauses?'

'He says a whole new will. The thing is, and it's downright embarrassing to say it, he's taken a fancy to his doctor's receptionist. She's a nice enough woman but well, she's about thirty. He's heading towards ninety-one; and he's worth a bit. It's quite possible he means to leave her the lot!'

'You suspect your father of being of unsound mind?'

'Jerry! The last thing I want to do is ask a court to find my dad totally incapable of understanding what he's doing. The trouble is I don't *know* what he's doing and he won't say. He just taps his finger against the side of his nose and says, "Wouldn't you like to know?" But he drops hints; and sits in his favourite chair with a silly smirk on his face, saying how every cloud has a silver lining. I've insisted the doctor visit him at home. I refuse to drive Dad down to the surgery. But that, of course, is what he wants me to do, so that he can leer at the receptionist and pay her fatuous compliments with everyone else listening!'

'Very trying,' agreed Jeremy. 'I dare say the receptionist understands. They must have other elderly patients who occasionally act oddly.'

'Those other old fellows aren't worth what Dad is worth. Losing my mother hit him hard. But it's been ten years since she died; and he's got us, and his grandchildren. Recently he's started saying he needs to update his will. Last night was the final straw. I was sitting with him, watching television. It was some commercial channel carrying an advert for a dating site that caters for the over fifties. It's one thing to be over fifty and quite another to be over ninety! But Dad got a dreamy look on his face and said, "It's quite right, you know. It's never too late for love." Jerry, you've got to come up here immediately, this weekend, and talk to him. He's not safe.'

So, instead of going home last Friday night, Jeremy had travelled by train to a windswept corner of the Lake District. He had dined '*en famille*' with his godfather, Marcus, and Marcus's wife, son and daughter-in-law. At the end of it they'd drunk an excellent port.

He spent the Saturday discussing business, and chatting to his client, his godfather. The old fellow had opened the conversation.

'Good of you to come all the way up here at the weekend, Jerry. Marcus has been bending your ear, I suppose?'

'He's naturally concerned about you, since your fall and the little problem with your heart.'

'It's not my physical health he's worried about. Thinks I'm potty, doesn't he? Marcus is a good fellow, excellent son and all that. But he's so bloody predictable. Does him good to have me stir him up a bit.' Philip Liddell chuckled.

'What's all this about a new will?'

'Oh, that . . . well, I thought I'd leave a bit to one of the donkey charities. Always been very fond of donkeys, plucky little fellows. Only a modest donation, mind you, couple of thousand. I leave it to you to find a suitable charity.'

'As you wish. Just the one new clause?'

'For now. The rest of the will can stay as it is.' Uncle Philip paused. 'At least, for the time being.'

'Is there any possibility you might remarry?' Jeremy asked as casually as he could.

'Oh, a bit late for me to take plunge again, Jerry. I'll let you know if ever I do!' Philip Liddell cackled merrily.

'In the meantime, I don't need a wife. Hester Wills is a tartar, but she is a very good cook.'

Hester Wills was his housekeeper, who came in daily. She was a formidable figure of entrenched opinions. 'I'm a plain woman!' she would say if anyone ventured to protest. She certainly was that. But her roast dinners were the stuff of dreams.

'You might consider setting Marcus's mind at rest.'

'Why? Watching him work himself into a frenzy is the only thing I've got to give me a laugh.'

Glad he's only my uncle, and the firm's client, thought Jeremy. I don't envy Marcus having him as a father. He really can be quite a spiteful old devil.

That evening they'd dined again, very well. On Sunday Marcus had loaned him some boots, and dragged him out for a healthy hike around the snow-decked scenery. During it, he grumbled about his father; warning his cousin not to be taken in by the old man's misplaced sense of humour, and demanding Jeremy 'do something'.

'Have you spoken to his doctor about his state of mind?' asked Jeremy.

'Much good *he* was! They ought to retire *him*.'

Jeremy interpreted this as meaning that the doctor had declared Philip Liddell perfectly clear in his mind. Having failed to get the medical profession onside, Marcus had turned to the legal brain of the family. Sadly, for him, he would be disappointed there too.

'Frankly, Marcus, your dad seems pretty clear in his mind when it comes to his estate,' Jeremy retorted, as he and his cousin battled uphill against a raging wind, under the sullen gaze of sheep huddled in the lee of a drystone wall.

'Indeed?' was the frosty reply.

'Look here, Marcus, have you considered that the old chap might be having a bit of fun with you?'

'FUN!' howled Marcus. The wind snatched at the word and whirled it away. The sheep pressed themselves even closer to their stone shelter.

'Well, you've made it pretty obvious you're worried. Uncle Philip isn't muddled, not in my view, anyway. He's pulling your leg.'

For a moment, Marcus had looked on the verge of a coronary episode himself. His face turned bright red. '*What has he asked you to do*? That's what I want you find out, Jerry! Is he going to leave her the lot? If he does, I shall challenge it in court.'

'Well, you know, a conversation between a solicitor and his client . . .'

'Don't throw the rulebook at me! Well, if you won't help, I shall have to hire a private detective. This femme fatale may have played this game before with other old gents!'

'For pity's sake, Marcus! Don't suggest that without any proof. Or the lady will take *you* to the cleaners, if you're wrong. But yes, if you're seriously worried, we could ask an inquiry agent to check out her background. She's probably married with half a dozen kids! All I can say is that he hasn't asked me to make any changes you need to worry about.'

'Humph!' said Marcus. 'I don't trust him.'

'Look here, have you considered that your father is a mischievous old devil, and what's more, he's bored.'

Marcus looked puzzled. 'Bored?'

'Let's face it, since his physical health has deteriorated and he can't go out much, of course he's bored.'

As advice, it wasn't what Marcus wanted to hear. But it had been Jeremy's honest opinion. Perhaps luckily, at that moment he'd put his foot into a snowdrift that had masked a ditch, and fallen in. Marcus had been forced to abandon family problems to tackle the practical one of pulling Jeremy out. They'd struggled back to the house in silence and spent an hour drinking hot toddies while Marcus brooded about his father and Jeremy contemplated the next day's long journey back to London and day at the office. Only after all that would he be going home in the evening. He'd be lucky to stay awake during it all.

'Randy old blighter!' said Marcus, gazing into the golden depths of his glass. 'Don't tell me he oughtn't to be in some sort of care.'

'Stop fretting, Marcus, or you'll have a breakdown.'

'I was relying on you!' retorted his cousin with a baleful glare.

Naturally, during his absence from home, Jeremy had phoned his wife. Laura had assured him no problems had arisen in his absence. She hadn't sounded too convincing, at least not to Jeremy. Years dealing with a variety of clients had fine-tuned his antennae in matters like this. Between Uncle Philip, Marcus, Laura and whatever ailed Rob, could things get any worse?

'Damn,' muttered Jeremy now, more loudly than he'd intended. The fellow doing the crossword glanced up and then, meeting Jeremy's eye, looked down again quickly. The train had slowed. The man opposite Jeremy abruptly closed down his laptop, stood up and retrieved his coat from the overhead rack. The attractive brunette, across the aisle and ahead a bit, was getting ready to leave the train, too, wriggling her arms into a dark-blue coat. She was a regular. Jeremy had seen her often on this train. She looked as if she were successful at whatever she did. But there was humour in the set of her mouth. The workaholic with the laptop, too, was a familiar sight, as was the overweight sweaty man asleep beside him. That chap was due to get off here and would miss his stop unless woken by a Good Samaritan. Jeremy decided to take on the role and tapped the man's arm. The guy awoke with a start, stared resentfully at Jeremy, then out of the window. They were entering the station, the end of the platform coming into sight. The train had slowed right down and the aisles had filled with those who were getting out here.

'Your stop, too, I think?' said Jeremy.

'Oh, right! Thanks.'

The three of them squeezed past the crossword addict, who scowled at them. They shuffled along the aisle in single file, the brunette, now buttoned into the blue coat, slightly ahead of them. Jeremy retrieved his overnight travel bag from the luggage racks at the end of the compartment. Then they all came to a stop to allow a younger man, who'd travelled with his bike in the open space by the doors, to get off first. They watched him tenderly lift his metal steed out and down to the platform. He was serenely unaware that he was any kind of obstacle to his fellow travellers, and probably would have resented anyone pointing it out to him. They all melted into the throng and jostled their way out of the station building into the car park. Apart from the cyclist, who had already turned into traffic going past the station and disappeared, nearly everyone was heading for a car. But the brunette had set off at a brisk walk away from the car park. She must live in the town itself, near enough to walk home from the station. That meant she lived in an older building, not in one of the outlying estates.

Jeremy lived a mile out of town at Abbotsfield. They'd bought the house when it had been one of a pair of newly converted barns and it had appeared, as they say, a good idea at the time. Their son was young. They wanted space, unpolluted air to breathe, country living. Or, as Jeremy now thought wryly, country living as depicted in glossy magazines. The people in the other barn conversion were called Baxter and ran a wine import business. They were away a lot, visiting vineyards on the Continent, or discussing business with producers there. For them, moving to Abbotsfield must have been ideal, because they didn't have to stay there all the time. OK, Jeremy conceded, I go up to London every working day. But it doesn't compare with wine-tasting in beautiful locations or spending time deciding where to lunch or dine in nice little restaurants.

The only other business in Abbotsfield belonged to a landscape gardener who was out nearly every day, presumably creating or maintaining gardens that were a delight to the eye. It was a pity he didn't take more care of his own place. When he returned, the fellow parked his muddy van in the narrow road before his cottage and left it there all night. This meant that when Jeremy set out on his drive to the station, quite early in the morning, his view was blocked as he pulled out into the road. There would have been room to park the van behind the cottage in the cluttered yard, if the gardener tidied the place up a bit, or got his shaven-headed henchman to do it. Jeremy had spoken to him, asking him not to park in the street, very politely, but to no avail. As for the muscular employee, he appeared to live nearby but Jeremy had yet to discover where.

Apart from the landscape business, Abbotsfield was quiet to the point of being comatose. Few people lived there, just a few old folk in some poorly maintained dwellings, and a fellow by the name of Finch who lived in the best of the cottages. True to his surname, Finch spent a small fortune stuffing the trees and bushes in his front garden with wire hangers. These, and a wooden bird table, Finch kept supplied with nuts and seeds for local birdlife. He was by occupation a maths teacher, said Laura, commuting to and from his school. If Jeremy wanted to know anything about Abbotsfield, he asked his wife. She lived there all the time. Jeremy, like the feathered friends that visited the maths teacher's bird table, flew in and out on brief visits. Otherwise, Abbotsfield was devoid of activity. He had Laura's word for that. 'Quiet as the grave,' she said. Each morning, Jeremy drove to the station in town, the bird-fancier drove off to his teaching post and Henderson to his gardens. The old people seldom showed their faces except once a week, a Wednesday, when, apparently, a volunteer-run bus service came to take them all into town to shop.

'They all shuffle out to their minibus, chattering like sparrows,' Laura had told him, 'and in the mid-afternoon come back laden with supermarket bags.'

Then she would add, 'Of course, Rob wants to spend his time somewhere livelier! You can't blame him for going off every evening to find his friends.'

Sure enough, when Jeremy had driven himself from the station that evening, the van with the legend *C. Henderson Landscape Gardening* was inconveniently parked as always, just where it would block Jeremy's view of the bend in the road the following morning.

'Hello, darling,' said Jeremy, hanging up his coat and walking into the kitchen.

Laura was arranging chops on the grill pan. She was wearing jeans and a floppy shirt and, from behind, looked like a teenager, instead of the forty-eight-year-old woman she was. She turned away from the oven to welcome him with a kiss. Her fine fair hair curled around her face and, when she smiled, dimples appeared in her cheeks. At moments like this, loving her was almost painful. He thought how absurdly young she still looked, at least to his eyes. It's like the portrait of Dorian Gray, Jeremy thought. She stays young and I age. Nevertheless, perhaps she did look a little tired around the eyes.

'How was life at Uncle Philip's?' she asked.

'Ruddy madhouse, but the old chap keeps a decent port, and Mrs Wills still dishes up first-rate nosh. Glad to be home. I see that wretched gardener has left his van blocking the view again.'

'His name is Callum,' Laura reminded him. 'He's very pleasant.' There was a hint of reproach in her voice.

That irritated her husband. 'If you get on with him so well, you might ask him about parking the van somewhere less inconvenient. When I tried, he just grinned at me and said, "Right you are!" After that he did nothing about it.'

'He leaves it there in the evenings because he walks everywhere,' said Laura.

'What do you mean, he walks everywhere?'

'In the evenings he likes a drink after work; and there's no pub here. He can't risk losing his licence, so he doesn't drive to a pub. He comes home, leaves the van, and walks across country to a place called the Black Dog, right on the edge of the town. He says it doesn't take him more than half an hour, across the fields.'

'Since when have you been so pally with him, anyway?'

'We're not *pally*! He's a neighbour, not a friend. We chat sometimes when he's around during the day. That cottage of his used to belong to his grandmother. He told me.'

'You don't chat to that scary guy who works for him, I hope.'

'Gus? No, Gus doesn't say much, not even to Callum. I don't see him much, anyway, only if he's helping Callum load the van or the trailer. How did your weekend gallivanting *really* go?'

'I found them all in good health and squabbling like sparrows over a crust. The views were splendid with all the snow. The house was like a fridge, so thanks for putting that hot-water bottle in my bag. The atmosphere round the table was a bit fraught. In a nutshell, Uncle Philip is full of mischief and running Marcus ragged. If anyone is likely to go round the bend, it's poor old Marcus. He thinks the old chap is planning to get married again to a much younger woman, and remake his will.'

'And is he?'

'Doubt it. He only wants a new clause in the will and it involves an animal charity, not a floozy. I told Marcus his fears were groundless. He now thinks I let him down.'

Laura laughed and turned back to her cooking. Jeremy looked down at the grill pan. 'Only enough for us, I see. Where's Rob?'

Laura kept her gaze fixed on the meat. 'He said he would be back too late for dinner.'

'I don't like him roaring round the country roads on that bike after dark. Ask your good neighbour Callum to show Rob the footpath to town across the fields.'

Now she turned to him, her face crumpled in despair. 'Rob wouldn't *walk*. I don't like him being out on that motorcycle so much, either. Of course, if he had a car . . .' she added tentatively.

Jeremy started to reach out and hug her, to tell her that, whatever it was, it would all be all right. Instead, he heard himself snap, 'I'm not rewarding Rob's idleness by buying him a car! Rob won't do a damn thing to organise his life; and it can't go on, Laura.'

He then did hug her and apologised for his bad temper.

Laura told him not to worry. 'Poor you, you must be worn out after such a hectic weekend; and spending such a long time in trains.'

This made Jeremy feel a heel.

They ate the chops in near silence. At the end of the meal, he pushed back his chair and helped Laura clear the table and wash up. It's now or never, he thought.

'I've been thinking,' he said tentatively, 'perhaps we ought to downsize.'

She turned to him, her eyes wide with amazement or shock, he wasn't sure which. 'Why?' she asked.

'The house is too big. The commute is getting to be too much for me. Abbotsfield is without any activities or shops or anything . . .' He faltered.

'It's a short drive into town. If we downsized, there wouldn't be room for my studio.'

She was a potter. Her studio was housed in a brick outbuilding to the rear of the property. It was one of the reasons for moving here. He should have thought about that and been ready with some answer, before he raised the possibility of moving away.

'I wasn't suggesting we move into a flat! I was only thinking that, well, you're pretty well alone out here most of the time. The Baxters are always going away. The other people here seem mostly to be retired. Except for

Henderson, I suppose, who drives all over the place on his gardening projects. Or that chap, Finch, who teaches in town, so he's away during the day in termtime, and doesn't seem to be around much at weekends.'

Jeremy paused, as he thought, I don't even know my neighbours very well. I come home here to roost, like a bird, and that's all. Finch ought to put me on his rare sightings list.

Aloud, he continued, 'But there's nothing here for Rob. You've got to agree with that. No wonder he roars off on that motorbike to hang out with who knows what company or where. He needs, he needs . . .' Jeremy faltered again. 'Rob needs some change in his life that will make him concentrate his mind and make some plans. He's just drifting.'

A steely light had entered her eyes. 'I know what this is about, Jeremy. You want us to move into some rabbit hutch where there's no room for Rob. He's our only child. I'm not throwing him out! Yes, he's got his problems, but making him homeless isn't the answer.'

Families, thought Jeremy sadly, what happened to domestic bliss? Or do we all like being at each other's throats? The tension following this conversation, perhaps 'spat' would be a better word, lasted into the evening before the atmosphere started to thaw.

'Oh, by the way, I've got some news,' said Laura a little later, over coffee. Her tone was casual, which made her news all the more shocking. 'There's been a murder while you were away.'

'What, here in Abbotsfield?' Jeremy was stunned. Was she serious?

'Of course not! In town. Callum found a body in the old churchyard on Saturday night. More coffee?'

Just like that! Jeremy asked himself. She's got some news. There's been a murder. That landscaper fellow found a body. Would I like some more coffee? How am I supposed to react?

'*Callum did*? While he was roaming round after dark like Count Dracula, I suppose. Whose body?'

'Oh, it's all right. It's no one we know. Callum didn't recognise him. He told the police. They've been searching the churchyard. It's been taped off and out of bounds to ordinary folk. That's annoyed a few people, I think. They like to cut through, or visit graves, and Basil is pretty purple in the face with indignation.'

'Basil? Oh, him over the road. Why?'

'Well, he is very keen on protecting the environment and he says the police are damaging the churchyard, trampling through it and disturbing everything in the hunt for clues.'

'*It's all right*,' Jeremy heard himself splutter. Anger flickered into life in him. 'Perhaps you should design a wall plaque, with a message,' he snapped. '*No Matter how Bad things are, they can always get Worse!*'

'Really, Jerry, that's in very poor taste.'

The brief flame of anger was quenched. 'Sorry! Bad influence of old Uncle Philip.' He added, 'Sorry, I'm tired. It's been a long weekend.'

She reached out and patted his hand. 'Poor you. You must be exhausted. Would you like a brandy?'

Alan and Meredith had also eaten, caught up on their respective days at work, and settled down to catch a bit of television.

'Is this it?' asked Alan suddenly. 'When the pair of us have retired, will we spend our time like this?'

He was slumped on the sofa with his arms folded and legs stretched out in front of him. On the TV screen, Monsieur Poirot was exercising the little grey cells again.

'I won't. I'm going to write that book. And you'll be happy out in your garden.'

'Keep telling yourself that!' he muttered.

Perhaps fortunately, at that moment the doorbell let out a screech. It was an old-fashioned type, of a period with the house, and it let everyone know there was a caller. A stranger might have thought someone had carelessly stepped on a cat.

'I'm going to dismantle that thing!' growled Markby.

'Then callers would have to knock. I'll go.'

'We can get a modern bell,' he was saying as she left the room.

Meredith opened the door and there was another woman on the doorstep. She looked much like the one who'd come on Saturday evening, not in features, but in general type. She was more sturdily built than the previous caller, but probably about the same age. She had similar fashion taste: a showerproof coat and, crammed on her grey hair, a woollen hat. The hat was hand knitted; and had a link to the first caller's beanie in a crocheted flower sewn to it. It was hard to tell what kind of flower it was. It looked as though it was red, but artificial light from the hallway behind them made it difficult to be sure. It could have been either a poppy or a rose.

'I am sorry to disturb you,' announced the visitor in a way that suggested she wasn't sorry at all. Her tone, if anything, was belligerent, as was her general stance. She stood with feet apart, balanced on her booted feet, like an artist's easel.

'Can I help you?' asked Meredith politely. 'This isn't the vicarage any longer. If you want the vicar, I can give you a card with his new address.'

'I don't want the vicar!' retorted the visitor. 'And I know this isn't the vicarage any longer. But my sister-in-law is woolly minded and she thought it was. She came to see you, didn't she?'

'I don't know,' said Meredith. She was aware Alan had joined her and was standing a few paces behind her, listening.

The woman stared hard at her. 'You must know. Her name is Felicity Garret. I am Melissa Garret. She married my brother, Charles.'

'I am afraid that name means nothing to me,' Meredith told her. She looked over her shoulder to where her husband lurked by the staircase. 'The name Felicity Garret mean anything to you, Alan?'

'Not a thing!' he replied cheerfully.

Melissa Garret stared at them both mistrustfully but didn't move. She seemed to be processing their replies. 'I dare say,' she said, 'that she didn't want to give her name.'

'Then we can't help you!' said Meredith promptly. 'I'm sorry.' She stepped back and made to close the front door.

'Wait!' ordered the visitor. 'I haven't finished. I want to know what she said—'

Markby stepped forward. 'Oh, but you have finished, Miss Garret. Good night!' He closed the door firmly.

As he did, a squawk of rage came from the caller. She remained on the doorstep for a few seconds before stomping off angrily down the path.

'Old dragon!' said Alan impolitely.

Meredith privately agreed but said aloud, 'We haven't seen the last of her or the other one.'

'I sincerely hope you're wrong,' Alan retorted.

'So do I hope I'm wrong. But I've got a bad feeling about it.'

Chapter Four

Markby looked up at the sound of a knock on the door to see Steve Kendal, brandishing a sheet of paper. His first thought was that Kendal looked more cheerful than usual. Perhaps the cuisine had improved in the canteen.

'Come in, Steve, and tell me your good news.'

Kendal looked slightly disconcerted. 'Well, I don't know that it's good news exactly, but it is progress. I think we know the identity of the victim.' He put the sheet of paper on Markby's desk. It was a printout.

'Aaron Hooper,' Markby read aloud. 'We thought our Unknown Male might have a police record.'

'He was London born, as you can see,' said Kendal. 'He was active in the general London area for most of the years we can account for, pushing drugs small-time, handling stolen goods, also small-time. He left London suddenly. Perhaps he upset someone dangerous. After a couple of months during which his moves are unaccounted for – I'd guess he was lying low – he turned up here. Been around this area for six months or more.'

Markby studied the photo that accompanied Hooper's record. It struck him that in life Hooper had not looked any more prepossessing than he had done in the morgue. His cheekbones were still flat. His lumpy nose still looked as if it been moulded by a talentless amateur and stuck on as best its creator could. His eyes had been as expressionless in life as in death, lacking any gleam of intelligence. The jagged scar on his cheek was the only thing that distinguished Hooper from a dozen other ne'er-do-wells of his type. Markby read the accompanying record.

'Not a mover and a shaker, was he?' said Kendal. 'He served a couple of jail terms for drugs-related offences and one for handling stolen goods. Also, he did a bit of time for a violent assault on a girlfriend. He wasn't Mr Big.'

'No, Steve, he wasn't, not going by this. He was thirty-seven at the time of his death and I'd guess a real non-achiever. We all know the type. They hang around in the shadows of the criminal underworld, waiting for someone bigger to give them a job. The only thing puzzling me is that there's no obvious reason why someone should rendezvous with Hooper in a burial ground here and kill him. He was well down the pecking order. Not a big-time drug dealer, just a gofer. At some point he had a fight, or was attacked, by someone holding, I'd guess, a broken bottle, and acquired a scar on his face to prove it. Yet, almost certainly, Hooper was in that cemetery by arrangement. It's tempting to assume drugs would have changed hands. But it's almost too easy. How did Hooper travel to the cemetery, anyway, at that time of night? Did he walk? Are there any unclaimed cars parked nearby?'

'By bike!' Kendal said smugly. 'We found it, pushed into the hedge.'

'A motorbike? Big thing to push into a hedge!'

'Oh, no, not a motorbike; just an ordinary pushbike. It was definitely Hooper's. His dabs are all over it. So are other fingerprints. More than one person seems to have used the bike in recent weeks.'

Markby sighed. 'A pushbike! Somehow that says it all. It would be pathetic if it weren't for the fact that he contributed to doing a lot of harm as part of the chain in a very nasty business indeed.'

'And it got him killed,' Kendal said.

'It got him killed, as you say, and I don't suppose there's a single person out there who mourns him.' Markby paused. 'On the other hand . . .'

'Sir?' asked Kendal as the superintendent fell silent.

'One never knows.' Markby tapped the printout. 'Let's not release too much information to the public yet. The whole town knows about a body, likely a murder. As yet, they don't need to know much more. Oh, except for that missing phone. He would certainly have carried one on him. Some kid may have found that, so we can put out that we're interested in hearing from anyone who's stumbled across it.

'It's been a couple of days and no one has come forward to report a missing male person. Perhaps no one is shedding any tears for him; but his absence must be worrying someone. That person may be trying to locate him. Put the word out that we're interested to know if anyone is asking about him – or anybody else – in the pubs. If he was part of a drugs distribution network, then a link in that chain has been broken. It's a small link, and it will soon be repaired. There's plenty of replacement material out there. Nevertheless, it will have inconvenienced the organisation and someone will be angry. In the meantime, all the public needs to know is that we have a body we suspect may be that of Aaron Hooper and we'd appreciate any information.'

When you live alone, as Callum did, it's easy to develop the habit of 'thinking aloud'. (That always sounded better than 'talking to yourself'.) The danger is that occasionally you find yourself saying something aloud in public that you'd rather have kept in your head.

Right now, at the end of the day, Callum was in his kitchen/office, with a mug of strong brewed tea in his hand, and 'thinking aloud'. What he was really doing, he knew, was talking to his late grandmother. Callum had spent much of his childhood with his grandmother, here in this cottage. She had been his friend, confidante and refuge. She'd also been his moral compass. Of course, he'd strayed from her standards somewhat, since growing up; but never without a feeling of guilt.

All his summer holidays had been passed in Abbotsfield, and a good part of his school years, too. Had he known of Jeremy Hawkins's opinion that there was nothing to do here, he'd have been puzzled. Callum had never been bored here. As a child he'd wandered freely over the surrounding fields and woods, discovering the paths and ancient tracks that he now used to get to and from the Black Dog. This meant he could find his way by moonlight without the need of a torch. But this evening, for the first time, he wasn't sure whether or not to go out at all.

'It's not because last time I went to the Black Dog, I found a dead bloke on the way home,' he told his grandmother (or her image in his parents' wedding photograph). 'It's because the cops have put tape all over the place and I can't cut through the churchyard easily.'

The expression on Grandma's face told him what she would have thought of making a short cut through the churchyard going or returning home from the pub. '*Serve you right, Callum!*' she would have said. '*Sooner or later, bad behaviour finds you out!*'

'Bloody nuisance,' grumbled Callum. ('*It's never necessary to use bad language, Callum! The English language is rich enough without that.*')

'I could do with a pint!' he told the photograph defiantly. 'I wonder whether Gus is over at his caravan.' He went to the back door, opened it and peered out.

There was a dim, tarpaulin-shrouded shape in the yard by the back wall. Gus's motorbike. That didn't mean Gus was in his caravan. Gus had an extensive acquaintance in a parallel society, much of it in the traveller and gypsy community. All manner of vehicles picked him up and drove him off to mysterious destinations. Callum never asked him about any of this because Gus was essentially a private person. He didn't tell you his business and he never asked you about yours. He was also barely able to read, wrote his own name with great difficulty and furrowed brow, and sealed any agreement with a handclasp that was like having your fingers caught in a vice. That handshake was sacrosanct. If Gus said he'd be there at eight in the morning, he'd be there. If sent off in the van to do some job, you could be sure he'd do it. Callum was happy to let him keep a key to the side gate, to get access to his motorbike. He sometimes wondered whether Gus had means of access to the cottage itself. It wouldn't surprise him. But there had never been any sign that Gus had been here when Callum was away.

An icy blast of air whistled through the door, threatening to destroy the warm fug of the kitchen. Callum closed it quickly. He didn't normally drink with Gus so it didn't matter. The night was so cold it seemed a bad idea to set off on foot across the fields, anyway. He balanced this against a need to see other people, living, breathing people; and the yearning for human contact won. He went to lace up his walking boots and wrap up in his thick jacket.

It was a cloudless night, lit by a silver disc that was the moon. That could mean frost by morning. As always, once he got out there, tramping along that ancient footpath that was a right of way across the fields to the town, any troubles he had were lifted from Callum's shoulders. Away in the distance he could see a string of moving lights that marked the motorway. Better communications brought more people. There were plans underway, he knew, to build new housing on the edge of town. Inevitably, this would creep towards Abbotsfield. Something swooped over his head, disturbing the air, and a silent winged shape was briefly silhouetted against the moon. An owl. It was night, but there was plenty of life out there, going about its business. He heard the distant yelp of a fox. You and me, Reynard, we like the cover of night.

It took him longer than usual to reach the pub, as he couldn't use his short cut through the churchyard. But at last he got there and the sight of it, its windows bright with the yellow glow, the murmur of voices and, when he opened the door, the sudden sense of being enveloped in a living world in which people were relaxed and happy, all cheered him immensely, wrapping him in a comfort blanket. Death and horror no longer had any place. They were outside and he was inside, in a different world.

It was certainly busy tonight. He'd noticed how full the car park had been. There were some new patrons here, notably a group over there in the corner. They sat round a couple of tables pushed together and something about them, their turned backs, their low voices, a differentness from the usual clientele, all told Callum who they were. They were off-duty police personnel, having a drink together for some reason. If he'd had any doubt about this, the presence among them of one person in particular would have told him their identity. It was the woman officer, the one who'd come to his cottage with Markby. She had a foreign-sounding surname. Santos, that was it.

As if she sensed someone staring at her, she lifted her head and saw Callum by the door, and smiled briefly in recognition.

He felt absurdly awkward and didn't know how to respond. He couldn't just grin at her without feeling like the village idiot. So he raised his hand briefly in greeting and then let it drop. Like blooming Hiawatha, he thought. Why not just say 'How!' and be done with it?

He went to the bar to order and saw that Mick, the barman, had been watching.

'Coppers,' said Mick quietly, wiping the bar counter with a cloth. 'Usual, is it?'

'Please.' Callum hunted in his pocket for the money. They all knew, didn't they? Every patron in the pub had identified the off-duty law. There was a kind of invisible dividing line between the group enjoying their drinks in the corner and the rest.

'Here,' said Mick, placing the filled glass on the counter, and leaning forward confidentially. 'You found the body, right?'

'I didn't plan it!' said Callum in dismay, struck by the lasting horror of it. The emotion wasn't down to the moment he'd realised that he was shut in a churchyard with an unburied corpse. It was the realisation now that his discovery would grow to legend as time went by. It would follow him around forever. He'd be the bloke who found the body. Worse, he'd be the bloke who'd found the body while walking through the churchyard at night, because that was what he, Callum, did. He'd never thought twice about taking his short cut. It had never struck him how weird it might seem to other people. What was he? Some kind of freak? Mick, for one, must think Callum a bit odd, to put it mildly.

'What were you doing there, anyway?' asked Mick, confirming his worst fears. 'Wandering about over there in the graveyard.' He peered at Callum from beneath bushy eyebrows, his brow furrowed.

'Short cut,' mumbled Callum, staring down into his beer.

'Rather you than me,' said Mick.

'I'd rather it had been you!' retorted Callum with a return of spirit.

He took his drink and moved away to escape further questions. Because the other drinkers had all taken the seats furthest away from the police party, Callum was obliged to sit on a bench just inside the door. It was famously the least desirable seat in the pub. Anyone, going out or coming in, brushed by you and, if it was raining, showered droplets all over you.

Fortunately, someone had left a copy of the local paper on the bench and he was able to open it and hide behind it. No use pretending that wasn't what he was doing. He found no comfort in it, because one article, spread across the centre fold, complete with map, showed where the new housing was being constructed. It was even closer to Abbotsfield than he'd realised. The time would come when he wouldn't be able to walk across the fields at night, because they would no longer be fields. They'd be streets and rows of identical builds with mock Georgian doors. If there were any back gardens, the owners would probably pave them over and make them into barbecue areas. Increasingly, as a landscape gardener and designer, Callum had found that clients asked for 'somewhere to entertain outdoors'. As if this country had the sort of climate that let you do that for more than a couple of months in the year . . . and it didn't rain so that everyone had to rush back indoors or squeeze into the mock-Alpine hut that was really a shed. In theory, an ancient right of way shouldn't be obliterated. But developers were adept at getting round that. They'd claim that it would still be possible to walk through the new housing, using the roads, so no one like Callum would be prevented from getting to the pub. The arrival of new residents would make new trade for Callum himself, and for the Black Dog. Mick the barman would be pleased about that. For many of the regulars, it would be a different tale. They, and Callum, would be displaced by a chattering bunch of bright-faced young professionals, their faces shining with the pride of being new homeowners. Perhaps the pub would extend its menu beyond crisps and peanuts, and start offering food. They might build on a proper dining room; turn themselves into a restaurant. Callum would have to find somewhere new to drink and he wouldn't be able to walk to it. His life, he realised despondently, was about to change for ever. Finding the dead bloke was but the first step into an unknown future.

He was aware that the group in the far corner was

leaving. He spread the newspaper out on the table and bent over it studiously as they brushed past him, their exit releasing a blast of cold outside air down his neck. But they hadn't all gone. One remained. He looked up and saw DS Santos standing before him. She smiled down at him. 'You haven't been put off drinking here, then?'

'No!' said Callum. It came out much more fiercely than he'd intended.

She looked startled. 'Fair enough,' she said and made a move to follow her colleagues out of the door.

He had not meant to sound as if he'd taken offence and he hadn't intended to give offence. He needed to say something more, and quickly, but what? So, to account for sounding grumpy, he found himself telling her what he felt about it all: the future development, the disappearance of the fields under brick and tarmac, the loss of all his childhood memories. As he spoke it became less an inspiration for the need to fill a conversational void, and more and more an outpouring of personal dismay at the prospect of loss.

He revolved the opened paper on the table so that she could read the article with the map of the proposed development. 'See that? That's what they're going to do! Here.' He tapped the paper. 'That's Abbotsfield. Only it's going to disappear one day soon.'

Santos hesitated, then came round the table and sat on the bench beside him. That meant he either had to twist uncomfortably to face her, or put up with her talking into his earhole.

'That wedding group in the photo over your desk, back at the cottage, that's your parents' wedding?'

It wasn't the question he'd been expecting. He did twist round and stare at her. 'Yes. Later they split up.'

'Sorry,' she apologised. 'It must have been a difficult time for you.'

Callum considered this. 'I don't remember them being unhappy when I was little. I suppose they kept up a good front for my sake; or because they were scared of my grandmother. My mum rowed with Grandma a lot. But if she was rowing with my dad, it was when I was out of earshot. I was twelve when they divorced. Out of the blue, or as I saw it. My mum remarried and moved south. My dad took off in the other direction and went to work on an oil rig in the north of Scotland. They both said I was "settled in school", that was the phrase, and they didn't want to uproot me and disturb my education; so, they left me behind.'

'How did you get to school from Abbotsfield? Did your grandmother drive?'

'Good grief, no!' exclaimed Callum, managing just in time not to use a less elegant expression. 'Well, she didn't need to then. We were still on a bus route. Baz and I used to catch the bus together at the crossroads.'

'Baz?'

'Basil Finch, he still lives in Abbotsfield.'

'The guy who is so worried we'll disturb the natural habitat in the churchyard?'

'That's Baz. He gets a bit worked up about it. You don't

want to take any notice. He was always like that, even when we waited for the bus together. The bus company axed the route a few years ago.' Callum frowned. 'Not economically viable. Anyway, to all intents and purposes, I lived with my grandmother. She left me the cottage in her will because she wanted me always to have a home somewhere. I saw both my parents from time to time during my teens, individually you understand? Not together. Then my mother and her husband went to live in Spain and run a bar. End of visits.'

Callum added hastily, 'I was perfectly happy with my gran. I suppose I should have missed my parents more, but I didn't. My dad has remarried now and is still in Scotland. They've made a success of their lives in new relationships. Good luck to them. So, you see, as things turned out, they didn't need me and I didn't need them. No hard feelings on either side. I don't feel sorry for myself, in case you were wondering.'

She had been listening closely and now asked, 'Are you still in touch with them?'

'No,' said Callum quietly. 'No point, is there?'

'I'm divorced,' she told him. 'But we didn't have any kids so we hadn't that problem to sort out. I'm glad you were happy with your grandmother.'

'Yes, well . . .' Callum mumbled, suddenly embarrassed and looking down at the newspaper. 'Didn't mean to ramble on like that. Sorry.'

'Don't be. I understand how you feel about Abbotsfield; and how you must feel about the proposed new buildings.'

85

She gave another of her brief smiles. 'I should go. I have to work in the morning.'

'So do I,' said Callum, folding the paper and pushing it aside. He stood up. 'It's not mine,' he explained, indicating the paper in case she thought he was a litter lout who discarded his rubbish anywhere. 'Someone else left it there. Or it might be Mick's, the barman's.'

Mick was busily polishing glasses and pretending he hadn't been watching them both the whole time.

'Do you mind if I walk out with you?' he asked, as he and DS Santos made for the door together.

'No problem. So long as you don't worry that your barman friend might think I'm arresting you! He knew we were all police officers, didn't he? People generally do.'

'Let him think what he likes.' Callum gave Mick one of his Hiawatha salutes in farewell.

Mick nodded acknowledgement and grinned.

Outside the pub, she asked, 'I've got my car. Would you like a lift home? I've only had one drink.' She glanced around them. 'Everyone else has left, no one to see us.'

'Thanks,' said Callum, 'but I'll walk back over the fields – while they're still there.'

Santos looked along the churchyard wall on the other side of the street. 'Where do you climb over? Right opposite?'

'Oh, no, just along here. It's a very old wall and the bigger stones stick out a bit, makes it easier to climb.' He led the way to the spot. 'See? That one low down is a bit like a mounting block. I just stand on it, reach up . . .'

In demonstration, Callum reached up to grip the top of the wall, and, using the rough stonework as improvised footholds, scrambled up and sat astride the top, looking down at her. 'Like that!' he said. 'You see, I really do climb over here.'

'I wasn't checking your story!' she called up, sounding annoyed.

'Didn't think you were.' *Like heck. Of course, she was, had been. I know it: and she knows I know it.* 'OK?' he called down.

In reply she reached up her arm. 'Give me a hand?'

Callum reached down his hand and gripped her wrist. A moment later she was seated atop the wall with him.

'Yes,' she said. 'It's pretty easy.'

'If you're fit, and obviously you are, being a cop.'

'Show me a villain and I'll chase him down,' she told him. She looked down into the darkness of the churchyard. 'I suppose there's a soft landing down there? Not a lump of marble?'

In reply, Callum simply swung his leg over the wall and slithered down to land on the turf on the far side. A minute later, with a thud, she landed beside him. They sat side by side on the wet grass, backs against the wall, surrounded by the dead.

'Tell you what, Officer,' said Callum. 'There's police tape all around here ordering Joe Public like me to keep out. You're OK. You're allowed.'

'You're with me,' she said kindly, adding, 'we're pretty well finished here, anyway.'

There was enough moonlight to show the ground ahead of them. Santos raised a hand and pointed. 'The victim was over there, wasn't he? Just in front of us?' She got to her feet, slapping her jeans free of grass, grit and frost.

'Yes. I thought he was sleeping it off.'

She was looking around them in the moonlight. 'I can see why you do it,' she said suddenly, 'why you would cut through here.'

'Do you?' asked Callum, surprised and grateful. 'I'm glad someone does. Everyone else thinks either that I'm barmy; or I'm one of those loonies who go out looking for ghosts. I hope Markby doesn't think that.'

'Shouldn't think so. You don't believe in ghosts, I take it?'

'No,' said Callum. 'Not the white-sheeted sort. I do feel my grandmother's presence back at the cottage, as if she'd never left. But not here. I believe in things growing, new shoots, and new life. I don't think some spectral form is going to rise from one of these graves and flap about. I told Markby. It's why I didn't run when I saw the dead fellow. I never thought he was an apparition taking a snooze on his own grave. I told you, I just thought he was a drunk.'

Santos said very quietly, 'We're not alone, Callum.'

'OK, if that's what you believe. As I said, I still think Grandma—'

She interrupted him impatiently but in the same low voice. 'I mean it literally. There is someone else in this churchyard, someone alive, and he's over there, beneath those trees, watching us. Don't make a big thing of it. Act casual. Give me your hand.'

'What?' asked the startled Callum.

'Do a bit of acting, can't you?' Her hand gripped his. 'You and I are just a couple taking a romantic midnight stroll. Just let's wander quietly and slowly in that direction, gazing at each other.'

'I feel like a twit,' muttered Callum as they set off.

'You say the nicest things,' retorted Santos. 'There, did you notice that?'

'Yes, I did. You're right. He's lurking over there under the trees.'

'I told you he was! I'm an investigating officer on the team in this case. I'm not trying to seduce you.'

If I were the clever sort who could think of suitable replies off the top of his head, thought Callum, I'd have an answer to that. But I'm not; and I can't. Damn!

They were almost at the clump of trees now. Their proximity successfully alarmed the target. He broke cover. For a brief moment they saw a thin wild-looking human shape, before the intruder turned and began to race away from them, leaping over obstacles and darting between the tombstones. He seemed to be heading towards the new cemetery.

'*Stop!*' yelled Santos in an ear-splitting voice. '*Police!*'

'Keep it down!' exclaimed Callum, clapping his hands over his ringing eardrums. 'They'll hear you back at the pub.'

But she wasn't listening to him. She had dropped his

hand (pity about that), and was in hot pursuit of the flying figure. What was he supposed to do? Chase after the pair of them, lending his support to the Law? By the time he caught up, she'd probably have the target in an arm lock. He decided he'd better run over there in the unlikely event she couldn't manage. After all, the last person who'd had some kind of encounter in this churchyard by night had been stabbed to death.

As it happened, the decision was made for him. Santos tripped and sprawled flat. The quarry vanished. By the time Callum reached her, Santos was sitting up, clutching her shin, and expressing her frustration in colourful language.

'You tripped over that,' explained Callum helpfully, pointing at a section of stone edging around a plot.

Santos fell silent for a moment, staring up at him. Then she erupted again. 'Of course I fell over that! Give me a hand up, can't you?'

'Take it easy, you might have chipped a bone.'

'I haven't chipped a bone! I'll just have a mega-sized bruise tomorrow.'

'You don't know. Look, there's a bench over there. Lean on me and sit down for a moment. It wasn't a good idea, you know, to go chasing after him in this place. Even I wouldn't have tried it and I know the ground better than you.'

'Callum!' she said in a suppressed voice. 'I know you were brought up by your grandmother, but you don't have to sound like her.'

'I don't!' snapped Callum. 'I'm just saying you did a daft thing.'

'I didn't do a daft thing! He wasn't supposed to be here. As you reminded me, there is police tape all the way round and notices advising the public this is a crime scene. He was an intruder and, when challenged, he ran.'

'I'd run if I had a crazy woman chasing me through a churchyard,' said Callum. 'There was a murder here the other evening, I'd like to remind you. He didn't know you were a cop. You could have been the killer, returned. Of course the poor bloke ran!'

They had reached the bench during this conversation, Santos hobbling and Callum supporting her. They sat down and she rubbed her shin.

'*He* might have been the killer returned!' she snapped. 'I had to challenge him.'

'If he was the killer, then he might still have the knife. There is,' concluded Callum censoriously, 'such a thing as common sense.'

Santos drew in a deep breath and said, in a venomous undertone, 'Don't tell me you don't sound like someone's grandmother.'

'Will you shut up about that?' retorted Callum, who'd had enough. 'I don't sound like my – or anyone's – elderly relative. I am making sense. You are not. And I don't care if you are a cop. It doesn't make you Wonder Woman.'

'Now you sound like my ex-husband!'

'Then I'm not the only one to think like it.'

'Ruddy men all stick together,' she muttered.

'It's called self-defence,' retorted Callum.

'Oh, ha, ha! Where was he making for over there, do you think?'

'Well, I'm not a trained detective. I'm only a bloke who designs and lays out gardens and public amenity areas. But that does at least give me a sense of location. He was running towards the new cemetery, wasn't he? So, my amateur guess is that he was making for the gap in the hedge over there. By now he's run through it and gone.'

There was a moment of silence.

'I'm sorry I said you sounded like your grandmother,' said Santos. 'I never met your grandma.'

'You'd have liked her,' said Callum, adding, 'and she'd have liked you.'

'A woman of taste and discrimination, then!' said Santos with a stifled giggle.

'Yes, she was a canny old bird.'

Another silence. Then Callum said, 'I know I found the body and I suppose that makes me a suspect. But, official business aside, I don't want to quarrel with you.'

'No need for us to fall out. I'm obliged to you for showing me how to climb over that wall back there.'

'I didn't know you were going to shin over it like greased lightning in the way you did. I thought you were just checking my story.'

'Yes, I was, you're right.'

'Fair enough. I also didn't know you were going to take me by the hand and lead me into chasing an unknown suspect through a maze of gravestones.'

'I do that sort of thing,' said Santos. 'It's my job.'

'Taking comparative strangers by the hand?

'No! And don't read anything into that.'

'I wouldn't dare,' Callum told her. 'But I feel that I should mention that there is another intruder coming towards us . . .'

'Mr Henderson!' she said warningly.

'And this one has a torch.'

'You're right!' gasped Santos.

'I am occasionally right. Sit tight. I'll handle this one. You're off the pitch, injured.'

A bulky dark form was approaching them from the town side of the churchyard. Callum stood up and Santos, with a squeak of pain, stood up as well. The newcomer reached them and a powerful beam of torchlight played over them, causing them both to blink.

'Well, well,' said a familiar voice. 'DS Santos and Mr Henderson.'

'Yessir,' said Santos miserably.

'Oh, it's you, Mr Markby,' said Callum. 'I suppose you heard the racket from your house.'

'You could hardly have advertised your presence better!'

'We were chasing an intruder, sir,' said Santos. 'I ordered him to stop and told him I was a police officer.'

'And you, Mr Henderson. I know you like wandering around this place at night, but were you assisting my officer in the execution of her duty? Or something else?'

'I showed the officer where and how I climbed over the back wall.'

'And we disturbed an intruder in the churchyard, sir. He was hiding under some trees.'

'And the officer has injured her leg,' said Callum. 'While in pursuit.'

'No, I haven't!' snapped Santos. 'That is, sir, I tripped and fell. I've bruised my shin, that's all.'

'Then you'd both better come up to the house and check out the damage to your shin, Santos. And you, Mr Henderson, can explain how you came to be giving my officer this guided tour of the churchyard, and irregular access to it, in the first place.'

They both began to speak at once, but fell silent as Markby turned away. They followed him back to the Old Vicarage where they were welcomed by a smell of coffee and Meredith in her dressing gown. She stared at them both in surprise.

'This', said Markby, indicating Beth, 'is DS Santos. Mr Henderson you may remember from when he stood outside in the middle of the night yelling about a corpse.'

'Sorry to have disturbed you again, Mrs Markby,' mumbled Callum.

'DS Santos is in need of first aid, I think.'

'I've only bashed my shin,' said Santos defiantly. 'I, um, was running and I fell over a bit of stone edging round a grave.'

If Meredith thought this in any way unusual, she didn't show it. 'You'd better come with me, and I'll see if it needs a dressing or some TCP or something.'

She led Santos out of the room. The unwilling patient

could be heard protesting, 'You aren't going to put something on it that will make it sting, are you?'

Markby shut the door on the women and addressed the unhappy Callum.

'OK, Henderson! Tell me about it.'

'It's like I said,' protested Callum. 'I went to the pub—'

'On your own?'

'Yes! On my own. We weren't on some sort of date.'

'I'm relieved to hear it. You may like strolling round the countryside at night. But do it alone! I am in charge of an official investigation and Santos is one of my officers. How did you come to be together?'

'I was telling you,' grumbled Callum, 'if you'd let me finish! Are you people all the same? You ask questions and then don't let anyone answer?'

'I apologise for interrupting you,' said Markby, his steely tone contrasting with the polite words. 'Get on with it.'

'I am getting on – oh, blooming heck! Listen, I went to the pub, on my own. A bunch of your blokes were in there, having a drink together. There were some women, too, I mean, some women officers, or I suppose they were women officers. One of them was –' Callum jerked his head in the direction of the door. 'Her,' he said.

'Yes?'

'So, we happened to leave at the same time. She – the officer – asked me to show her where I climbed over the wall. So I did. And we both climbed over the wall.'

'That was taking it a stage further,' observed Markby mildly.

'I only meant to show her how I climbed it. But she hopped over it too.' Callum paused. 'She's very fit, isn't she?'

'It's a requirement of the Force. We need to know our officers keep in good physical shape.'

'Well, you don't have to worry about that one. When we'd both jumped down into the churchyard, we, or rather your officer, realised someone else was there.'

Markby leaned forward and asked, with a renewal of interest, 'Sure?'

'Absolutely sure. That is to say, I didn't notice him, but she spotted him. Then he saw we were on to him, and he ran.'

It would be best, thought Callum, to leave out the handholding bit.

'You are sure it was a man?'

'He was fairly tall and took long strides. He covered the ground pretty quickly and seemed to know where he was going. I mean, I supposed he was making for that gap in the hedge in the new cemetery.' Callum paused to reflect. 'Mind you, she's got a fair old turn of speed, too, hasn't she? Your officer, I'm talking about. She went haring after him, leaving me standing. But it's an obstacle course in there. You can trip over easily. She did. We already explained this.'

'You didn't chase after the intruder yourself?'

'No! I had no beef with him, whoever he was. He was probably just cutting through, like I do. But I thought I'd better follow her, in case she had trouble. Not that she couldn't handle it, trouble, I mean.'

'DS Santos seems to have impressed you, Mr Henderson.'

'She terrifies me,' confessed Callum. 'I don't know what she's going to do next.'

Markby made no comment on this. Instead, he turned his head and looked towards the door into the hallway. 'I hear them coming back. This is what we're going to do. I take it you walked to the pub on one of your nocturnal rambles?'

'Yes. I understand the officer drove herself there and she's left her car in the car park.'

'Then I will drive *both* of you to the pub car park where Santos can collect her vehicle and drive herself home. Then I will drive *you* back to Abbotsfield. I want,' added Markby benignly, 'to know you've got home safely, Callum.'

'Oh, all right!' muttered Callum. 'Much obliged, I'm sure.'

Jeremy had awoken a little before two. Perhaps, even asleep, a corner of his mind had been anticipating the sound of Rob's motorcycle returning, He heard the tyres crunch across the gravel before the house; and the head-lamp's beam briefly lit the window before it was switched off. Faint scrapes and bumps from below meant Rob was now indoors. Laura's breathing remained regular. She didn't move. Jeremy slid cautiously out of bed, pulled on his dressing gown, felt for his bedroom mules with his bare feet, and let himself out of the room.

There was a light on downstairs. Rob must be in the kitchen. This made Jeremy even angrier. Their son couldn't get home in time to eat with his parents, and now he was probably making a sandwich down there, scattering crumbs across the cleaned worktops, shoving his plate, mug, cutlery, whatever he used, into the freshly emptied dishwasher. He drew a deep breath and pushed open the door.

His son was seated at the kitchen table. Predictably, he was staring at his mobile phone. I suppose, thought Jeremy, those things are going to be part of our lives evermore. Rob had been eating but hadn't troubled to make a sandwich. Whatever it had been, it had come in a plastic cup and left a faint odour of curry. Steam rose from the electric kettle in a lazy curl. His son's face had a thin, haunted look and his hair was lank. Just as Jeremy had wanted to fold Laura in his arms earlier that night, but hadn't, so now he wanted to hug his son as he might have done when Rob was a toddler. Ask the boy what was the matter, so that Daddy could make it all come right. But had he ever done that? Laura had been the comforter, the sticker-on of plaster dressings on scraped knees, had listened to infant tales of woe.

Rob shut down his phone at the sight of his father and said, 'Hello, Dad,' in a defensive sort of way.

On the way downstairs Jeremy had told himself that he must NOT rush in and demand to know where his son had been. So he asked, 'What was that?' and nodded towards the empty plastic container.

'Pot noodles,' said Rob.

Against his own expectations, and certainly against his son's, Jeremy heard himself laugh. Rob looked astonished and then offended. I must be nervous, thought Jeremy. Guffawing like an idiot. Pull yourself together! he ordered himself silently.

'I like them,' Rob said defiantly.

'What? Oh, I just thought of Hester Mills, Uncle Philip's cook. She would have some strong views on eating reconstituted food of any sort.'

'Oh,' said Rob. 'Suppose so. The old dragon still cooking for Uncle Phil, then?'

'Oh, yes, he eats very well. Your mum was cooking chops when I came home last night.'

'I told her I wouldn't be in to eat!' Rob said defiant.

'Did you eat at all? Or was that it?' Jeremy indicated the pot noodle container.

'Got a burger from the van in the square, does it matter?'

Things were going downhill conversationally already, thought Jeremy, and he'd only walked through the door a couple of minutes earlier.

Perhaps Rob was thinking the same thing because, after a moment's silence, he asked 'They all OK?'

Jeremy failed to make the necessary leap of mind and replied, 'Very nice.'

Then he realised that, of course, Rob was asking about his weekend trip north, not whether he'd enjoyed the chops. 'Oh, yes, all very well, for the most part.'

'Sorted, then?' asked Rob.

I'm going to need a translator soon, thought Jeremy. 'Yes, I managed to sort everything out, thank you.'

'Old bloke is worth squillions, I suppose?' said Rob in that lacklustre way, fiddling with the phone in his hand.

Whom was he texting at this time of night? wondered Jeremy. When I walked in just now. Or was he just catching up on messages?

Then he found the words; not the perfect ones, perhaps, but something approximate.

'I do understand,' he said, 'how bored you must be out here at Abbotsfield. Frankly, I'm sorry we ever bought this house. We had some idea about fresh air and country peace and quiet. A place for your mum's studio. But, of course, at your age you don't want peace and quiet. You want a bit of life.'

'This isn't leading up to asking me if I've thought any more about going for a university place next year?' Rob stared at him with suspicion. 'Because I haven't.'

'Why not?' asked his father.

'Studying what?'

Jeremy indicated the silent mobile phone in his son's hand. 'Some sort of technology.'

'Not my scene, uni,' said Rob.

Jeremy suddenly felt very tired. Tired from his weekend excursion, from his day in the office, from his wretched train journey, from life generally. From sorting out problems at home and problems other people had at their homes or in their businesses. Too tired to cope any longer with any of it.

'OK,' he said. 'Well, I'm off back to bed. Goodnight.'

He walked out of the kitchen, vaguely aware of Rob's surprised expression, but not caring.

He had been mistaken in thinking he hadn't woken his wife. The bedside light was switched on and she was sitting against propped pillows, waiting for him.

'I was just—' he began feebly.

'Leave him alone!' she interrupted fiercely. 'You'll make things worse.'

'What things worse?' he retorted, suddenly angry. 'How can it be any worse?'

'He needs time.' She twisted to thump the pillows behind her. 'He doesn't need interrogating by you.'

'Laura, he's got to understand—'

'No, *you've* got to understand. If you're going to start jumping out from behind doors in the middle of the night, the moment he gets home, he'll . . . he'll leave!'

'Leave and go where?' retorted Jeremy.

'That's just it, isn't it? We don't know. As long as he's here, we know where he is and, eventually, we'll get this sorted out. He needs time.'

Laura lay down, with her back turned to him. 'Switch out the light!' she said in a muffled voice from the pillows.

Jeremy switched out the bedside light, as bid. When I was a little kid, he thought, I was afraid that some faceless, nameless threat lurked out there in the darkness. It was shapeless, that was one of the worst things about it. I didn't even know what it looked like. All I knew was that it was there and watched me, waiting. I would switch on the light and see for myself it wasn't there. But it is *still* there. I can sense its presence and almost make out its hovering shape. Just as I knew it was there when I was five years old, I have no doubts now.

Chapter Five

Sometimes in winter there is a brief moment when the weather seems to forget where it is with regard to the calendar, and allows a few hours of unseasonal sunshine. This was the case this morning. Callum had brought outstanding paperwork up to date. This was a resented necessity as far as he was concerned. But he'd done it; and was rewarding himself with taking a break for a cup of coffee. The wind was still cold, so he wore his jacket; but sat in his yard with his back to the wall of the cottage, mug in hand. The sun had warmed bricks behind him and the heat permeated his jacket pleasantly. He felt reasonably at peace with the world for the first time since he'd found the guy in the churchyard. It had only been a few days ago, but it seemed as though it had been longer because so much had happened since then. It had been a hectic and confusing time and he appreciated the moment of tranquillity.

He didn't require Gus's help today, and the shrouded form of his helper's motorbike was missing from the yard.

This meant Gus was out of Abbotsfield somewhere about his mysterious other activities, or just visiting any traveller friends who'd turned up in the neighbourhood. Callum didn't care where he was. Gus would reappear when needed. Callum leaned his head back against the brickwork behind him, and closed his eyes.

He was doomed not to enjoy his moment of leisure for long. The gate to the yard scraped open and someone came through it, invading his space. He'd heard no car so it was someone local, and as it wasn't Gus, that left a very short list of possible visitors. He had a pretty good idea who this was, so kept his eyes shut and waited for the caller to make the first approach.

'Callum?' asked a voice tentatively.

'Yes, Rob?' replied Callum, still with his eyes shut. 'What can I do for you?'

'I thought I'd just call round . . . but if you're busy . . .' Rob's voice tailed away.

'As you can see, I'm taking a break. But if you want to make yourself a cup of coffee or tea or something, and find a chair, you're welcome to join me.'

I'm stretching a point, he thought. He's not welcome. He's a nuisance. But he was going to turn up sooner or later; and it saves me going to find him. Eventually, I'd have to do that. He sipped his coffee and waited.

Rob was a noisy blighter. He rattled the kettle and dropped something on the draining board, scraped the legs of a kitchen chair along the tiled floor and through the back door, banging it against the frame, and eventually arrived beside Callum. 'You haven't gone to sleep, have you?' he asked anxiously.

Callum opened his eyes. 'Chance would be a fine thing, the racket you make! If I'd nodded off, I'd have dropped my mug.'

'Oh, right, yes.'

Callum waited for his caller to continue, but there was only silence, so he had to open his eyes and acknowledge Rob's presence formally. The young man perched awkwardly on the chair and was staring at Callum in a mix of dread and supplication. His dark hair was long enough to cover his ears and make a ragged fringe along his jawline. His skin had an unhealthy pallor and he was, in Callum's opinion, seriously underweight. He hadn't shaved in a few days and there was a smudge of dark hair along his upper lip.

'You look a wreck,' said Callum without rancour, 'and please tell me you aren't growing a moustache!'

'What?' His visitor looked startled. 'No!'

'That's something, I suppose. What do you want?'

'Well, I, it's a bit difficult. I need to talk to you.'

'Yes, you do,' agreed Callum. He drained the remains of his coffee and set his mug on the ground beside him. 'Go on, then.'

Rob drew a deep breath. 'You had the cops here a couple of days ago, didn't you? I mean, they came to see you. Mum told me.'

'Yes, they did. And you nearly ploughed into them on that bike of yours. We don't get much traffic through

Abbotsfield, but we do get some, so don't roar out of here as if you're in some kind of race. Be more careful.'

'Did you tell them it might have been me, my bike?' asked Rob nervously.

'No. If you do it again, I shall.'

'Right, well, thanks, anyway. You found that body in the churchyard, didn't you?'

'I did. I'm not giving you the gory details. The cops are investigating and I'm keeping shtum on their orders. But that's not what's brought you, is it? Well, you're curious, that's fair enough. But something else is worrying you.'

Rob said nothing so Callum drew a deep breath and went on, 'There's a question you want to ask me, but you're afraid of saying more than you should.'

No reply.

'OK, let me ask you a question. What on earth were you doing hanging about in the churchyard last night, around eleven thirty, just before the pubs turn out?'

'You recognised me, then?' Rob asked miserably.

'Of course I recognised you! Who else runs like a demented spider, when disturbed?' Rob opened his mouth but Callum continued, silencing him. 'Before you ask me another daft question, I didn't tell the police I thought it might be you. But you have used up my entire store of good will as far as you're concerned. Anything more and I report the lot, in detail, to the Law.'

'I'm grateful,' mumbled Rob.'

'So you should be. I've got enough on my mind without having to cover up for you. Don't kid yourself I've done that because I'm worried about you, or care a hoot what you do. I'm not. I'm worried about your poor mum, who is a very nice lady and deserves better than having you cause problems. You should think about her.'

Stung, Rob flushed and snapped, 'Well, all right! But I didn't know you and your girlfriend would be making out in the churchyard at night. Downright kinky, if you ask me.'

'First of all, I don't ask you. Secondly, she's not my girlfriend and thirdly, we were not "making out" as you choose to call it.'

'You were holding hands. You were wandering among the graves like a couple of extras in an *Addams Family* film. How weird is that?'

'She'd already spotted you lurking under the trees and the hand-holding was to avoid spooking you. But you bolted, anyway. You're lucky she didn't catch you. She's a cop, quick on her feet, and trained to deal with fleeing suspects.'

'*You* didn't chase after me!' said Rob astutely. 'You left the action stuff to her.'

'Not my job. It *is* hers. But if it happens again, I will happily lend a hand. What on earth were you doing in the churchyard that late, anyway?'

'What were you?'

'I was assisting the Law in its inquiries. You were lurking on the wrong side of a police cordon.'

'Well, there's been a murder, hasn't there?' retorted Rob defensively. 'It's not like we get a lot of those around here. I was curious to see where you found the body, but the cops have the place all taped off, like you said. I couldn't go there in daylight. I had to go after dark.'

'Oh, right! It's OK for you to prowl around among the dead at night, but not for me to take a short cut through there, is that it?'

'I was just *curious*. Well, thanks, anyway, for not saying anything to the police.'

'Just don't forget! Next time I will tell them whatever I know. And if it becomes necessary, I'll also tell them I suspected it might have been you last night. So, keep out of trouble.'

Rob stood up and went into the kitchen to leave his mug on the draining board. When he came back, he hovered for a few moments by Callum's chair.

'What else?' growled Callum.

'Mum and Dad want me to try for university.'

Callum stared at him, nonplussed. 'This has something to do with me?'

'No, only, I'd rather do something else, like you.'

'I'm not having you work with me! I've got Gus and I don't need anyone else.'

'OK,' mumbled Rob and shambled off.

Callum sighed and got up to go into the kitchen. 'You know something, Grandma?' he told the wedding photograph. 'Life is getting far too complicated.'

Marcus Liddell rang Jeremy at his office. That annoyed Jeremy even before the conversation began. Why did his cousin assume Jeremy could just drop whatever he was doing and listen to Marcus's woes?

'Don't mind me ringing you at work, do you?' Marcus asked in a perfunctory sort of way.

Jeremy wanted to shout down the line, 'Yes!' Instead he asked, 'All well at home now?'

Marcus's sigh was audible in his ear. 'I really wish I could say it was, Jerry.'

'Look, Marcus old chap,' began Jeremy. 'I can't come haring up to the Lake District again so soon—'

'Oh, no, no! Of course you can't. I really appreciate it that you took the time to come recently. Fiona is very grateful, too.' Fiona was his wife. 'You know what the situation is, so I can't talk about it with anyone else.'

'I'm afraid there's not a lot of time I can give you now,' interrupted Jeremy. 'A client has an appointment at eleven and I need to prepare . . .'

'Oh, I quite understand, Jerry. It's just that there's been a development of sorts.'

'Regarding the doctor's receptionist?'

'Oh, no, no! He's given up that idea, if it was ever in his head. No, the crafty old blighter has found another way.'

'Another way to do what?'

'Find a wife.'

'Marcus,' Jeremy said patiently. 'Will you just consider the possibility that Uncle Philip is *not* trying to launch into matrimony again?'

'I think I know my father. And I know what he's up to!' was the testy retort.

'So, what other way has he found?'

'Ah!' said Marcus in triumph. 'He's got himself coopted on to the parochial church council.'

'Didn't know he was regular churchgoer.' Jeremy couldn't conceal his surprise.

'He hasn't been. He's been a church festivals attendee. Christmas, Easter, All Souls, when he goes along to light a candle in memory of Mum. That sort of thing. But he's realised that church is a good place to find widows.'

'You make him sound like a serial killer.'

'And on the parochial church council are a couple of fine examples: strong-minded ladies of respectable background, comfortable means and steely intent. The only thing lacking in their lives is a man to organise. They're all terrific organisers. They've got their eye on him. He's got his choice. Just you wait and see, Jerry! He'll pick one of them and marry her.'

'Then I shouldn't worry, Marcus,' said Jeremy ruthlessly. 'It sounds as if either of them would be excellent. Now, I've really got to prepare for the client. He'll be here in twenty minutes. Love to Fiona. Goodbye!' He put the phone down.

'You are a thoroughgoing pest, Marcus,' he told the empty room. 'As if I haven't got enough to worry about.'

The walk from the railway station to the Old Vicarage took Meredith about ten minutes. To take the car wouldn't cut much off the time because of the one-way system affecting part of the drive and the time to find a parking space. In the evening, as now, when every home-travelling commuter was trying get out of the station exit at the same time, there were the traffic lights to contend with. All in all, it was easier to walk. Good for your health, too, so walkers awarded themselves gold stars.

Meredith's glow of satisfaction at having done the right thing faded as she neared the front door of the Old Vicarage. There was someone waiting near the doorstep. They were reliant on the street-lighting at this time of a winter evening and that had to contend with the over-looming shadows of the churchyard yews beside and behind the house. This meant she couldn't make out the identity of the would-be caller. The waiting figure was a male, she was sure of that. He was a small man and he stood in a very neat and tidy way, not lounging, or 'hanging about', but stiff and still like a small sentry. The house behind him was dark. That meant Alan wasn't home yet. He wouldn't be long. He hadn't contacted her to let her know he would be late. But with all that had been happening recently, that small dark silent figure was disconcerting, even alarming. Instinctively, she slowed her step. He didn't move, just stood there like the toy soldier he resembled. She wondered if, when she finally reached him, he'd salute.

She stopped a few feet from him and waited. He didn't salute but he did speak. 'Mrs Markby?'

'Yes,' Meredith said. She hadn't intended to say anything more. But all those years of consular training kicked in and she added, 'Can I help you?'

'My name is Charles Garret,' he said. 'I believe both my

wife and my sister have called on you. I came to apologise and to explain.'

'Felicity and Melissa,' said Meredith. She repressed a smile. Relief at realising who he was made her want to grin like the Cheshire Cat.

'That's it,' he said, more brightly. He sounded grateful that she'd remembered.

People do like you to remember names, she thought. Fear of rejection is so often preceded by a worry that you won't know who they are, or have met and forgotten them, which is worse. Then they will have to explain their identity before they can even begin to explain the problem. As an ex-consul, she knew that, too. It made her realise that for both their recent visitors, Felicity and Melissa Garret, coming to the house had been an ordeal. Meredith felt sudden embarrassment and regret for the way both women had been turned away.

A chill wind blew a gust of icy breath around them, and dead leaves from the churchyard trees were caught up and tossed towards them, rattling around their feet as they fell to the pavement.

'You had better come inside, Mr Garret,' she said. 'Have you been waiting long?'

'Oh, no, no,' he assured her. 'Only a little while, perhaps half an hour.'

Half an hour on a cold evening standing doggedly by the front door of an empty house, waiting. Suddenly, Meredith knew that whatever it was that troubled little Mr Garret, it was serious.

'Then you'd like a cup of tea,' she said. 'I know I would.'

He followed her into the house, repeatedly apologising and thanking her for her kindness.

'My husband will be home shortly,' she said, as a way of calling a halt to all this. As she spoke, she wondered what Alan would make of coming home to find the Garret family – or its troubles – had progressed from the doorstep to the large Victorian drawing room.

The room, once filled with knick-knacks and solid nineteenth-century furniture, and with oil paintings on its walls, was now filled with the motley collection of furniture and objects gathered by Alan and herself over the years before they married. Its hearth, where a blazing fire would once have been tended by a parlourmaid, now housed a gas fire. Meredith lit it.

'It'll warm up the room pretty quickly,' she told her visitor. 'It's very efficient, even if it's not in keeping with the house.'

'They're very expensive to keep warm, old houses,' said Mr Garret sadly. 'I own such a building. Mine is actually Regency, you know. My great-great-grandfather acquired it as nearly new. It has been lived in by our family ever since.'

'Goodness,' said Meredith genuinely impressed. 'It's rare for one family to occupy a house from new, for so many generations, I mean.'

'Mine is the last,' said Mr Garret. 'Felicity, my wife, and I have no children. My sister Melissa, of course, never married.' He paused. 'It's difficult to decide which of those two things have caused the most problems.'

He sat on the sofa, still wearing his coat. Meredith could now see it was a very dark grey gabardine, almost black. It was buttoned up to his neck, the white collar of his shirt just peeping above it. His posture was upright and unmoving, knees together, feet in well-polished shoes neatly placed one beside the other, his hands folded in his lap. His complexion was very pale, his grey hair cut very short. He wore rimless spectacles. She suddenly found herself wondering whether, by profession, he was or had been an undertaker. She looked at his clasped hands. They, too, were very white and the skin looked soft. She started thinking about embalming fluid and was relieved to hear the sound of Alan's key in the lock.

'Here's my husband,' she said to the visitor. 'I'll just let him know you're here and then I'll get that tea.'

Alan, in the hall, was taking off his coat. He turned from hanging it up to look at her with raised eyebrows. She realised he'd heard her talking to a third person.

'Who's here?' he asked in a low voice.

As quietly, Meredith told him, 'Charles Garret.'

'Felicity and Melissa?'

'Felicity's husband. I think he's come to apologise.'

'If that's all it is . . .' murmured Alan.

'I'll fetch the tea. The poor man had been waiting outside for half an hour before I arrived.'

When she returned with the tea tray, Charles Garret had been persuaded by Alan to unbutton his coat, even if he hadn't taken it off. The room was much warmer already, the gas fire's jolly orange glow brightening the whole area, except for the far corners that remained obstinately shadowy. Beneath his coat, she could now see that their visitor wore a dark grey pullover. It was impossible to rid her mind of the notion that he must be or have been an undertaker.

'Mr Garret,' said Alan, 'has just been telling me that he was born in the town and has lived here all his life, in a house his family has owned since the early eighteen hundreds.'

This gave Meredith her chance to ask. She had to know. 'Are you also in business in the town, Mr Garret?'

'Oh, I'm retired now!' he said quickly. 'It's meant I am at home so much more and I've realised . . .' His voice tailed away. 'I should have realised before,' he finished. 'I blame myself; I really do.'

'What line of business were you in?' Meredith asked. It would bother her until she knew, and she wouldn't abandon the opportunity to find out.

'What? Oh, I was a butcher,' he said.

'A butcher!' exclaimed Meredith. It came out more loudly than intended, and she saw Alan glance at her in surprise. She couldn't help looking at the soft white skin of his hands as she handed the visitor his cup of tea. A butcher. A lifetime spent handling bloody cuts of meat. That was why the skin had that texture, the fresh blood so much more efficient than any hand cream. Wasn't there once a mad Austrian countess who'd bathed in it to preserve her fine skin?

'The shop is still in the town,' the visitor was saying. 'Still with our name over the door. But it's a charity shop now.'

'Oh, I know it!' exclaimed Meredith. 'But I didn't connect the name. I should have done.'

'Oh, no, no reason at all. We are not the only family by the name of Garret in the town. Although none of the others, as far as I have been able to establish, is related to us.'

He then began to sip his tea and didn't speak again until the cup was empty. He set it down and resumed his tale.

'Melissa and I were both born in the house. We also had an older brother, Edward, but he later joined the Army and left the area. He died a few years ago. His wife predeceased him. They had no children. I married later in life than is usual. I brought Felicity to the family home. Melissa naturally remained. She'd always lived there, never married, and had nowhere else to go. It's always been her home.'

How quickly, thought Meredith, can a family with three children and every prospect of future generations carrying the name forward be reduced to three elderly people dwelling together in one house! She wondered whether Charles was thinking the same thing. He had fallen silent and appeared unsure how to continue.

To help restart the conversation, Meredith asked, 'How did you meet your wife?'

'Oh!' Charles Garret blinked as if he'd dropped off and been suddenly woken. 'Oh, yes, met. Well, at the local

Drop-In. It's a sort of club that meets during the day and it's for pensioners, really. But anyone getting on a bit can drop in – that's how it got its name. The visitors don't *have* to be drawing the old age pension or any other kind, just getting on, and needing a bit of company, get out of the house . . . meet new people. It's not easy when you're older. At the Drop-In they can make new friends, chat, have a cup of tea. From time to time, we run a little event: a whist drive, something of that sort. I have been involved in the running of it for some years. That's how I got to know Felicity, my wife. We got along very well. It seemed a good idea to become a couple. And it was, still is, a good idea.' He faltered. 'Or perhaps it wasn't.'

Markby, who had been listening closely, now asked, 'The fly in the ointment, as you might say, did that turn out to be your sister?'

Meredith was startled because it wasn't like Alan to be tactless. All those years questioning witnesses and suspects, she thought.

Charles hadn't taken any offence, nor did he appear to be startled at the question. Instead, he almost appeared grateful to be asked.

Meredith saw that she had misjudged her husband. This is something Charles wants to tell us about, she thought, but he didn't know how to broach a delicate matter. Alan realised that and helped him out. He was quicker on the uptake than me.

'It hasn't been all her fault!' Charles leaned forward to emphasise the words, his hands still on his knees. 'Perhaps, before I married, I should have given more thought as to what that would mean to Melissa. You see, following the death of our mother, a very long time ago, my sister had always run the household. Seen to the meals, decided on colour schemes if any redecorating was to be done, kept it tidy . . .' He fell silent.

'And when you brought your new wife home, your sister felt threatened,' Meredith said. 'And your new wife was longing to take the house in hand and personalise it. Am I right?'

He looked at her gratefully. 'Yes, that's exactly it! I wasn't blind. I was aware of it. But I trusted that, in time, they'd sort things out between them. I was working then in the shop, so away all day. Besides, if I am honest, and I must be honest, I hid my head in the sand. I didn't want to know about any problem. But once I'd retired, of course, I couldn't escape it. They just didn't get on. Frankly, I believe that Melissa's resentment progressed to actual hatred of Felicity, though it is very hard to say such a thing of my sister. But she always had a – a very strong personality. I've sometimes wondered whether it would have been a good thing if she, as well as Edward, had joined the Army.'

'So, Melissa never worked?' Alan asked. 'From the financial viewpoint, that must have been – a problem.'

'She was a dressmaker,' said Charles. 'She was always clever with her hands. She made wedding dresses. Her reputation was high. But then, a few years ago, she developed arthritis in her fingers. She had to give up the dressmaking. She could still do odd bits of crochet, that sort of thing. But working with fine, expensive materials, that was out of the question. No longer a free hand in the house, no longer making the wedding dresses. The dress-making had brought her into contact with customers; given her a link to the outside world. I did understand that. When I retired from the shop, I also missed the customers and the chats with the regulars. But I now had a few shared interests with Felicity to replace it. When Melissa couldn't manage the scissors, or the fiddly decoration that had to be stitched on by hand, beadwork and so on, well, that was that. She had nothing. If Felicity weren't there, she'd have had the house entirely to herself, and she'd have looked after me. But that had also been taken from her.'

He sighed. 'My sister isn't one to suffer in silence. My wife doesn't have the same strong personality, although in her own quiet way, she doesn't give up. It's been awful. I should have put my foot down. Since I've been at home all day, after retirement, and seen how Melissa bullies Felicity, I do try to intervene. But I'm just not very good at it. But I have told them both that things must change!' He looked at them apologetically. 'I think that's why Felicity came here. She thought it was still the vicarage. She thought she could talk to the vicar; or he'd know someone she could talk to about it. I do apologise. Melissa came because she found out Felicity came. I have spoken to her very strongly.'

Meredith repressed the urge to say, *It's a bit late for that.* 'We do understand, Mr Garret,' she said.

'Well, thank you both for the tea and for listening,' he said. 'I mustn't take up any more of your time. I just wanted

119

to explain.' He was buttoning the gabardine coat. 'I wish you both a pleasant evening!'

And then he bustled out.

'I suppose,' said Meredith when they were alone, 'I ought to feel some sympathy for him, but I don't. He's been wilfully blind to the situation when he should have been standing up for his wife.'

'Perhaps he should have married a wife like mine?' suggested Alan. 'More than able to stand up for herself!'

Chapter Six

'Yes, yes!' agreed Markby a little testily, 'take it down by all means.'

'It' was the blue-and-white tape fluttering around the border of the churchyard.

Steve Kendal asked, 'What about the notice, sir?'

Markby stared morosely at the sign asking members of the public to contact the police if they had noticed anything unusual or suspicious recently in the area. 'Anyone been in touch?'

'So far, no one reports seeing anything on the night of the murder, I'm afraid, sir. Two sets of local undertakers are anxious to know when burials can recommence in the new cemetery,' added Kendal. 'That local nature group I told you about is giving me grief. That bloke, Finch, is upset because they had planned a winter ramble through the old churchyard. I ask you, who goes for a ramble in winter, hoping to find interesting creatures? It's full, so Finch tells me, of fauna and flora. His idea of "flora" is what most of us call weeds. But one man's meat is another man's poison, as they say. Same goes for the "fauna". Not everyone views the wildlife as he does, mind you! Several people have complained to us about the mice and rats.'

'Rats?'

'Yessir. They say there is vermin "overrunning the place", in the area of the old churchyard in particular.'

'Why are they complaining to us? We're the police. We're not a firm of exterminators.' Markby shook his head.

'I tell them that,' said Kendal morosely. 'But they say they've complained to the church and to the council and had no joy. Oh, and an elderly woman name of Benton, living in that house over there –' Kendal pointed across the churchyard to a tall, narrow, Victorian villa bordering the far boundary – 'she complained about courting couples chasing one another around the graves. The words are hers, sir!'

'And when was this?' asked Markby mildly. From the periphery of his vision, he could see Santos fidgeting about and trying to look inconspicuous at the same time. She wasn't being successful.

'Two nights ago,' said Kendal.

'This woman, Benton, didn't see anything on the night of the murder, by any chance?'

'No such luck, sir. She was interviewed the next day when we conducted a house to house. That's when she complained about the rats. Then, yesterday, she called out to me from her doorstep as I was going past; and told me she'd once again seen courting couples *up to no good*.

The words are hers, sir. I don't know if she really saw anyone. The thing is, people start to imagine things, once something like this has happened. Especially as I told her I wasn't interested in the mice and rats. In a couple of days' time, I shouldn't be surprised if she doesn't contact us to say she's seen a flying saucer.'

'Just so long as we make a note of it, whatever it is and however nutty it sounds. As regards the police tape, I dare say it has served its purpose. But leave the notice in place, reminding people we are still interested in information. Someone may yet come forward.' Markby paused. 'I am worried, I admit, that we haven't found the victim's mobile phone. We know Gus Toomey saw him using one in local pubs. No phone. No murder weapon. I have a nasty feeling that someone has been ahead of us and done a pretty thorough clean-up of the scene.'

Kendal reddened. 'It's a big area, sir. We've had a lot of men on it. But when you look at the place, the state of it . . .' He gestured around at the jumble of trees, grass and weeds, graves, flowerpots and general debris. 'It's like the needle in the haystack.'

'I know, Steve. Take the tape down and pray that a member of the public eventually comes forward.'

Kendal set off to organise removal of the blue-and-white tape, and Markby turned to Santos.

'You still seem to be favouring that injured leg, Sergeant.'

'Am I, sir? It's not really troubling me. It's come out in a nice purple bruise, but that's it.'

123

'Get it checked out if it continues to bother you.'

They had been moving towards the main gates of the churchyard as he spoke. They had not been unobserved. The door of the house indicated by Kendal opened and an elderly woman descended the steps to the pavement. She was tall and thin with grey hair untidily pinned up in a knot; she wore a baggy jacket over a sweater and an equally baggy skirt. She approached them in a stately manner, slow but purposeful, and appeared to be holding out something in her hands, like an offering. Markby's heart sank. He recognised the type. To his alarm, she recognised him.

'Ah, Superintendent Markby,' she said. 'You remember me? Celia Benton. I'm your nearest neighbour, now that you have moved into the old vicarage. I never approved of it being sold off. But at least respectable people such as you and your wife have moved into it.'

The problem was, he didn't remember her, or not just at this moment when he was concentrating on something else.

She'd reached them where they stood and halted. The object she was holding in her hands could now be seen to be a pottery ornament, a bowl of brightly painted roses. He wondered whether he was supposed to take it from her. But why she should think he'd want such a thing he had no idea.

'Although one sees very little of your wife!' she finished. Her tone was part curiosity and part reproach.

'She works in London and commutes every weekday.'

Markby knew he sounded rather brisk, but they had had

enough random callers at the Old Vicarage so far. In addition, he was beginning to wonder whether Mrs Benton was slightly eccentric. She still held out the pottery roses.

'Mm,' she said. 'I suppose that is necessary. Two of your officers came to see me,' she continued briskly in an abrupt change of subject, 'with regard to the dreadful event that took place in the churchyard. I believe this young woman was one of them.' Her gaze switched abruptly to Santos and there was challenge in it.

'Yes, I was,' agreed Santos, sounding as official as she could.

'I remember you,' said Mrs Benton, now gazing at her thoughtfully.

Santos chose not to reply to this and Mrs Benton returned her attention to Markby. 'I did not see anything on the night of the murder,' she said regretfully. 'Or I should have raised the alarm.'

'Quite so, Mrs Benton,' he told her.

'Although things are always going on in there.' She half turned towards the gates of the churchyard and extended the pottery roses towards them. 'I did tell the other officer, the inspector, that courting couples frequent the place. It is quite inappropriate.' She bent a stern eye on Santos again. 'Disrespectful,' she said. 'There was a couple there just the other evening, fooling around, chasing one another, despite the police tape.' She pursed her mouth and subjected Beth to renewed scrutiny. 'One of them was very like your officer here in build.'

'Inspector Kendal made a note of your complaint,' said

Markby smoothly. 'But we are conducting a murder investigation and lesser problems such as you mention should be reported elsewhere.'

'In any case,' continued Mrs Benton determinedly, rolling over any protest he might make, 'that is not the matter I wanted to ask you about.'

Santos suppressed a sigh of relief. Markby wondered what was coming now.

'Both of my late parents are buried in the churchyard,' announced Mrs Benton. She leaned forward confidingly and added with a definite note of pride, 'They were among the last burials before the purchase of the new cemetery. I look after the plot but at this time of year, there is no point in placing flowers on it. They wouldn't last five minutes. So, when I saw this, in the florist's window, I thought it would be just the thing to put there until the weather gets warmer.' She held up the pottery flower group for their closer inspection.

'Very nice,' Markby said, privately thinking it lurid. 'Well, Mrs Benton . . .'

'But there is police tape around the area warning the public to keep out. So, am I permitted to place this bowl of flowers on my family plot? Or must I stay out?' she concluded defiantly.

'Oh, please go and place your tribute. The tape will be taken down later today, anyway,' Markby told her. 'Now, if you will excuse me . . .'

'I should not like to be told I am interfering with a scene of crime!' she told them fiercely.

'Quite. Look, DS Santos here will go with you and explain your presence to anyone who asks.'

It was Beth's opinion that the superintendent then bolted. He certainly walked away very quickly.

'Come along, then!' Mrs Benton ordered her.

Santos followed the woman resentfully. Across the churchyard she could see Steve Kendal in conversation with a couple of constables. He was presumably telling them to take down the tape.

'Here!' said Mrs Benton and stopped so suddenly that Santos almost cannoned into her. 'I've brought a trowel, too, in case there are any weeds. They do grow, even in cold weather.' She produced the tool in question from her pocket. 'The only way to tackle weeds is to keep them down all the year round.'

'I understand a local naturalist thinks some of them are of interest. He has already expressed concern to the officer in charge here, about our search,' said Santos.

There was something about Mrs Benton's hectoring manner that made her want to start an argument. 'We've assured him we are treating the churchyard with the greatest respect, as hallowed ground.' Well, if Kendal hadn't exactly said those words to the outraged Finch, Santos was reasonably sure Markby would, if Finch appeared again with his protests.

'I suppose you're talking of Basil Finch,' said Mrs Benton brusquely. 'I knew his grandmother. I understand he has quite a reputation as a naturalist. He contributes articles to magazines. Well, I dare say there are many spots in the area where there are interesting plants. But, whatever Basil's opinion, this is not one of them.'

Santos's momentary interest in picking a fight with Mrs Benton had flickered out. 'Which is your grave?' she asked, more to be polite and soothe the old bat than out of real curiosity.

'It's not *my* grave,' snapped Mrs Benton pedantically. '*I'm not dead!* And when I do die, I am told I shall have to be buried over there, in the new cemetery. It's very annoying.' She flung out the hand that was not holding the pottery flowers, and pointed into the distance.

'Oh, dear,' said Beth, gaining a suspicious glance from the lady.

Mrs Benton's late parents' resting place was among the tidier burial spots with a layer of marble chippings over it, contained within the granite border. It was very similar to the one that had been, literally, Beth's downfall. For a moment she had been worried it would prove to be the same one. But no, she decided in relief, this plot was a double one. The one she'd caught her foot on had been a single one.

'All right, then?' she asked the woman brightly. 'I'll leave you to it. I see my colleagues over there.' With that she set off determinedly towards the figure of Kendal.

'Who's that?' asked Kendal suspiciously as she reached him.

'She's placing a bowl of pottery roses on a grave. Mr Markby said she could.'

'She can do what she likes,' said Kendal, 'as far as I'm

concerned. This lot's coming down, anyway.' He indicated the tape.

'She's coming over here!' called out one of the constables with Kendal. 'She looks a bit upset. She's waving something.'

Kendal and Santos turned to see what was happening. Mrs Benton was indeed approaching at a much faster pace than Beth would have thought natural for her. She seemed to be agitated. Her hair had escaped from the pins holding it into a bun, and fluttered around her head. She held both arms in the air and in one hand she was clasping an object.

'Bloody hell!' exclaimed the constable. 'The old girl's got a knife!'

'Stop there!' shouted Kendal. 'Just stand still and drop your weapon!'

'It's not mine, you silly man!' yelled Mrs Benton. 'It was in my family plot. I dislodged it when I started weeding. Someone had pushed it down among the chippings. I told you, all sorts of improper behaviour goes on in here!'

'Forensics have the knife at the moment, sir,' said Kendal. He'd come to Markby's office to report the churchyard now open to the general public again.

'Well, it may turn out to be the murder weapon, or it may not,' Markby replied. 'Let's suppose, for the time being, that it is. Why did someone make an attempt to hide it among the marble chippings on that grave? It would have to be that woman Benton's family plot,' he added gloomily, 'and she would have to pick it up and handle it, removing it from the exact spot. Did you take her fingerprints, Steve?'

'After some argument, sir, she agreed to come to the local station. We had to keep assuring her she was not a suspect. We just wanted her dabs for elimination.'

'Now I shall have her ringing my doorbell every evening, wanting to know the latest news of our inquiry. I'll soon have to put a notice on my door, asking people to form an orderly queue,' grumbled Markby.

'She's making a terrible fuss,' said Kendal. 'I think you should know, because she's talking of contacting the chief constable and her MP. Normally, I wouldn't take much notice of that. I'd just put it down to her being potty. But she's the sort of person who would know all those people socially.'

'It's not our fault if the murderer, or any other person, hid a knife among the chippings,' said Markby.

'It's not so much that . . .' Kendal was looking uncomfortable. 'It's because after we found the knife, we cleared all the chippings from the grave to make sure there was nothing else hidden among them. We put them all back. She stood over us and made sure we did. But she's very upset and says it was desecration.'

'Well, I can't help that!' said Markby briskly. 'She can complain until she's blue in the face, and she probably will. But we had to make a thorough check. Tell forensics the matter is urgent.'

'I was hoping we'd find the murdered man's mobile phone,' said Kendal. 'But it's not turned up. We could, I suppose, search all the other graves with those marble chippings on them, just in case the murderer hid the phone the same way he hid the knife – if it is the knife.'

'Remember that the killer had very little time before Henderson appeared on the scene. I'd be surprised if he had time to hide the phone as well as the knife. But you'd better get back to that churchyard and check out the other graves with a layer of chippings for a mobile phone. Oh, ask Santos to come and see me, would you?'

Kendal withdrew, his expression showing both surprise and suspicion.

'The superintendent wants to see you,' he told Santos. 'What's it all about?'

'I don't know,' lied Beth. She had a good idea, but she wasn't going to share it with Steve Kendal. It would lead to the whole escapade of the chase through the churchyard becoming public knowledge to everyone who worked in the building. She'd never be allowed to forget it.

Markby greeted her with, 'Just close the door, Beth. Then come and sit down.'

She did so, and when she turned back towards his desk he was leaning back in his chair and surveying her calmly enough but in a way that made her feel more than a little nervous. She remembered to sit down, as requested, and being at a lower level made things worse. He knew that, of course.

'Is it about that Benton woman, sir?' she asked. Get in first; that was the first rule of defence. 'We had to search all the chippings.'

'Yes, you did. I've already been through that with Steve

Kendal. What I want to go through with you is your midnight escapade with Henderson in the churchyard.'

'With respect, sir, we went through all that in your kitchen, the same night.'

'That was before the discovery of a knife hidden on a grave plot. Of course, we don't know yet whether it's the murder weapon, but forensics should be getting back to us on that today or tomorrow. In the meantime, we're working on the assumption that it is the murder weapon and something led to the murderer hiding it in the way he did. Doesn't that strike you as odd?'

'Yes,' admitted Beth.

'The killer and his victim meet in the new cemetery near the gap in the hedge where there used to be a stile. There's a confrontation and a stabbing. The victim staggers off into the old churchyard, following the line of the wall, and collapses on a grave, propped up against the headstone. There he dies and is found very shortly afterwards by Callum Henderson, on his way home from the pub. Henderson climbs the wall as part of his usual route back to Abbotsfield, and nearly lands on the victim. We know the rest.

'But the killer has also left the scene, or we must assume he has. Henderson saw no sign of anyone else. Why didn't the killer take the murder weapon with him? He could then have disposed it somehow, hidden it, well away from the scene of the crime. Any comments, Sergeant?'

'Perhaps the killer didn't leave the scene immediately, sir,' Beth offered. 'Perhaps he followed the victim to make sure of him. But he sees the victim collapse, or he sees Callum – Henderson – climb the wall down into the churchyard. So he turns and makes off. He's more worried about being seen by a witness than anything else.'

'If he's still carrying the knife, he can ward off an unarmed man,' Markby pointed out.

'Yessir, but Callum will have seen him. OK, it's at night, but there's moonlight. If he's close enough, he knows Callum will get a good look at him.'

'Well, yes, but I doubt an identification made in those circumstances would stand up in court.' (Unless, thought Markby uneasily, the killer has reason to think Henderson might recognise him, even in such poor light.)

'The killer doesn't stop to reason that out, sir. Or can't risk it.'

'All right, let's go with that. What does the killer do next?'

'He doesn't want to be caught with the weapon still on him and he doesn't want just to throw it away to be found, so he hides it quickly among the marble chippings on a grave. His intention is to return at a later date to retrieve the murder weapon and dispose of it somewhere he feels is more secure.'

'Which brings us neatly to the person you saw hiding under the trees while making your midnight visit to the churchyard with Henderson. There's police activity over the whole area during the day. Our killer can't get back immediately to retrieve the knife. As he waits, he grows increasingly nervous. The police are searching. He doesn't know how thorough they'll be. Instead he decides to return during the night. But either he couldn't remember which grave it was he used to hide it, or before he found it, he saw you and Henderson climb over the wall. By then he must be thinking that churchyard is one of the busiest places for miles around. He hasn't time to do more than take to the shadows under the trees.' Markby allowed himself a brief grin. 'But he hadn't counted on a lynx-eyed police officer conducting her own investigations with the help of the finder of the body.'

Santos spoke quietly. 'Perhaps he avoided Callum catching sight of him. But he may have caught sight of Callum – and he may have recognised him. Callum doesn't work in an office unless he has to. He drives around all over the area. He works out of doors where people pass by and see him. Or he may have done some landscaping work adjacent to wherever the killer works.'

Markby considered the possibility. 'You may be right, Santos. If you are, then sooner or later, he'll seek Henderson out.'

Steve Kendal had a visitor. To that point he'd been puzzling over what kind of confab the superintendent was having with a junior officer. 'Why not me?' he muttered. 'What's he got to talk to her about that I can't be present?'

The sound of someone uttering a discreet cough interrupted him and he looked up.

'Someone downstairs at the desk asking about a missing person, male,' said the uniform standing there.

'I understood you wanted to be told if anyone came in asking that sort of question.'

'Yes, well?' urged Kendal.

'She's a woman called Kylie Hooper.'

'Hooper?' exclaimed Kendal, leaping to his feet. 'Are you sure?'

'Yes, Inspector. She's down at the front desk and wants to talk to someone about her brother. He's missing, she reckons.'

Kylie Hooper was a sullen-looking, lank-haired, sturdily built woman. Kendal judged her to be in her thirties. As soon as he saw her, he knew this had to be Aaron Hooper's sister. She had the same flat features and lumpy nose. She wore a grubby anorak, leggings and scuffed boots. She stood before him, hands thrust into the pockets of her anorak, and scowled at him.

'My brother's missing. His name is Aaron and he lives with me. Well, for the past year he has, after he came down from London. He left in a hurry. London wasn't healthy for him, he said. He turned up on my doorstep, like a regular bad penny. He wanted to stay for a few weeks, but it turned into months.'

Kylie glowered across the desk at Kendal. 'Of course, I knew it wouldn't be just for a few weeks. Not if he was in any trouble, and he'd got people looking for him. I reckon they were; and he was afraid. It's always been the way with Aaron. He never had no friends, and he was always crossing the wrong guys.'

She sat back on the wooden chair in the interview room

and stared moodily at the cup of tea with which she'd been provided.

'These people who were looking for him,' said Kendal. 'Was he afraid they'd find him here in Bamford?'

'He was hoping they might forget about him, if he'd left London. They don't know about me, so wouldn't look here. That's why he came. I didn't want him living with me. He's always been a bloody nuisance, ever since he was a kid. Always in trouble. But he turned up and what can you do? He's family. So, I rented out my back bedroom to him, put all the kids together in the other room. Well, it's a bit of extra money, isn't it? I can always do with that. I got three kids and my boyfriend left us just before Christmas last. I don't know where he's gone. Christmas Eve he went, left me with nothing to cook for Christmas dinner but burgers and chips, with a box of mince pies for afters. I bought all the kids' presents in charity shops. I reckoned my boyfriend had got someone new. I'd suspected it for a while. She's welcome to him. He was always useless. I don't want him back. But it's left me pretty skint. I only got what the social gives me and the kids' allowance. So, when Aaron turned up, I told him he could stay if he paid me rent. At the time, I didn't know how long he was going to hang around, nor that he'd more than likely get himself murdered.'

What a family, thought Kendal. 'And you think your brother Aaron is the murdered man?'

'You got his body, ain't you?' continued Kylie.

'Well, we do have *a* body . . .' Kendal said cautiously. 'We're investigating a murder.'

'And you want anyone with information to come forward, don't you? It's in the local paper, out this morning. My neighbour give it me. Here.' She withdrew her right hand from the anorak pocket and handed him a folded sheet of newsprint. 'I tore it out and brought it with me,' she explained unnecessarily.

'You're quite right, Ms Hooper,' said Kendal. 'We do have, as you say, a body. We suspect it may be that of your brother. Would you be willing to make an identification?'

'What? Go and look at him?' she grumbled.

'Yes, we'd be obliged.'

'I ain't got no transport. I come on the bus.' She retrieved the sheet of newsprint and stuffed it back in her pocket. 'And I got plenty of other things to do. He was always a nuisance, like I said. And if this stiff you've got is Aaron, then he's still being a nuisance now he's dead. Besides, he's taken my son's bike. You haven't got that, too, have you? Because I want it back.'

'We'll drive you to the morgue,' Kendal said.

'It worked, sir!' said Kendal triumphantly to Markby, later. 'Someone was missing him and eventually came forward. Kylie Hooper has now identified the corpse as that of her brother Aaron, who has been living with her as an undeclared lodger. We thought he was Aaron Hooper, from the records. Now we have a member of the family confirming it. Plus, we know he was in hot water when he left London and there were people wanting to find him.

His sister says Hooper was "always crossing the wrong guys". Maybe those guys found him.'

'I'm not convinced, Steve,' Markby said. 'I'm sure his sister is correct in saying "people" were looking for him and he was hiding here. But if so, those were definitely not people he'd arrange to meet at dead of night in a spot as deserted as a burial ground. *If* he wanted to meet those old acquaintances, he'd want it to be in broad daylight with plenty of witnesses around. Much more likely, he'd have gone on the run again to avoid meeting them.'

'But we can release the victim's name now?'

'Go ahead. His sister will already be spreading the word.'

Chapter Seven

Callum was frying sausages and debating whether to open a tin of beans or put some frozen chips in the oven, or both. One of the things his grandmother had omitted to do was to teach him basic culinary skills. He'd been allowed to mash potatoes, he remembered. Frozen chips would never have featured on his grandmother's menu. But, even given that task, he hadn't taken to the art of the mashed potato with any enthusiasm. It had seemed a lot of work for such a bland result. It hadn't been oversight on Grandma's part that had left him dependent on the frying pan and tins. It was simply that, as a woman of her generation, she had assumed that the adult Callum would find himself a wife. She would have been more critical of his failure to do that than his inability to follow a recipe.

A knock at the back door coincided with one of the sausages bursting and spitting hot fat in his face. He jumped aside, swore, pushed the pan off the hob and stomped off to answer the knock, wondering who might want him at this time of the day, out of working hours and before any recreational trip to the pub. He opened it to find DS Beth Santos on his doorstep.

'Hello,' he said, with sinking heart. 'I didn't expect to see you. Come in, I'm cooking my supper.'

'I didn't have you down as a chef,' she said, following him back to the kitchen.

'I'm not, that's it!' He pointed at the frying pan. 'Do you want some?'

'I haven't come to beg a meal. I've come to tell you that we've confirmed the identity of the dead man you fell over in the churchyard. His name was Aaron Hooper. Mean anything to you?'

'No,' said Callum. With this athletic woman copper hovering at his shoulders, he decided to skip the oven chips. She'd probably lecture him on his diet. He settled for opening the can of beans. 'I've got nothing to add to my previous statement,' he added over his shoulder. 'That's police-speak, isn't it?'

'Do you know anything about drugs going down in the town?'

'No.' Callum shook the opened can vigorously over a saucepan and the beans fell out in an orange-brown lump.

'But it wouldn't surprise you to know that drugs were supplied around the town?'

'I'd be more surprised if you told me they weren't. They're on offer everywhere, aren't they? But they're not my scene. Do you mind if I eat while we talk?'

'Go ahead. I've come at a bad moment, obviously.'

'It's not a bad moment,' said Callum. 'But I'm hungry. You can sit there and talk as much as you like. Just let me eat while you're yammering on.'

'Only you seem to be a bit out of sorts,' Beth told him.

'*Out of sorts?*' Callum paused, fork mid-air. 'I'm more than out of sorts! I'm fed up to the back teeth. First, I find a dead bloke. Then I'm caught by Markby, with you in the churchyard in the middle of the night, and he gets the wrong idea.'

'I have explained to him about that,' Beth apologised.

'Now he sends you out here after I've had a day wrestling with paperwork and – various other problems.'

'He didn't send me,' she admitted. 'I've finished for the day, too, and I just came out to tell you we know who the dead man is. I thought you'd like to know.'

'Thanks! But I don't want to know anything. I don't want to be involved any more than I am already. Put me in the category of innocent bystander.'

'And because Markby thinks that the murderer might still have been nearby when you found the body.'

'Don't think that hasn't occurred to me,' said Callum indistinctly. 'And I told your boss so at the time.'

'The killer might have seen you. OK, you didn't see him. But, well, he might have got a good look at you. And, incidentally, you're not an innocent bystander. You're an important witness.'

'I'm being persecuted, that's what I am. Police harassment! If I ever have the misfortune to find another body anywhere, I'll keep the information to myself.'

His visitor looked towards the stove on which the frying pan still sat, with two sausages remaining in it. 'Actually, I haven't eaten yet, and if you really don't want those sausages . . .'

'The offer still stands,' said Callum with dignity. 'Help yourself. But you'll have to open another tin of beans. You'll find one in that cupboard.'

'I don't much care for baked beans, thank you,' she said from the stove. 'I'll just make a sandwich with these. You do have bread?'

'In that bin. And while you're there, you might as well put the kettle on.'

When they'd eaten and drunk the tea, Santos asked, 'I hope you're in a better mood now.'

'I wasn't in a bad mood when you came,' argued Callum. 'I was hungry, like I said. And I wasn't expecting you. I'm all right now.'

'Because I've got a favour to ask.'

Callum groaned. 'I knew it! I knew you hadn't driven out to Abbotsfield just to tell me the dead bloke's name. It'll be common knowledge already, I should think. Will be tomorrow, at least. What really brought you?'

'I thought you might be going out later to the Black Dog for a pint; and you'd be walking over the fields to get there, using the old right of way.'

'So what?'

'So, can I come with you?'

Callum stared at her. 'You're looking for a midnight stroll across the fields by the light of the silvery moon?'

'Yes, but just a straightforward walk. I promise I won't try and hold your hand again. Come on, Callum! No one would see us. Markby won't know.'

'And after we reach the pub, do I get a pint? Or have I got to turn round and escort you back immediately?'

'Of course you can have your pint, or two or three. You won't be driving. I won't come in with you. You needn't worry the barman will see you with a copper.'

'Oh, I'll be OK,' said Callum. 'But, if I stay in the Black Dog, how are you going to get back again to your car which is parked outside in the street here?'

'Easy. I can walk back myself, once you've shown me the track of the right of way across country.'

'You'd get lost on your own,' argued Callum.

'I've got a torch. I'll make a note of any landmarks.'

'You won't be able to do that by moonlight or even with a torch. What makes you think there will be any landmarks? It's open countryside. It's dark! Listen! I don't care if you spend all your free weekends orienteering. You'd get lost if you tried to find your way back to Abbotsfield alone. It's a mediaeval right of way; and it's hardly used. It's not a nicely laid out gravel path with signposts along it!' exclaimed the exasperated Callum.

'*You* find it,' she argued.

'I've been walking it since I was a kid. In summer, a couple of people from the cottages over the road might use it, during the day. Like our resident nature-lover, Basil Finch, on one of his guided rambles.'

'How can anyone "guide" a ramble?' asked Santos,

diverted. 'It's a contradiction in terms, surely? Ramble suggests roaming freely. Guiding—'

'I don't know,' said Callum, interrupting. 'And I don't care. Take it up with Basil. He calls them rambles.' He paused and grinned. 'You should see them in the summer. Baz at their head with a clipboard hung round his neck, pointing at goodness knows what, and his merry band following behind with their cameras and notebooks.'

'Which is his bungalow? The one with the rubbish in the front garden? I saw there was a supermarket trolley amongst all the rest. That could qualify as theft.'

'Only if you spend your life seeking out crimes and misdemeanours. How do you know whoever lives there didn't find the trolley already abandoned in a ditch?'

That annoyed his visitor. 'I didn't come here about that, anyway. I wouldn't be here at all if you hadn't managed to fall over a dead body,' she snapped.

'All right, all right! Basil lives in the first cottage you get to when you reach Abbotsfield, coming from town. It's got a couple of trees in the front garden, hung about with those wire containers for nuts, for the birds. But if you're thinking of asking him to guide you, forget it. Even Basil isn't barmy enough to go out at this time of year, and in darkness. You've only got the moon to help you. On cloudy nights, you're blind. The only other person I know who uses it sometimes is Gus. He's like me. He doesn't need a map or a torch. Instinct and experience tell him where he's headed.'

'I've got my mobile if I get lost.'

'You probably wouldn't get a signal.'

'You know, Callum,' she said seriously. 'I never had you down as a negative sort of person.'

'I am not negative!' denied Callum with dignity.

'So why are you making so many objections?'

'I am giving you practical advice.'

'Thanks. Advice noted. Now will you let me walk with you as far as the pub across the fields?'

After a brief silence, Callum asked, 'Why?'

'Why what?' She had a mulish look on her face. She wasn't going to give in.

'Don't act dumb with me. You're not dumb. Neither am I, by the way. Why do you want to do this? If you don't tell me the truth, I'm spending my evening sitting here watching telly. I'll give the pub a miss. You can go across the road and ask Basil to show you the way; and in the morning, I'll head up the search party to find you both.'

She heaved a sigh. 'OK, I've been thinking and I've drawn a rough map.' She dug into her pocket and withdrew a sheet of paper with a plan sketched on it in pencil. She placed it on the table and smoothed it out. 'Of course, I've had to work it out from my own observations. There are no security cameras covering the site. Nor have I taken any actual measurements. I've estimated it all.'

'How long did it take you to draw that?' asked Callum, interested – even impressed – despite himself.

'Never mind that! Now then, look.'

'I'm looking,' growled Callum. He knew he was going

to have to give in, and walk with her across the fields, but he was going to know why first.

'This square shape I've drawn,' she began, 'represents the churchyard. Now, that's a very big area. There must be a couple of hundred graves there at least. That's only counting the ones still visible and still clearly marked. I mean, with some sort of headstone letting you know who's in them. There are other signs of graves which have lost their markers. Some are now just sunken areas and some are more like hummocks.'

'They've been burying people there since the Middle Ages,' said Callum. 'What do you expect?'

She ignored the interruption. 'The shaded area on the right, on my map, is the new cemetery. It's much smaller; and was formerly a field. Down here under the bottom line of my diagram runs the road into the town centre. This is Markby's house, the Old Vicarage, on the right. The main area of the town is to the left. Got your bearings?'

Callum wanted to reply that yes, he had his bearings. He was beginning to wonder whether his visitor had hers. However, sarcasm on his part would not be welcome.

She was chattering on merrily. 'Abbotsfield, where we are now, is over here to the right of the town on my plan, and in between are the fields you walk across.'

'Until they build on them,' said Callum gloomily.

'Do you want me to explain or not? The Black Dog pub is behind the churchyard. See? In the lane of the same name which runs along the back of the churchyard. *You*, on your nightly visit to the pub, have to walk cross-country to this side of the churchyard, by which time you're in the town's fringes, among buildings. Then you climb into the churchyard over the wall around here somewhere, by my reckoning. There's a wonky little hut there. The maintenance men use it to store stuff. We opened it up when we were searching the area, or Steve Kendal did. He said it's got some really old tools in it, including a scythe. I shouldn't think anyone would still use that to cut the grass, do you?'

'Absolutely not!' muttered Callum. 'Need your head seeing to. It would take for ever.'

'Well, that hut would give you a bit of cover as you jump down.'

She tapped the paper. Callum made a sort of growl.

'Then, I guess, you cut across the corner of the churchyard between the graves, and climb over the far wall of the area to drop down into Black Dog Lane.'

'The cops don't need tracker dogs, do they? They've got you! What else am I supposed to do?'

'Well, returning to Abbotsfield, you take the same route, but in reverse. See? You have to climb two walls. One, to get into the churchyard. Another, to get out into the lane on the far side. On your homeward journey, you follow the same route in reverse. You climb into the churchyard, as we did the other night, from Black Dog Lane. Then you cut cornerwise, through the graves, to the other wall, nip over that and through a few houses on the other side and then – well, bingo! There's nothing between you and home but fields. Agreed?'

'Yes . . .' said Callum warily. 'Of course, I have to climb

147

two walls, one to get into the churchyard and one to get out.'

'So, it follows someone else could do the same.'

'If they wanted to, but I can't speak for anyone but myself. And I found the stiff by the *far* wall, opposite the pub. Your police mates have searched the whole churchyard. They haven't found anything of any interest by either of the walls you reckon I have to climb over to get into, and out of, the churchyard, or anywhere else. You'd have said if you had.' He frowned suspiciously. 'Have you?'

'We found some broken flowerpots and we think they mark where the attack took place. And a member of the public found a knife hidden in marble chippings on one of the graves.'

Callum looked up sharply. 'Which grave?'

'I probably shouldn't tell you. We don't know if it's the murder weapon, anyway!' she added hastily. Then, when he didn't reply, she added, 'What's the matter?'

'Nothing!' snapped Callum. 'OK, I'll show you the way cross-country to the pub. Then I'm all out of favours, right?'

'I still don't know why you insist on doing this, Sergeant,' he added later as they set out. 'There's snow coming. You'll have to put your best foot forward. I don't want to fight my way back in a blizzard.'

'You're not going to call me "Sergeant" all the way, are you? I'm off duty and my name is Beth.' Santos looked uneasily up at the sky. 'Do you really think it might snow tonight?' She shivered and pulled the hood of her parka over her head.

'Wouldn't be at all surprised. We've been lucky so far this year. If you're off duty, what are we doing out here, checking out that ground plan of yours?' After a pause, he added, 'Beth – that's short for Elizabeth, I suppose?'

'No, it's short for Bethan. I might not sound it, but I'm mostly Welsh by descent.'

'Where does the Santos bit come in? That's not Welsh.'

'No, it's Portuguese and it was my grandad's name. He was a seaman and he got left behind in Cardiff when his ship sailed.'

'He jumped ship, you mean?'

'Not really. He'd met my grandmother and forgot the time.'

Callum burst into laughter. 'So, is he still alive, still hiding out in Cardiff?'

'No, he got homesick and talked his way on to another ship. Grandma always said it was because he couldn't manage the Welsh language. You see, her family spoke nothing else at home. She had to translate all the time and his English wasn't that good, either. I suppose it put a downer on the marriage. But then, I'm no marriage expert. I'm divorced. I told you that.'

'You didn't take your husband's name when you married? Was he a copper too?'

'Yes, he was, and no, I never changed my name. It was too complicated, altering everything and so on. And it would confuse people as we worked together. Anyway, we weren't married very long. We realised pretty soon it wasn't a good idea. We had no real life outside of work. Most of our friends were also either police officers or other personnel connected with the job. But we parted in a civilised sort of way. Obviously, though, one of us had to move away. Otherwise, seeing Gary every day would be like still being in a relationship. So I moved on, came here. How about you?'

'Oh, I've never tried being married,' said Callum firmly. 'All the girls in my life have eventually got fed up and cleared off. Mostly, I think it was the mud. That always upset them.'

'Mud?'

'I do landscaping and that sort of thing. Generally, it involves a lot of mud. They start going on about taking boots off and leaving them outside; and don't like it when I bring work indoors. They always want to *organise* a bloke,' added Callum gloomily. 'I don't like being organised.'

'I had noticed.'

'What does that mean?' asked Callum, offended.

'Well, your kitchen is a bit of a mess. I know you use it as an office, too. Everything being all over the place can't be helpful. Perhaps if you planned it out? You plan gardens. Planning a work area with a kitchen corner ought to be a doddle.'

'There you go, you see? You can't wait to organise me. I have that effect on women. They put me down as a slob.'

'I didn't say I thought you were a slob. You're very easily offended.'

'No, I'm not. I'm a very easy-going sort of guy, just so long as no one tries to organise me.'

'All right, all right! I won't try to do it again. You're very touchy, aren't you?'

Callum stopped walking and turned towards the direction of her voice. 'If you think I'm touchy, then how about this? Another word out of you, and I'll go back and leave you here in the dark. See how you get on then, Sergeant!'

'Not another word, promise. Aargh!' This exclamation as something swooped low over her head.

'It's only the owl,' said Callum. 'It's often about the place at night, just hunting for its supper.'

'How am I supposed to know that?' Beth retorted with ruffled dignity.

'Join Basil Finch's ramblers.'

After that they proceeded more or less amicably until they reached the outlying houses of the town and threaded their way through poorly lit streets to emerge from an alley between a closed hairdressing salon and a betting shop. Across the road stood a solidly built wall of large, mossy rough-hewn blocks. Trees on the other side stretched branches over it; and the pitched roof of the maintenance men's hut was just visible in the gloom, above the topmost stones. There was no lighting on the further side and it was very quiet.

Callum led the way across the road to stand by the wall beneath the pitched roof of the hut, looming above them on the further side. He patted the stone beside him.

'Here we are then. Up you go, if you want to check out how I climb over it, like you did with the Black Dog Lane wall.'

Beth was examining her map by the light of a small torch. She put it and the folded diagram away in her pocket; and ran her hand over the uneven surface of the obstacle before them, poking her fingertips into gaps.

'Where are the handholds? You showed me last time,' she said.

'Work 'em out for yourself. Oh, all right. Put your foot in this hole between the blocks down here, see? Then scramble up and when you get to the top, you can reach out and grab the tip of the hut's roof. Use it to steady yourself, then sort of roll over it and drop down. It's a soft landing, just a pile of dead leaves that have rotted down to compost. A bit squishy and wet, nothing worse. Oh, you might disturb the rats. They tunnel under the hut to nest and are probably huddled up in there for warmth. But one might have come out to look around.' When Beth seemed frozen, he added, 'OK, I'll go first, you follow.'

Callum scrambled to the top of the wall with the ease of practice and stretched down his hand. 'OK?'

'Can you see or hear any signs of rats down there?'

'No, of course I can't. They're quiet creatures, and more scared of you than you are of them. Are you climbing up or not?'

'Yes, of course.' Beth scrambled up to join him and they both dropped down into the churchyard.

'There you are!' said Callum a little smugly. 'And not a

rat in sight.' When she made no reply and didn't try to get to her feet he added anxiously, 'Are you OK?'

'Callum,' she whispered, 'there's someone else here, beside me.'

'Can't be!' snapped Callum. 'Look, you did this to me last time we came here at night. You found an intruder.'

'I tell you, there is.' She turned away from him and was prodding at something. 'Hang on, let me find my torch.'

'It'll be a sack of garden trimmings.' Callum was on his feet now and peering past her as he spoke. 'Gimme that torch. Oh, my G— You're right!' he gasped.

The torch beam made its way down the clothed body of a woman. A casual glance in the poor light might indeed have mistaken her for a sack of garden debris, half buried in the pile of damp, dead leaves. But the pitiless glare of Beth's torch, gleaming on white legs and feet in clumpy ankle-high winter boots, dispelled any hope Callum might still have that this was all the shape might prove to be.

This – this object was not anything so workaday as rubbish; but a woman. She was fully clothed in a coat, skirt and the boots, and lay on her side, her face hidden by the leaves and by the beanie hat pulled over her head. Some sort of crocheted flower was attached to the hat. It's meant to be a poppy or a rose, Callum guessed, the gardener in him coming to the fore even at this moment of horror. He stretched out his hand.

'Don't move her!' Beth warned. 'Just let me check for a pulse.' She stooped to place her fingers against the base of the woman's neck. 'I'm sure she's dead. I'll have to call this in. Oh, and you have to stay with me until the police get here. I know you don't want to be involved in the finding of another corpse, but bad luck. You are. You'll have to make another statement.'

'Do you think I ought to go over to the vicarage and tell Superintendent Markby?' whispered Callum hoarsely.

Beth hesitated. 'Yes, OK, but if he's not there, come straight back here.'

Callum turned back towards her as he was about to move off. 'Will you be OK here on your own? If you like, I'll stay here and you go and tell Markby. I mean . . .' He looked around them. 'There might be someone hiding here, the – er – attacker . . .'

'I'm the serving officer. I'll phone it in and stay by the body,' she told him sternly. 'You go and tell the superintendent. Before you say anything, I chased off the intruder we spooked the other night, and I can tackle another one. Oh, and if there's a rat, I'll hit it with my torch. Go on, hurry up!'

'Mr Henderson!' exclaimed Markby on opening his front door. 'Prowling around the churchyard again? You're getting to be quite a fixture of the place.'

'Sorry to disturb you again, Superintendent,' said Callum nervously. 'I do realise you must be getting fed up with me.'

'Believe me, Callum, if it's about my garden, it would be a pleasure to see you, even at this hour of the night. But I've a nasty feeling it isn't. By the way, is DS Santos with you this time?' He peered past Callum into the gloom. 'I trust not? Because, I can tell you now, I don't approve of any further developments in that situation. Cast your roving eye in another direction, not towards one of the officers investigating the case.'

'She is with me,' admitted Callum. 'I mean, we came together, but she's waiting over there beside the maintenance men's hut. We – we've found another body. Sorry!' he added.

Meredith had appeared in the hallway meantime. '*Another* one, Callum?'

'Yes, Mrs Markby, it's a woman's body this time. Beth – Detective Sergeant Santos – is phoning in a report to your lot, Superintendent. She did check for a pulse and she's sure the woman is dead. I said I'd come and tell you and get back to her. I think we ought to do that, get back to Beth ASAP. Just in case, you know . . . the murderer, if there is one—'

Markby interrupted him to say briskly, 'Tell me the whole sorry tale later! Meredith, where's that key James Holland left here, the one for the churchyard's main gates?'

'In this drawer somewhere.' Meredith pulled open the top drawer of a small bureau in the hallway and produced a large, antique-looking key, with a label attached.

'Do me a favour? Go and open them up, would you? Before the cavalry arrive with vehicles and equipment? Thanks! OK, Callum, lead on.' Markby was struggling into his Barbour as he spoke.

They made their way to where Santos stood over the

body, signalling in their direction with her torch.

'Sorry, sir,' she said apologetically as Markby reached her. 'Scene of crime is on its way and the doctor.'

Markby had also brought his torch and shone it on the dead woman's head. 'Difficult to tell,' he muttered. 'I'm sure I've seen a hat like that . . .'

Movement behind them told them Meredith had joined them. 'Gates are open! Is that – oh! Shine the torch on her head again, Alan.'

'It would be better if you went back to the main gates and directed . . .' Markby's voice tailed away as he realised his wife had no intention of leaving the scene before she'd had a good look at the body. 'There!' He directed the beam on to the dead woman's head.

'Alan,' Meredith whispered. 'That's Melissa Garret.'

A rustle in the compost broke the momentary silence that followed her words. From beneath the body, a rat crept out and scuttled away to safety beneath the hut.

Chapter Eight

After that, the customary wheels were set in motion. If Mrs Benton was concerned about activities in the churchyard, she had plenty to occupy her that night. On top of everything else, by the time they were ready to move the body, the pubs had turned out. Word had passed quickly round all the pubs and bars; and even drinkers who did not normally use this route to go home made a diversion to the immediate area in the hope of seeing something interesting. The home-going patrons of every hostelry in the town, so Markby estimated, had gathered to watch from as near a standpoint as they could reach. Keeping them back was occupying three officers who might usefully be engaged on checking the rest of the churchyard.

Speculation among the onlookers was wild. Two murder victims had now been found in the churchyard within a relatively short space of time. There was a murderer on the loose, haunting the churchyard at night. He might be out there in the darkness, even now, watching. Worse, he might be mingling in the crowd itself, enjoying the attention his handiwork had caused.

At the moment, the leading theory running round the onlookers was that this was the work of a maniac, a ghoulish fiend who stalked the local burial sites and killed indiscriminately. Inevitably, someone contacted the local press, and a local stringer for the national dailies had turned up and was speed-dialling every newsroom number he had. This was the sort of story readers loved. Too late for the first editions, perhaps; but headlines were being reset and, by the later morning editions, the story would be nationwide. A second explanation was also whispered: black magic rituals; although, thought Markby ruefully, neither of the victims would have qualified as sacrificial victims as normally imagined by fiction writers and film-makers.

'What is it about murder?' asked Steve Kendal in genuine puzzlement. He had been on the point of going to bed when the call had reached him. Now he stood by Markby and looked on gloomily. 'Why can't that lot down there –' he indicated the spectators behind the nearest barrier – 'why can't they just go home and read about it tomorrow? They can't see anything from where they are. It's not ruddy entertainment! Isn't there anything on the telly?'

'Sadly,' Markby told him, 'for them, it's better than the telly. It's an adventure.'

'They must lead very quiet lives,' snarled Kendal,

glowering at the crowd. 'Oy! Constable! Move them further back!'

'They do lead quiet lives, compared with ours,' Markby remarked.

Kendal muttered something he couldn't catch. Then he said, more distinctly: 'It's that landscaper again, then? Found this body, too?'

'That's right.'

'We need to take a closer look at him, sir,' advised Kendal. 'If the same person keeps "finding" stiffs, that's not just weird, it's suspicious.'

'Technically,' Markby told him with a sigh, 'the body was discovered by DS Santos, who, as far as I can make out, fell on it.'

'Fell on it?' squawked Kendal.

'Yes, she was climbing over the wall with the aid of Henderson. When she jumped down into the darkness behind the wall, next to the groundsmen's hut, she all but landed on the stiff, as you describe the victim. Don't let the public hear you refer to the deceased like that.'

This image successfully silenced Kendal for a full minute. Then he asked indignantly: 'What is it with her and Henderson! Can't they find anywhere other than a churchyard?'

'Let me handle that little problem, Steve,' warned Markby.

Kendal snorted, and marched off down the road to the barrier to insist again that the crowd not only be moved, it should disperse. But that proved a vain wish. The crowd members were on home ground. They knew every street and alley around the area. They shambled off, grumbling, in a variety of directions; and slowly returned to reassemble further back. 'It's like trying to clear away a liquid spillage with a broom,' lamented one officer, tasked with the job. 'It oozes its way back.'

Kendal returned to inform the superintendent that they needed more officers. 'Only I don't know where we're going to get them from at this time of night,' he added.

If the barriers in the street could only serve to keep away the curious pedestrians to a certain distance, they were more successful in blocking any motor traffic wanting to use the street, and sending it off on hastily improvised diversions. Inevitably, any such unexpected barrier to normal routes had a knock-on effect through the town and as far as its outskirts. This was the time of night when long-distance lorries, heading for or coming off a nearby motorway junction, must pass through the edges of town. Thus, the crime scene, a specific location in theory, spread out tentacles of disruption into the whole area.

A new source of fascination arrived in the shape of a cloaked figure in clerical garb. Someone had phoned the news to Father Holland.

'All we need!' snapped Kendal. 'A priest turning up with bell, book and candle!'

James Holland didn't have any of those when he arrived on the scene a few minutes later. He pushed his way through the crowd to where the two senior police officers stood. Mobile phones snapped his progress, skirts of his cloak flapping. He was clearly in a very agitated state. 'This has to be stopped!' he urged Markby.

'I agree. Neither of us wants any murders,' Alan told him.

'I mean all this talk of sacrificial victims. You'll have to put a twenty-four-hour guard on the churchyard, you know! There will be all kind of loonies in there looking for evidence of rituals and souvenirs.' James groaned. 'I'll have to tell the bishop. I'll phone him now. He'll go ballistic. This sort of thing attracts the nutters. They'll come from far and wide to indulge their hobby. They'll be dancing naked in there, you'll see!'

Markby started, as a cold wet finger seemed to touch his face. Then another touched his nose.

'Blast!' growled Kendal, on the other side of him. 'It's starting to snow. It'll hide all the evidence. We won't be able to see a thing by morning.'

'Thank goodness,' said James Holland, who had his own priorities. 'If it's too cold, and better still, if it's snowing, that will put paid to any naked pagan rituals.'

When Markby finally got back home it was well after three in the morning. The snow was falling fast now and already banking up in drifts under the stone walls of the churchyard. They'd placed tarpaulins over the actual murder scene to preserve footprints or any other clues. It was a good try, thought Markby, but Steve Kendal was right. A fingertip search of the crime scene when dawn came would be well-nigh impossible. Everywhere was unnaturally quiet, the snow muffling even the sound of the police vehicles. At least the crowd of onlookers had dispersed rapidly when the snow began.

There was a light on downstairs in the Old Vicarage and he wasn't altogether surprised to find his wife sitting on the sofa with her legs tucked under her, a shawl round her shoulders and a half-empty mug of cocoa clasped in her hands. She was staring at the television weather forecast in a way that suggested she wasn't paying any attention to it, but was deep in her own thoughts. He recognised the kind of wakeful sleep with which he was familiar from many years in his profession, induced by its long hours, its responsibilities and those nightmares that make you fear slumber. In sleep, the slaughtered dead rise up and advance remorselessly towards you; and you can't fight them off.

I know I'm tired out now, he thought. It's training that makes me put it aside and carry on; that and long habit. I've been outside on a perishing cold night, stumbling around a crime scene in a damp churchyard. Following that, I was back at base setting up a murder investigation team. Now I've gone beyond being tired. Some people call that getting your second wind. It's not what it is, because that suggests a new input of energy. Instead, it's the complete absence of it and everything else. It's being suspended in a void. It's a dangerous time because this is when mistakes can so easily be made; and errors of judgment at the outset of an investigation can damn the whole process. As a younger man I might have had hidden resources. I suppose I must have done. Tomorrow, the lack of sleep will kick in and I'll feel lousy. Of course, I'm ready for retirement. I'll miss it all. I resent it. But it's a younger man's game.

He walked across, gently removed the cocoa mug from his wife's hand and put it on the occasional table beside the sofa. 'You should have gone to bed,' he said.

She stirred and swung her feet stiffly to the floor. 'Wouldn't have slept,' she mumbled.

'You've got a job to go to in, let's see,' he glanced at his watch, 'in under four hours' time. If the trains are running, which I doubt. It's snowing quite heavily now.'

'I was planning to ring in sick, anyway. I'd be useless at work. All I see is the image of poor Melissa Garret, lying dead. I know she seemed a bit of a battle-axe; and, from what her brother told me, she could be difficult. All the same, no one should end life like that. Tossed down like rubbish on a compost heap.'

'No,' he agreed, 'no one should.'

'Want a mug of cocoa?' Meredith made to stand up.

'I've had several cups of tea, thanks. I'm fine. Shall I switch the telly off?'

'What?' She started. 'Oh, yes, sure . . . I'd forgotten it was on.' As she spoke, a map appeared on the scene showing which parts of the country were the most affected by the snow.

'If you're planning to travel into work by rail,' warned the presenter smugly, 'it would be advisable to check with train companies first. Widespread disruption is expected. Road conditions round the area may vary and—'

Markby picked up the remote and pressed the off button. The weather chart for the day ahead disappeared in a flash. Trouble ahead on all fronts, he thought wryly.

'Alan?' Meredith asked. 'How did she get there?'

'On the compost heap? In the churchyard? I have no idea. Not as yet, anyway. It isn't so much a compost heap, more a pile of sodden rotten leaves.'

His wife ignored this quibble. 'She looked as though someone had just thrown her over the wall like – like an unwanted Guy Fawkes dummy. But the wall is constructed of stone blocks, and it's high, fairly wide. The effort required would have been extraordinary. But if she wasn't thrown over the wall, then how did she come to be there? The main gates were locked. The only opening into the whole area was far away, over in the corner of the new cemetery where there's a gap in the hedge. Getting in that way would mean carrying her, all the way across the new cemetery and old churchyard, like a sack of potatoes. Wouldn't more than one person be needed? Dead bodies are heavy, aren't they?'

Alan nodded. 'Dead weight, as they so rightly say.'

'In the time that would take, they'd risk being seen – either by one of us looking out of a back window in this house or by Mrs Benton on the watch for misbehaviour of another sort among the graves.'

'Oh, yes, I told you about that, didn't I?' Markby muttered. 'That reminds me. Callum Henderson and one of my officers appear still to be carrying on a curious sort of courtship among the graves. I thought I'd made it clear to Santos that I thought it inappropriate. I warned off Henderson as tactfully as I could the first time. Perhaps I should have avoided tact and used plain speaking the first time. Henderson is the most important witness we have so far, the first to arrive on the scene of Hooper's murder, and now, it appears, one of the two people to find this body.'

'If it's only inappropriate, they'll work it out for themselves,' his wife said. 'Callum will probably be the one to cry off. He's had enough of tripping over corpses, I think. And if it's serious, well,' Meredith considered. 'That could work out well for both of them.'

'Oy! This isn't love's young dream, you know. Apart from the fact we're investigating murder, and she ought not to be hobnobbing with witnesses out of hours, Santos is not long divorced. She has recently torn up her previous life and moved to a new location to be among strangers. She's vulnerable. I had to send them both back to Abbotsfield in a police car because DS Santos's vehicle was parked outside Henderson's cottage. I shall be having strong words with her about that.'

'OK, she's one of your team. But you don't have to play agony aunt! She doesn't strike me as vulnerable. Pretty tough cookie, I'd have thought,' objected his wife.

'I formed much the same opinion of you when we first met.' Her husband managed a smile. 'Strong-minded woman, if not downright fierce! Fanciable, mind.'

'Aw, Superintendent! You say the sweetest things.'

'Callum is vulnerable, too, in his own way.' Markby sat down beside her and put his arm round her shoulder. 'He's too wrapped up in the world he's made for himself, outdoor, lots of hard work, his own boss. He doesn't take into consideration there's another kind of world, more complicated, involving emotions. Finding the first body was a terrible shock for him. But, you know, it struck me then that, after the initial shock, he was more annoyed than anything else. It forced him out of his comfort zone into a world full of things he prefers to shut out. Finding a second body . . . even if, technically, Santos found it. Poor old Callum's world has turned topsy-turvy.'

'Then he needs someone like Beth Santos.'

'If he does, he hasn't yet worked that out,' warned Markby.

There was a silence, then Meredith asked soberly, 'How did the Garrets take the news? Did you break it to them?'

'Yes, I could hardly send someone else to do it, after Charles called here, and both his sister and his wife had been at the door. That made it rather personal. I took a victim support officer with me. It's a remarkable house although most people probably walk past it every day and don't notice it. It dates from eighteen hundred, must have been built by a wealthy citizen, I imagine, and has that kind of solidity houses of that period have. Everything about the exterior speaks success and standing in the community, solid and immovable, built to proclaim the first owner's status and belief that he'd made his mark and would be remembered. Sadly, no one remembers him now, but the house is still there, so perhaps he had the last word in a way.'

Alan sighed. 'As you can imagine, the Garrets were understandably very shocked. They'd just finished washing up the dishes from their evening meal when we arrived. They had done it all by hand. I saw no sign of a dishwasher. I think they would find such a machine unnecessary. There wasn't even an electric kettle, just a battered old copper kettle that sat on the gas hob. The whole house, not just the kitchen, is stuck in a time warp. As for a washing machine, surely they must have that! But I couldn't see one. Perhaps there's some sort of outdoor building that's been adapted into a wash-house.'

'Their great-grandfather bought the house, so Charles told us,' Meredith reminded him.

'The original furniture has gone, or I didn't see any. But what is there now is very old. I suppose it was furnished between the two world wars, say around nineteen thirty, and nothing's been replaced since, unless absolutely necessary.

'At any rate, you could open it up as a museum. Charles opened the front door to us with a tea-towel still in his hand. He led us back into the kitchen where Felicity was putting the dried plates back in the rack over the cooker. She recognised me, of course, because she'd met me when she called at the Old Vicarage. But a policeman of any kind turning up unexpectedly at the house is always alarming.

She turned as white as a sheet and I was concerned for her. I was painfully aware that, at her age, the shock of the news I was bringing could have a devastating effect.'

Alan paused and frowned.

'What is it?' Meredith asked.

'I don't know. I've had to pay this kind of visit before, many times, and it never gets any easier. But on this occasion it's really got to me. Perhaps because the whole place was so odd? There was a real monster of a tabby cat prowling around, looking disgruntled. It gave me a dirty look and sat down to stare me out. Sort of creature you'd try to pet at your peril. I made the mistake of trying to be friendly. I said something daft like "Hello, puss!" But it was having none of it! It stood up, arched its back, all its fur bristled making it look even bigger, and it swore at me.'

'You'd invaded his territory,' Meredith said. 'Just as Melissa believed Felicity had invaded hers. Same reaction.'

'It could have seen off any dog, believe me! Anyhow, I told them we'd come about Melissa. But at first they thought I'd come to speak to her. Charles said, "Oh, dear, I'm afraid you've missed her."

'He explained she'd eaten with them and then gone out to some book club meeting in the town. They were expecting her to return between nine thirty and ten. They hadn't been worried about her. She generally got a lift home with one of the other booklovers. She was her own woman with her own life. She had her own key to the front door. They'd planned to turn in early. "Nothing on the telly!" said Charles Garret. "There never is!" He had difficulty in understanding that his sister was dead. He insisted we must be mistaken. "No, no, she's gone out to her book group meeting and she'll be home later."

'His wife kept nodding away in the background without saying a word. All this was still taking place in their kitchen. Charles hung on to the tea towel, waving it around as he spoke. I realised it was the ordinariness of the setting that made what we were telling them sound so – so outlandish.

'I persuaded them both to move to the sitting room. Even then, Charles took time to hang the towel up neatly on a hook. Felicity spoke up at last and asked, "What about Jasper?" Unsurprisingly, it turned out Jasper was the cat. He was still holding his ground in the middle of the kitchen glaring at us. Charles said, "Leave him to me. We had fish for supper. He can still smell it."'

Alan paused again and frowned. 'But I felt it wasn't just the smell of fish that made Jasper so defiant. Perhaps he sensed something had happened to his owner. Or he knew the weather had turned unpleasant? At any rate, when Charles opened the back door and tried to shoo him outside, Jasper clearly had no intention of being put out in the snow! It proved impossible. He hissed and looked really scary. Charles showed great enterprise. He dropped a hand towel over the animal and, while it was struggling to free itself, he scooped it up and threw it, towel and all, into the downstairs cloakroom; and shut it in.

'Once we were in their sitting room, I started again explaining why we were there. I went through it all. This time they seemed to understand. Up to a point, that is. If I said Melissa was dead, she must be dead because we were the police and we should know. But their minds still rebelled against the news.' Alan heaved a sigh. 'We got them to realise it at last. Then the real shock set in.'

'They went to pieces, I suppose?' Meredith asked sympathetically.

'It would have been better if they had, or cried, asked questions, anything. But they sat there on the sofa just frozen in horror, white faced. They both looked ill now and Felicity was gasping for air. I wondered if I ought to send for the doctor to come out. Telling the family is always bad in cases like this.'

Meredith said, 'I guess it's something altogether out of their experience.'

'The Garrets were practically catatonic. Charles's action in dealing with Jasper gave way to a total inability to make any decisions. As you'll understand, interviewing them hasn't so far produced a great deal for us to go on. We'll try again later. I'm worried about Felicity Garret. She was trembling when we left, and her husband was doing his best to soothe her, but he wasn't in a much better state himself. They wouldn't hear of having the victim support officer stay with them. Both she and I tried to make the case for her staying there, but no. Charles actually said, "I'm sorry, but we can't manage a stranger in the house just at the moment." There was no arguing with that. He said it so formally, apologetically, but resolved. I might as well have suggested they take in a paying guest. There was nothing we could do but leave them to it for the time being.'

'I think I understand,' Meredith said slowly. 'They're both of an age when dealing with such a catastrophic event in their lives bewilders them as much as anything else. They don't understand it. I don't mean they just don't understand why it's happened. I mean, I suppose, that their quiet existence has no place in it for such a violent event. It's as if, at their age, they'd almost completed the jigsaw of their entire lives. Now something has burst in and thrown all the pieces up in the air. They've got to re-assemble them and they don't know how. They've lost the original picture. There's nothing to guide them. Time isn't on their side.'

Markby nodded. 'Charles Garret is seventy-four. His wife is sixty-nine. Melissa was sixty-eight: three elderly people, pensioners, sharing a house. All right, not always sharing it harmoniously. There were squabbles, as in all households. But, as you say, it was the picture of their lives and they mostly got on with it. Until now.'

'I feel . . .' Meredith hesitated. 'I feel we let them down, or I let them down.'

'How?'

'Well, all three came here, one at a time, to consult us, or one of us. Yes, they had all three been living together. The two women probably squabbled a lot. But I feel as though something had changed recently, some new element must have come in. We sent all of them away. Felicity Garret was the first to call here. I wonder what she wanted.'

'Felicity wanted the vicar. He doesn't live here now. As for letting her, or any Garret, down? No, of course we didn't.' He sounded offended. 'I've been a police officer all my working life. I am not a priest like Holland, nor have I ever thought of the priesthood as a career. When Felicity came to this house it was because she thought this was still the vicarage. She was seeking moral or spiritual advice. I'm not, wasn't then, equipped to give that.'

Seeing Meredith still looked unconvinced, he went on more energetically, 'Look, I told Felicity I was a police officer; and she was pretty dismissive of it! She actually said she didn't want a policeman. As for Melissa, whatever bee was in her bonnet, we couldn't have helped. I'm as shocked as you are to have her turn up murdered out there.' He gestured in the general direction of the churchyard. 'But it gives us a case to solve and it's a practical matter for us – my team and me – now.'

'Any idea how she died?' Meredith asked.

'She was stabbed. Carla Hutton will have to carry out an autopsy to find out any more.'

'Another stabbing?' Meredith looked dismayed. 'Just like the first fatality, the body Callum found! Is it the same killer, do you think?'

'We don't know,' he said firmly.

'Same location, same type of weapon,' she pointed out.

'But it's not enough to make us go leaping to conclusions. There's more than one reason for being stabbed; and more than one kind of weapon will serve the purpose. Let Carla do her job. Nor do we know if the two deaths are connected.

Aaron Hooper was a nasty little drugs-peddler who'd left London for reasons unclear. His sister reckons someone was after him. But I doubt she knows very much about it. She's mostly concerned with retrieving her son's bike. Hooper appears to have borrowed it to keep the fatal rendezvous in the new cemetery. Melissa was a respectable single woman who had always lived in this town. Not likeable, perhaps, but not involved in anything criminal. This isn't going to turn out to be *The Case of the Deadly Dressmaker*. There you are! There's a title for your first whodunit.'

Markby heaved a sigh. 'And now do you think we might get some sleep? You can phone in and take a day off. I'm going to be very busy indeed!'

Meredith still hesitated. 'When both Felicity and Melissa came here, they were looking for the vicar. Fair enough. They weren't looking for either of us. But when little Mr Garret came, it was specifically to see me. I can't get the image out of my head: that small, neat figure, standing like a sentry at his post, waiting on a cold, dark evening and determined not to leave until he'd achieved what he'd come for. If you've no specific objection, I'd like to call at his house tomorrow to give him my condolences and make sure he's all right, and his wife. I think he'd appreciate it.'

'Call on them by all means, but I suggest you call in the late afternoon. They won't have had much sleep. We'll be talking to the Garrets again.' He smiled. 'So don't be tempted to play detective.'

'I'm allowed to have ideas, I suppose?' His wife was offended.

'Hey! Don't get me wrong. I'm always grateful for your input. Anything you notice that I might have missed or . . . any feeling you might have about the place.'

'Do you think you missed something?'

'It wouldn't be the first time. Perhaps that cat gave me the heebie-jeebies!'

After a moment, he asked, 'You wouldn't have time to call on James Holland, would you? He came to the church-yard gates when word reached him. He's anticipating trouble with the bishop. Crazy rumours are already spread-ing about pagan sacrifices.'

'I'll call on him, too. Anything you'd like me to ask him?'

'Well, perhaps you could just ask if any member of the Garret family had been in touch with him, before all this happened.'

'I'll ask tactfully. Alan, I've been thinking while I've been sitting here, waiting for you.' She paused.

'OK, let's have it. What's your theory?'

'Well, I realise that we have to wait for Carla's autopsy report. That will show whether the body was moved or not? Postmortem lividity and all the rest of it. Right?'

'Yes, Carla will be able to tell us that.'

'Until then, anything is just a possibility. My idea – and when I tell you about it out loud, it will sound pretty impossible, but this is it: suppose Melissa was *alive* when she entered the churchyard?'

'Through locked gates? Please don't suggest she climbed over the wall! I know Callum and DS Santos managed to do that. But Melissa Garret? And alone?'

'To deal with the last objection first. She wouldn't have been alone, even if she didn't know it. Her killer was there. He'd either followed her or was waiting for her. Of course, I'm not going to suggest Melissa managed to climb the wall. She suffered with arthritis, so it's out of the question. She came in through the gap in the hedge in the new cemetery. Like you, she remembered when the so-called new cemetery was a field full of sheep, and where the stile had been, but now there's just a gap. So did her killer. She crossed the cemetery under her own steam and either waited by the workmen's hut by arrangement or she was being followed and she wanted to hide. She may have hoped the hut would be open or she could squeeze behind it, or that she just wouldn't be visible, huddled in a corner between the hut and the stone wall. It's dark there, even when there's a moon. The trees shield it.' Meredith paused. 'But he did find her.'

'What made her go there in the first place? She was supposed to have gone to a book club meeting. If she went to the churchyard instead, that was a deliberate change of plan! But why? Here we have a lady of mature years, unmarried, drawing an old age pension, utterly respectable, perhaps not much liked. What takes her out on a cold night to roam around a churchyard?' he asked.

'Dunno.'

'Fair enough. I "dunno" either! Come on, let's get some

rest. Tomorrow is going to be a very busy day.'

'I have a couple of days' leave left to me,' Meredith said thoughtfully. 'I'll tell them, when I call work tomorrow, that I'd like to take them now. I can't see how they could object.'

'There aren't any trains at the moment, Ben,' she told her colleague over the phone. 'Even if they run one later, I don't know I could get back home tonight. Besides, there's been another murder in the churchyard by the house.'

'Another body?' Ben Owusu's baritone voice, normally as reassuring as warm treacle, rose a note or two in pitch in astonishment. 'What's going on down there in your neck of the woods?'

'Believe me, Ben, I wish I knew. One corpse turning up in what's almost my back garden was bad enough. Now there's been another. Alan's running the investigation, of course. That's nothing to do with me. But what with that and the wretched weather, no trains and so on, I think it's a good moment for me to take my remaining leave. I'm in shock!' concluded Meredith firmly.

'Shock? You? Never! But take the days owing and a couple extra if needed. Then you can dig yourself through the snowdrifts, come back and tell us all about it. And hey! I'll want all the details.'

The snow had ceased, the sky was ice-blue, and under the sparkling white blanket the town presented an idealised Christmas-card picture. There was police activity in the churchyard, but the streets were quiet and almost deserted. Meredith decided to make the first call at the new vicarage.

'Meredith!' exclaimed James Holland eagerly. 'Have you got any news? The verger was here earlier and I thought he was going to have a stroke. The diocesan office keeps ringing up and the bishop is livid. Come in. I'm just about to make coffee.'

'Can I help?'

'Thanks, but no, I can manage boiling a kettle. Go and sit down and I'll be there directly.'

Meredith pulled off her wellington boots, left them in James's porch, and padded in socks into his welcoming, if untidy, sitting room. It was warm and cosy. She thought ruefully that he was probably much more comfortable here than he had been when he'd lived in the vicarage, rattling round on his own, with only the aged and erratic Mrs Harmer as his daily.

Mrs Harmer's exact age had been a closely guarded secret. It was only when she had died, a couple of years earlier, that she'd been revealed as being well into her eighties. Even then there was some confusion about the year of her birth. She'd insisted on 'taking care' of the vicar almost until the last. She'd always taken any suggestion that she retire as an insult. It was only when she had become physically infirm, unable to move about without the aid of a walking frame, that she'd reluctantly relinquished her duties to a cleaning company.

'It was the end of Mum,' said her daughter sadly, at the funeral. 'Looking after Mr Holland, that was her life, you see. She said it was her duty. Then the firm of cleaners replaced her and, well! She never accepted the idea of foreigners in the house. She said they were all Russians. She reckoned taking over the cleaning of the vicarage was only the first step. "They're all set to take over everything!" is what she said.' After a moment's reflection, the daughter added, 'I don't think they were Russians, myself. I think they were Poles.'

James came in at that moment, carrying a tray with two coffee mugs and a plate of Jaffa cakes. 'Here we go.'

'I'm sorry it's taken this to bring me to your door. But I've been meaning to call round for ages,' Meredith told him apologetically. 'Since we first moved here into your old home.'

'How are you getting on in my old vicarage? Or how were you getting on before all this began? It's a bit of a barracks of a place. But I expect you and Alan were managing there well enough before . . .'

James concentrated on handing her the plate of Jaffa cakes, but his hand wobbled even so.

Meredith reached out and took the plate from him. 'We were doing fine, thanks, before all this. Alan has plans for the garden. We had a new kitchen put in. But all that sounds so trivial, now these deaths have happened.' She tried for a smile, knowing it probably looked more like a gargoyle's grimace. 'Feel free to say it would never have happened in your time there, James.'

'Fortunately, in my time nothing like that did. You've no idea what trouble this is making for me. Sorry if that sounds selfish, but you probably don't know the bishop!'

'Can't say I do.'

'He's a thoroughly decent sort, fairly young as bishops go, and he's got a lot of progressive ideas about creating a church for the modern-day worshipper. Between you and me, frankly, this has knocked him for six. The churchyard is consecrated ground. When all this is over, there will have to be some sort of ceremony. He seems to think that, if there were any pagan rites going on in there, I ought to have known about it. But in all the years I was living in the vicarage, there was never any sign of such a thing.'

'Alan says the police don't think it has to do with any pagan rites or black magic. These are murders for which there will turn out to be very humdrum reasons, and they are probably not even connected. But he has asked me to inquire whether you've received a visit lately from any member of the Garret family. There used to be a butcher's shop of that name in the town.'

'Just about remember it,' muttered James. 'But I don't know any Garrets personally. Tell me why Alan wants to know.'

Meredith did, starting from Felicity's visit to the Old Vicarage, under the impression it was still actively the vicarage, to Melissa's appearance at their door, and finally Charles Garret's. 'What I'd like to ask, if I may, James, is whether Felicity Garret came to find you here, at the new vicarage. I did give her one of those cards you left.'

'No,' said James quietly. He got to his feet and began to wander about the room. The dimensions weren't overlarge and James himself was tall and strongly built and, despite his age and the streaks of grey in his beard, still a powerful presence.

He had come to a halt before the window and was staring out into the street. 'This is very distressing news,' he said. 'This second body, do the police know who it is?'

'Oh, yes, and Alan doesn't mind my telling you. It'll be all round the town by now. The body is of Melissa Garret, Felicity's sister-in-law. She was the second visitor who came to our door and, I'm ashamed to say, was turned away. I was about to tell you that bit, but – but I was leaving it to the last.'

'Always leave your audience with a memorable phrase to take away and reflect on,' muttered James, still staring into the street. 'You'd write a good sermon, Meredith.'

'I'm beginning to wonder if I could write a good anything. I've been thinking that, when I retire, I'll take up writing whodunits.'

'You'll be a natural.'

'James, I really think I let her down, all three of them. I let them all down.'

He turned round. 'No, you didn't. You can't see into the future any more than any of us.'

'Felicity Garret didn't come here, then?'

'I'm not avoiding giving you an answer, Meredith. I don't know if she came or not, is the best I can say. She didn't ring the doorbell and ask to see me, as she did at your place. But there was a woman standing outside one afternoon recently. I think, trying to work out exactly when, it must have been the day after you say the woman calling herself Felicity Garret came to the Old Vicarage. I don't know how long she'd been standing there when I saw her. She was very small, elderly, wore one of those funny little hats, handmade.'

'A crocheted beanie?'

'If you say so.'

'It could have been her.'

'Look, I'm used to people being nervous about ringing at my door. I often open it to find an unexpected caller. It's fine if they are members of the congregation and expect me to recognise them. I've got a good memory for faces. If they're not regular church attendees, it's different, and they can be nervous, shy . . . I thought perhaps she might be one of that kind of caller. So I went to the front door, and opened it. But she'd already taken fright and was scurrying off down the road like a disturbed beetle. Given what has happened, it's something I shall think about a lot. She isn't the murder victim, you say, which is a relief. But it's hard to dismiss the idea that whatever she wanted to tell me about, it had something to do with it.'

'Yes,' said Meredith, 'I think so, too, James. I'm going to call on the Garrets briefly later on, this afternoon. Just to express my condolences, you know.'

'Let me know how you get on, if you would? And whether you think they'd appreciate a call from me?'

'Will do, James, thanks for the coffee and Jaffa cake.'

* * *

'It is very good of you to come, Mrs Markby,' said Charles Garret.

Meredith remembered Alan had talked about the house being in a time warp. Charles ushered her into a small, neat room that could only be called a 'parlour'. Every surface was polished and gleaming to a standard she could never hope to achieve at the Old Vicarage. There was a grandfather clock in a corner, not working, and some decorated plates on the walls. A television was an anachronistic intruder. The contrast with James's untidy sitting room couldn't be more marked. It was half past four in the afternoon and already the light was failing. A couple of table lamps had been lit.

Charles gestured her towards a cretonne-covered armchair. 'Please sit down. Felicity, dear, I am sure Mrs Markby would like a cup of tea.'

Little Felicity Garret looked much as Meredith remembered her at the front door of the Old Vicarage: small, anxious and dowdily dressed. Only the absence of the beanie hat made a real difference because now her hair could be seen. It was grey, tidy and much like the rest of her. Her eyes were reddened and there was a dull red patch on one cheek. Meredith wondered if she had been scrubbing away the tears. She felt desperately sorry for her but in the face of grief there is often little one can say or do. Charles probably had the right idea in giving his wife a practical task to carry out.

'Oh yes, of course!' Felicity said and scurried away on her errand.

Meredith was reminded of one of the squirrels seen about the churchyard in warmer weather. She opened her mouth to say she didn't wish to cause any bother, but Charles Garret was ahead of her.

'Gives me a moment,' he said confidingly, 'to have a quick word with you, while she's out of the room.'

He had taken a seat at the end of the sofa, facing the visitor, and leaned forward to emphasise his words. 'She's very distressed,' he whispered.

'Of course, she is – and you are, too,' Meredith returned apologetically. 'I should have waited a day or two to call.'

'Oh, no, no! That's not what I meant at all. I am really very glad to see you. It distracts Felicity. She's been crying a lot. It's the shock, of course. Do you think I ought to phone a doctor?'

'It wouldn't do any harm to seek advice. A doctor should be able to prescribe something, perhaps to help her sleep. Or he could put her in touch with a bereavement support group. Perhaps you both—' Meredith stopped and apologised. 'Sorry, I don't mean to interfere. Of course, you won't come to terms with what's happened for a very long time. Sometimes just having someone to talk to is helpful.'

'I will never come to terms with it!' said Charles gloomily. 'Melissa was six years younger than me. That meant, when we were children, our mother expected me to keep a watchful eye on her. Keep her from harm . . .' His voice faltered. 'I did my best to keep her from harm even after we grew up. We spent all our lives together and in this house. I know that sometimes she could be difficult; but that was only because she missed the dressmaking. For a while she could still do little bits and pieces. But, these last months, even that was beyond her. It was taking her longer to finish even a small piece. All the little mats you see in here, they are all Melissa's work, and all done before the arthritis became so bad.'

Meredith looked around the room. Every surface seemed to be bedecked with some kind of lacy disc or runner. That's tatting, I suppose, she thought. I never had the patience to master any skill like that.

Charles was silent, lost in thought. He spoke at last in a way that suggested he'd reached a conclusion. 'All the time she could sew or do the other things she was happy. Yes, yes, I am sure her life was not unhappy. Or, at least, until I married. I should have given more thought to that and what it would mean to her. They didn't get on, you see, my sister and my wife. But you knew that, didn't you? I did try and explain when I visited you at the vicarage.' He heaved a sigh. 'I didn't think it would end like this. I've always tried to be optimistic. One does, doesn't one? It's human nature. Now everything is so confused . . .' His voice tailed away and he looked round the room as if some answer to his troubles might be found there. But there was nothing to comfort him.

Meredith felt desperately sorry for him. 'I expect the police will have asked you a lot of questions,' she said aloud.

'They have asked us questions; but we can't answer them,' was the doleful reply.

'But you knew she had left the house yesterday evening?'

'Yes, we did. I told your husband she belonged to a book club. The members meet at seven at the house of one of them. She went out to attend that; but the organiser has told us she never arrived. They didn't see her at all and she sent no message to say she was unable to come. They thought that unusual. I suppose we should have realised she hadn't returned. But sometimes the book meetings went on quite late. Felicity and I turn in early. Melissa had her own key. She never made much noise when she came home late. But I should have realised . . . I feel responsible, somehow.'

'She walked home late at night alone, at this time of year?' Meredith asked in surprise.

'Oh, no, she only walked *to* the meeting! One of the other reading circle members always brought her home by car. If that wasn't possible, she'd have phoned me; and I'd have got the car out and driven over to get her. So I wasn't at all worried about her coming home late. I just assumed she'd get the usual offer of a lift. But one ought not to take anything for granted, should one?' Charles rubbed his hands over his head. 'Oh, dear. Oh, dear, I feel so responsible. I shouldn't have assumed . . .'

A rattle of wheels announced the arrival of Felicity with a tea trolley. Charles jumped to his feet to help his wife. Meredith found herself wishing she hadn't come, or not so soon.

They drank their tea in an awkward silence. Meredith longed to ask Felicity if she had indeed gone to the new vicarage and waited outside for some minutes. James Holland would want to know. But it wasn't possible to ask while Charles sat there.

As she was leaving, Felicity put a hand on her arm and whispered, 'Thank you for coming. It's helped so much having someone here, other than the police, of course. Although they have been very polite, and a woman – a victim support officer, they called her – offered to stay here for a while with us. But we refused. It just seemed worse, having her here, because it was so – so official; and she wouldn't be here, if Melissa weren't—'

She produced a handkerchief from her sleeve and snuffled into it. Meredith noticed a long scratch on her forearm. It looked recent. She remembered Alan's warning that Jasper was not a cat to be petted. Luckily, Jasper wasn't to be seen. He was probably sulking because so many strangers had invaded his house.

Tucking the handkerchief away again, Felicity went on: 'For Charles, being able to talk to someone else, not the police, about his sister . . . it will have helped him enormously.'

Meredith hoped that was true. 'I wonder,' she said, 'who runs the book club? Because I've been thinking of joining one.'

Felicity brightened. 'Oh, she's a neighbour of yours. Not a next-door neighbour exactly, but probably your nearest, because her house is the first one you come to as you walk into town. It's just past the church itself. Celia Benton lives there. She's the organiser.'

Meredith didn't know it, but Markby had made his own way to Celia Benton's front door. He could, of course, have sent Kendal or Santos or another officer. But from his previous encounter with that lady, he understood that she would appreciate a call from an officer of suitable rank. That meant Superintendent Markby himself. Besides, he didn't want her taking another close look at Beth Santos.

'Ah, Superintendent!' said Mrs Benton as soon as she opened the door. 'I've been expecting you. Come in!' It was an order, not an invitation.

'You do realise,' she continued, 'that I have had no sleep virtually all night?'

'Nor have I, madam,' murmured Markby, as he followed her into a room that, as in the Garrets' house, was full of well-polished furniture. The walls were hung with Victorian watercolours of amateurish style; every available surface displayed some china ornament. The effect was like walking into an antique shop in a small town on the tourist trail. The whole room was dominated by a large oval frame hung above the fireplace. It housed the photographic portrait of a gentleman in army uniform, who kept a beady eye on Markby as he sat down.

He had prepared an apology for Mrs Benton's disturbed night. Not, of course, that any of it was his, or the police force's, fault. He was cut short before he could finish.

'Naturally you wish to talk to me about poor Melissa Garret.'

'Actually,' said Markby, 'we haven't released the name of the victim yet.'

'That doesn't mean no one knows who the poor woman was,' Mrs Benton returned quellingly. 'If the dreadful news isn't all round the town already, it soon will be.'

Damn right! thought Markby gloomily. 'You were expecting her, I understand? Her brother told us she had left for her book club meeting.'

'Quite right. It was the evening of our regular meeting. Melissa did not turn up. We waited almost ten minutes before we began, because we were surprised that she'd sent no message to let us know she'd be absent. I thought she might be ill, so this morning I rang the house. Her brother answered. The poor man is in a terrible state, naturally. It's an unspeakable business. But I can hardly say it came altogether as a surprise.'

'It didn't?' exclaimed Markby, startled.

'There has already been one murder in the churchyard, hasn't there?' declared Celia Benton fiercely. 'Once such a dreadful example has been set, there's no knowing where it will lead. I have complained time without number about the general bad behaviour I have observed in there. It is shocking, Superintendent, shocking. We are none of us safe! The members of our book club will be very unwilling to come out on a dark evening, as it is at this time of year, if they fear they are going to be attacked by a maniac.'

'Well, yes, I understand that. Perhaps it would be a

good idea to suspend the next meeting. Just a precaution, of course. But I must insist that we, the police, are not thinking in terms of a maniac.'

This didn't go down well. Mrs Benton leaned forward and glared at him. 'Of course, it's a maniac! Who else would attack an inoffensive woman like Melissa Garret?'

Markby had only encountered Melissa once, and that briefly. But she hadn't struck him as being entirely inoffensive. Quite the reverse. But if all the people who were ill mannered or aggressive were to be murdered, it would make a sizeable dent in the population.

'Now then, Superintendent! The question is, what are you going to do about it?' the lady continued.

Between the challenge in her eyes and tone and the stern observation of the military gent in the photograph, Markby felt himself up before some kind of disciplinary committee. He drew a deep breath.

'We are making exhaustive investigations into both deaths. Now, about Melissa Garret, you say you expected her here as usual?'

'Naturally, we had expected to see her. I've just told you so. She is – or was – a regular attendee. We had been reading *Emma*. Jane Austen, you know. We were all looking forward very much to discussing it.'

'Quite,' said Markby. 'Had Melissa Garret missed other meetings?'

'Rarely!' said Mrs Benton firmly. 'And never without warning, as I have already told you. Shouldn't you be writing this down? I am a witness, making a statement.'

'Well, not exactly a witness. You didn't see—'

'I am a witness to the character of the victim. She was very reliable. On one or two occasions, when she couldn't come, she sent a message to that effect, as I also told you. If you wrote things down in a notebook, I would not have to keep repeating my answers. Policemen used to carry notebooks and wrote information in them. As in so many things, Superintendent Markby, the old ways were the best.' Celia sighed and looked, for a moment, genuinely sad. 'Perhaps I should have realised there and then that something must be terribly wrong. People such as Melissa do not break the habit of a lifetime other than for a very serious reason. I should have rung her brother last night, as soon as it became clear she wasn't going to arrive. We could have reported her missing and a search party could have been formed. To think of her lying dead in the churchyard while we sat here and discussed *Emma*. We shall all miss her.'

'You didn't hear anything from the direction of the churchyard last night?'

'The officers who came earlier asked me that. I didn't hear anything, partly because I was not expecting to hear anything. That makes a difference, you know.'

Markby opened his mouth to point out that it was when no noise was expected that a sudden yell, for example, would be most noticeable. But he said nothing, because he had observed the lady wore discreet hearing aids. Probably, when she was alone, she took them out of her ears.

The remainder of his visit didn't contribute anything further to what he already knew. He thanked her and took his leave. Unlike his wife, he didn't even get a cup of tea.

If elsewhere the shocking news of a second body was spreading fast, it had yet to reach the residents of Abbotsfield. (Other than Callum, of course.) Otherwise, Abbotsfield remained as usual during the morning, showing little activity. The only change to the landscape was the light covering of snow.

Robert Hawkins, awoken earlier than normal by the brightness of the light, got out of bed and peered through the curtains at the snowy view. Following that, he wrapped himself in his old school dressing gown. It was too small and still bore a tape sewn into the neck band reading *R J Hawkins*. He emerged cautiously from his bedroom, listening for sounds that would let him know where his parents were. His father, having established that the train service was likely to be erratic, had announced the previous evening that he would be working from home, and was closeted in his study. Rob could hear his voice, speaking on the phone. He checked, as far as he could, where everyone else was. The owners of the wine import business were away again, not touring the vineyards of France at this time of year, but apparently on some winter vacation. Skiing in the Dolomites, rumour had it. The occupiers of the dilapidated bungalows couldn't have pointed to the Dolomites on the map, but wouldn't have worried about that. The light covering of snow had made their junk-filled front gardens almost picturesque. They themselves were nowhere to be seen, but then, thought Rob, they seldom were.

Callum's van, with the landscaping legend along the sides, remained parked outside the Henderson cottage. The yard behind the cottage was empty and silent. Rob wondered where Basil Finch was. When he wasn't guiding little groups of enthusiasts around sites of natural interest, Basil taught mathematics at a local school, and drove off early. But this morning, Rob had noticed that Basil's car was still parked in its usual spot. Snow had put a stop to school.

He opened the kitchen door cautiously. It had been quiet downstairs for a while and he hoped that meant his mother had gone over to her studio, a separate building. Peering through the kitchen window, he spied a line of footprints from the back door to Laura's workshop, indicating that was so. A Post-it note stuck to the tabletop further confirmed this. It also read, *Make yourself something to eat, if only cereal!* He didn't fancy cereal, but he was hungry, so he made toast and spread it lavishly with strawberry jam. Then he settled at the table with a cup of instant coffee, and was about to begin his late breakfast, or elevenses, whatever they might be called, when he was interrupted. Someone with a heavy tread was approaching the back door. It couldn't be his mother. She had long ago, in Rob's opinion, perfected the art of creeping up on him unheard. There was shuffling in the little porch outside. Someone was kicking off boots. Then came a knock at the door. Laura must have left it on the latch, because it swung open, before Rob could get to it, and Callum Henderson walked in.

'Oh, it's you,' said Rob. 'Mum's working. Dad's home, working in his study. He doesn't like to be disturbed.'

'I've come to see you,' said Callum. He sat down opposite Rob at the kitchen table, and placed his clasped fists on the surface. He was a man who worked with his hands, and as a result they were broad, muscular, suntanned and sprinkled with small white scars from mishaps while plying his chosen trade.

Rob couldn't avoid looking down at his own pale, thin hands; and felt such a moment of deep shame that he had to resist the urge to put them out of sight. He wished he wasn't still in his dressing gown. It was impossible not to see derision in Callum's gaze as he cast a critical eye over it. 'If you'd like some coffee, help yourself,' he muttered.

'I'm fine. You carry on.'

There was nothing Rob wanted to do less while Callum just sat there. But he had no choice.

Callum watched Rob eat the toast with a sort of detached interest, as if watching some form of wildlife, like the birds that flocked to Basil's hanging wire feeders. Rob found it more and more disconcerting. The toast snapped in two when he bit into it. One half fell on the table. He wished he hadn't chosen to spread strawberry jam on it. It reminded him of blood.

'What's this about?' he asked, attempting some sort of

self-possessed nonchalance and failing dismally. 'Can't work today and lost for company?'

'Thought we might have a chat. You know, a follow-up call to the one you paid on me.'

'Oh?' Rob couldn't keep the unease from his voice. 'This is about me in the churchyard again?'

'Not about the night you were chased across it by Detective-Sergeant Santos, if that's what's worrying you.'

Rob's face burned scarlet in anger and embarrassment. It didn't matter that no one else knew he'd been that fleeing figure. Callum knew. Callum, who had been fooling about among the headstones with a policewoman! Why didn't Callum feel embarrassment or shame? Because, an inner voice replied in Rob's head, Callum has no need to feel either. He's confident in what he's achieved, his business, his independence, in being his own man. Callum isn't me and . . . At this point Rob forced away the last part of the sentence because it would have been, And I'll never be like Callum. He told the inner voice he didn't want to be like Callum. But he didn't want to be himself, either, that was the problem.

Callum was speaking again. 'I've come about last night, as it happens. You obviously haven't heard the news yet, out here.'

'What news?' asked Rob suspiciously, reaching for his coffee mug. 'And if you've heard it "out here", as I suppose you mean Abbotsfield, why haven't I?'

'You've only just crawled out of your bed, haven't you?' He rolled over an indignant reply to that from Rob, suggesting it was none of Callum's business. 'There's activity in the churchyard in town. The police have cordoned off the area again.'

'Whaffor?' demanded Rob, over the rim of the mug. He couldn't even keep it steady and the coffee slopped about.

'Another body's been found. I thought I should tell you.'

Rob set down the mug with a thump and the remaining contents spilled over the table-top. He felt sick; and trapped into some sort of recurrent nightmare. Callum must have it wrong. 'Where? Not in the churchyard? Can't happen twice!' His denial sounded squeaky to his own ears.

'Well, it has.' Callum nodded towards the puddle of coffee spreading across the table. 'You need to mop that up before it drips on the floor.'

Rob, brain frozen, unwilling and unable to absorb this news, pushed back his chair and fetched a paper towel from a roll on the wall. Moving like a zombie, he wiped up the spillage, then stood for a second or two with the damp paper in his hand as if unsure what to do with it next, before disposing of it in the pedal-bin.

'Who found it? Not you again?' he demanded belligerently. *Stand up for yourself! Go on the offensive.* He was issuing the orders to himself in his head.

'Strictly speaking Beth Santos found it, but I was with her so, in a manner of speaking, yes, I was there when it was found.'

Rob stared at him in disbelief, then horror, before he rallied and attempted to follow his own mental instructions and take the initiative. 'What is it with you and her? Can't you find anywhere else to meet?'

'Why *we* were there doesn't matter. What matters is that *you* don't go skulking round the churchyard again. You were lucky last time. Markby didn't catch you. He only caught me and Beth.'

After an uneasy pause, Rob asked, 'Do they know who it is? I mean the identity of this new dead person.'

'An elderly woman by the name of Melissa Garret.'

'Never heard of her!' snapped Rob.

'Don't suppose you have. Neither had I. I believe she's a member of the Garret family that used have a butcher's shop. It doesn't matter. Just stay away from the cops and the churchyard, right?'

'Sure,' said Rob, after a pause. He hoped Callum, having delivered his news, might now leave. But Callum stayed where he sat, his folded hands still resting on the table. He was staring down at them now, not looking at Rob at all. Rob didn't know what was coming next and if this would be better or worse. Worse? How could it be worse?

He burst out, 'And that's why you came, is it? Just to bring the news and warn me off, because you think I've got something to do with all this; and, although you don't give a damn about me, my mother is a nice person in your opinion?'

'Both your parents are decent people. But they have a problem.'

'Me, I suppose?' Rob's face had reddened further and

the anger crackled in his voice. 'Well, my relationship with
my parents has nothing to do with you!'

He would have said a lot more, because now the words
came bubbling up and longing to burst out.

But Callum was shaking his head slowly from side to
side. 'No, you're not really the problem.'

'OK, so what is?'

Still gazing at his clasped hands, Callum began slowly,
'It's really that because they're decent people, your mum
and dad don't know how to deal with bad people.'

Rob saw an opening for defence and leaped into it.
'Then there you're wrong! My dad is a top-notch solicitor
with a leading firm in London. He's come across all kinds
of crooks. If you went up to his study, and told him he
didn't know about that sort of thing, he'd laugh at you.'

Callum sighed. 'I'm not talking about white-collar
fraudsters, neighbours arguing over property lines, and
greedy relatives who get old ladies to change their wills.
I'm talking about the professional criminals running the
drugs trade, and so on. They probably keep up an outward
show of being successful businessmen. As far as anyone
can see, they are respectable members of the community,
or act as if they are. But they are crooks, just like the people
they employ, from the mules who bring the stuff in, the
slick book-keepers who move the money around, the
pushers peddling the dope, down to the small fry out on
the streets, the runners. Your dad could look through all
his law books; but it wouldn't help if an enforcer sent by
one of the big fish came knocking at the door.'

'I've no idea what you're going on about!' snapped Rob.

Callum shook his head but still studied his clasped hands. It was clear, from Rob's own expression, that the refusal of Callum to look up was unsettling him more and more.

'I'm not saying that basically decent people don't get mixed up in bad things. But generally, it worries them stiff when they do. They can't wait to get back to being decent and honourable, because that's what Basil would call their natural habitat. Now the really bad people, they're rotten through and through, don't know how to be anything else. Pity, I suppose, but you need to stay away from them, Rob.'

Rob was now bright red in the face. 'Since when have you been a shrink or a priest or whatever?' Earlier his voice had trembled with nerves but now it shook with anger.

'Never have been, never will be!' returned Callum simply. 'I've not got the brains for it, I suppose. But I was brought up by my grandma; and she understood a thing or two about good and evil.'

'She was of a religious turn of mind, was she?' snapped Rob.

'Believe me, if she'd seen the Devil walking down the street, she wouldn't have been surprised. That was because she knew Evil existed, and whatever shape it took, it was roaming about looking for prey. She'd have told you not to mix with bad people. You know, she once said to me, "One bad apple will make the rest rot." Another time she said, "You can't make custard with milk that's on the turn." She had a way of putting it in words, so as you remembered.' Callum fell silent.

'Well, you've certainly remembered, but that's all rubbish,' Rob retorted angrily. 'And your old granny knew nothing!'

Callum at last raised his gaze from his clasped hands. He looked Rob full in the face, and smiled. Rob had been angry but the smile really scared him. It showed in his eyes and in the beads of moisture forming on his brow beneath the fringe of dark hair.

'OK, Rob, let me ask you a question.' Callum's tone was amiable but that didn't fool Rob.

'You can ask what you damn well like. I don't have to answer.'

'No, you don't,' Callum agreed.

'Well? What is it?' Rob was so agitated now that he scrambled to his feet, pushing against the table so that its legs scraped on the tiled floor.

'You know what it is,' was Callum's aggravating reply. 'But, all right. Let's go back to that night DS Santos and I disturbed you in the churchyard, and you ran for it.' His tone was almost casual. 'Had you been looking for the knife? Or had you just hidden it?'

Without waiting for an answer, he got to his feet and turned to stroll out.

Shocked to the core by the accusation and by the casual way in which it had been phrased, Rob leaped to his feet.

'Hang on, there! I didn't kill that guy! I had nothing to do with it. Like I didn't kill this woman, Garret! You can't just toss questions like that at me or anyone else. I had nothing to do with any of it.'

Callum paused and turned back. 'I didn't say you killed him. But I do think you had a reason for skulking about the churchyard that night, and it wasn't the feeble one you gave me. Just be more careful, right?'

'Have you shared these bright ideas of yours with your girlfriend?' Rob asked uneasily.

'If, by girlfriend, you mean Beth Santos, why should I? She's the detective, not me. She's quite capable of getting there on her own. By the way, you've got strawberry jam on your chin.'

Callum left.

Chapter Nine

Rob remained seated at the kitchen table before a cold cup of coffee, on which a skin had formed, and the scattered breadcrumbs of his toast. He could hear Callum striding away across the flags of the patio outside. But then the heavy stamp of his work boots stopped and Rob heard his mother's voice. Panic rose in Rob's chest. Surely Callum wouldn't repeat any of their conversation? But his mother sounded calm enough until, suddenly, she gave a loud cry. Callum's voice again, sounding reassuring, followed by Laura's, anxious. Callum's, insistent. He's told her about the new body in the churchyard, thought Rob. Ruddy man! Why didn't he leave it to me to tell her? Callum's heavy tread could now be heard retreating and the kitchen door opened to reveal his mother, white faced.

'It's all right, Mum!' Rob scrambled to his feet and went to put a reassuring arm round her shoulder. 'Callum's told you the news. I suppose. I wish he'd left it to me.'

'But I don't understand.' Laura looked frightened.

'Who would do such an awful thing?'

'I don't know, Mum.' They stared at one another for a moment. Then Rob went on, 'Did you come in for coffee? I'll make some fresh. I had made some for myself but I spilled it when – when Callum came out with his news. He was actually there in the churchyard again. Did he tell you that? He found the body, just like last time, or his girlfriend did. They both did.'

'Has Callum got a girlfriend?' asked his mother, frowning.

'Yes, she's a copper, a detective sergeant. Mum, are you all right?'

His mother had sat down with a bump on the nearest chair. 'What? Yes, I'm fine. It's just the shock. Callum didn't say he'd *found* the body. He just said there'd been a murder. Do they know yet who the victim is?'

'All my information comes from Callum. He says the dead woman was a Melissa Garret. He said something about a butcher's shop, an old one, used to be in the town.'

'Oh, yes.' Laura nodded. 'I remember Garret's butchers. It was still in business when we first came here. But it closed, oh, years ago.' She looked up as Rob set down the cup of coffee before her and put out her hand to grip his arm. 'Rob, I'm not asking you any personal questions. But promise me, please, that you'll stay away from the churchyard and anywhere else in the town that's deserted after dark. I don't want you in any trouble, Rob.'

You and Callum both, thought Rob, but didn't say

aloud. What he did say was, 'What's Callum's angle in all this?'

'Has he got what you call "an angle"?' Laura pushed back her hair nervously. 'What sort of angle?'

'He's got some sort of interest. That's a better word. I don't think it's just that he's taken to hanging out with that detective female, and they share a liking for churchyards at night.' Rob pulled a face. 'Well, he's always prowled around at night, hasn't he? Callum, I mean. He walks all over the fields when there's nothing out there but foxes and other wildlife. I could understand it if he were like Basil, interested in that sort of thing. What else is he looking for, prowling around out there?'

'He doesn't prowl,' said his mother. 'He just walks to the pub; or I think he does.' She sounded nervous, moving her hands about as if searching for something on the table. 'No, no, no,' she said abstractedly. 'No, no, no . . .'

'Mum? What are you looking for?'

She stared at him wide eyed. 'Looking for? Nothing.'

'Then stop fidgeting about, making those movements with your hands.'

'Oh, sorry.' Laura stared down at her hands and then folded them in the way Callum had done. 'I've got a bad case of the jitters.' She forced a smile that didn't reach her eyes. 'Callum gave me quite fright with that awful news. And then you told me Callum himself found the body with this girlfriend of his, the one I didn't know he had.' She looked bewildered. 'How can he keep finding bodies?'

'Bit of a dark horse, old Callum, if you ask me,' opined

Rob. 'And I'm not just making a bad joke.' He saw her expression and added hastily, 'Don't worry about it, Mum. But perhaps, you know, you ought to be a bit careful, not so pally with him.'

'I'm not pally!' she defended herself, her old energy returning. 'I only pass the time of day with him sometimes. And I never chat with Gus.'

Rob laughed. 'Oh, the Incredible Hulk! Yes, he's another mystery man. I wonder what he gets up to.'

Laura began to sip her coffee and then said, much more calmly, 'Perhaps you ought to get away for a bit, Rob. The Lake District must look beautiful at the moment, with everything under snow, and quiet without the summer visitors all over the place. Why don't you go up and stay with Marcus for a week?'

'Thanks,' said Rob firmly, 'I'd rather not.'

'Marcus is worried Uncle Philip is going to marry a strong-minded woman and change his will,' said Laura. She managed a weak smile that wasn't reflected in her eyes.

'Then I'm definitely not going anywhere near him,' Rob told her. After a pause he added quietly, 'I can't go now, Mum. Not with all this happening. Dad's usually in London all day. You're more or less alone out here in Abbotsfield. Callum's got his work and Basil drives off into town to teach those kids maths. The Baxters are always going away, either wine-buying in France or taking expensive winter breaks. I know you've tried to watch over me. Now it's time for me to watch over you.' He paused and repeated, 'I will look out for you, Mum, I promise.'

'Of course, dear, I know you will.' A veil seemed to pass across Laura's expression. 'We're a family and we look out for each other. For a start, I'm going to take Dad a cup of coffee. Unless you want to take it up? He'd like that.'

Rob shook his head. 'One of us is going to have to tell him about this new body in the churchyard. That had better be you, Mum.'

She stared down at him, coffee cup in hand. 'All right,' she said at last.

'Not interrupting, am I?'

'Of course not, darling.' Jeremy looked up at his wife and smiled. 'Ah, coffee! Just the ticket.'

'Been working hard?'

'Well, reasonably,' he told her evasively. The fact was, he'd spent almost as much time staring out of the window at the scene of snow-dusted countryside as he had concentrating on work. In truth, he didn't like working here in his own house where the domestic problems seemed to be queueing outside his study door, like a gaggle of unruly pupils who'd been sent along to see the headmaster.

'I heard Rob,' he said, 'and another voice. Who was that?'

'Only Callum,' Laura told him. She tried for nonchalance but it didn't work. She sat down on a nearby chair.

'What did he want?' asked Jeremy suspiciously. 'Not cadging coffee, I hope.'

'Oh, no, he never does that!' she told him. 'He, um, brought a bit of news.'

Jeremy raised his eyebrows. To himself, he was thinking, *This is going to be bad . . .* But when she told him, he was speechless. Just sat there, he thought afterwards, goggling at her.

His wife was talking and he managed, belatedly, to find something to say. 'What do you mean, another murder?'

'Well, just that. Another body.'

Jeremy scrabbled around in his head for words. 'Where?' Then, when she told him, '*What?* No, no, Laura.' He waved his hands around as if batting away a wasp. 'There can't have been another murder in the churchyard!'

'Yes, there has.'

'Callum's got it wrong.'

'He can't have done. He found it. He was there with a woman police officer, a detective-sergeant.'

Jeremy's bewilderment gave way to anger. 'What the hell is Henderson playing at?'

'I don't think he's playing at anything. He's really upset. I could tell.'

'We're all upset!' stormed Jeremy. 'Who is the victim this time?'

'Well, that's the really awful thing. You probably don't remember a butcher's shop called Garret's. It was one of the old town businesses and still there when we first came here. I used to buy meat there when I went into town. Then it got easier to get it from the supermarket. Although . . .' Laura was sidetracked. 'The supermarket meat wasn't so good, still isn't. But Garret's has gone now. The dead woman – it's a woman this time – is one of the Garret family, quite elderly.' Laura shook her head miserably. 'It makes no sense.'

'Look here, Laura!' said her husband. 'I've had clients who've waffled on like this instead of getting to the point. What is it you don't want to tell me?'

'Nothing! Only, well, Rob says this woman police officer is Callum's girlfriend. And they were in the churchyard and found – found the dead body.'

'Damn Callum Henderson!' snapped Jeremy. 'Why can't he take his girl to the cinema or a disco or something. Why is he always damn well hanging round graveyards like some sort of ghoul?'

'I don't know!' Laura burst out and he realised belatedly that she was near to tears. He put out a hand to take hers.

'It's OK, sweetheart . . .'

She clutched at his hand. 'Jerry, listen! I know that when you mentioned moving away from here, I was cross. You took me by surprise. I've had time to think about it and perhaps you're right. We ought to sell up. The time has come to leave Abbotsfield. There's nothing here, just as you say. It's not been good for Rob. I did try, earlier this morning, to persuade him to go and spend a few days with Marcus. But he wouldn't even consider it.'

'Frankly, I don't think Marcus and all his troubles are the answers to our troubles,' muttered Jeremy.

But what troubles? He wished he knew. The other evening, he thought, I remembered how afraid I was as a kid, afraid of some unseen monster in the dark bedroom. That monster is out there somewhere now. It's prowling around at dead of night, and its path is coming ever closer to me and my family.

'We'll talk about it in the spring,' he said soothingly to his wife. 'That's the time to go house-hunting.'

Markby had also had a visitor that day. At least this one didn't ring the doorbell late at night. This one was official and arrived mid-morning; following a brief phone call to let him know he was on his way. Hooper had only been a small-time drugs pusher; but any reference to drugs distribution tugged one end of a long string to ring a bell elsewhere.

The newcomer's name was Turner. He was a tall, strongly built officer with reddish-blond hair, a nose that looked as though it might have been broken more than once, and a crooked, disarming smile that didn't quite match the sharp look in his blue eyes. Today he wore a sheepskin jacket, because of the overnight snowfall, Markby supposed. It was unfortunate, perhaps, that it increased the resemblance he bore to a large and powerful animal.

Markby had met him before. He liked him, but was slightly wary of him, as he was of all personnel from specialised departments and agencies. They came to him because they wanted his help. They never told him more than they had to. They were dedicated officers doing a dangerous job; they were also persistent and single minded. If Markby were asked to describe today's visitor in a phrase, he would have said Turner was a likeable, intelligent thug.

So he wasn't surprised when his caller opened the conversation with, 'Thank you for taking the time to see me, sir. I believe you've got a body we're interested in.'

'It's not my body,' parried Markby. 'It's the coroner's body.'

'Sure,' replied Turner comfortably. 'Of course it is.' He grinned disarmingly. His front left tooth was chipped.

'In fact, we're investigating two deaths,'

Turner raised a bushy eyebrow. 'I was told only of one.'

'The other body was found late yesterday evening. In the churchyard again,' he added unwillingly. As Turner still sat there, waiting, Markby found himself impelled to explain the circumstances of the discovery and say they knew the identity of the victim.

A gleam entered Turner's eyes when he learned of the presence of a serving officer at the time of the discovery, but then it disappeared, switched off like a light bulb. Otherwise, Turner absorbed the information and then shrugged away Melissa Garret's death. 'I'm not interested in that one, the old lady. I'm here about the earlier one, the bloke. We hear you've identified him as Aaron Hooper. The name isn't unknown to us.'

'I'm not surprised to see you,' Markby told him. 'I thought either you or one of your colleagues would be around here soon for a chat. We knew Hooper was connected with the drugs scene locally, but we had him down as small fry.'

'Oh, yes,' agreed Turner. 'Very small fry. Unpleasant little creature but with his place in the scheme of things. Bit like a dung beetle.' The chipped front tooth flashed into view briefly. 'But follow the trail of the small pests, and with a bit of luck it will lead you to the bigger beasts. Any idea who killed him?'

'No,' said Markby. 'It's a pretty odd scenario, really. He was found in a local churchyard, sitting on a grave. I saw the body in situ myself. He was propped up against a gravestone.'

'Very apt!' approved Turner. 'Pity he wasn't under it.'

Markby chose to take this remark pedantically. 'Oh, there have been no burials in that old churchyard for donkey's years. If you die now and your family choose a traditional interment, it will be in the new cemetery, alongside the old burial ground.'

Any preliminary fencing over, Turner leaned forward and placed his clasped hands on the desk. 'Anything special or unusual, apart from where he was found?'

Markby hesitated. 'It may not mean anything. But the palms of both hands were scored with knife wounds. Not the sort he might have got trying to fight off his assailant. These were mostly likely inflicted while he sat there dying or immediately after death. The pathologist agrees with me. There's no indication he tried to avoid what the assailant was doing to his hands. It's in the report.'

'What about the guy who found the body? Could he have decided to decorate the hands?'

'Henderson? No, highly unlikely. When he found the

body, he came racing to my front door. I live in what used to be the vicarage, alongside the churchyard. It was pretty dark out there, just the moonlight. It wasn't until I played my torch beam over the body that I saw the cut hands, and when I looked more closely, that's when Henderson noticed them. Upset him even more than he was already.'

'What was Henderson doing in the churchyard at that time of night?' asked Turner and sounded genuinely, not merely professionally, curious.

'On his way home from the pub. Short cut. He takes that route every time. He lives in Abbotsfield. It's a village, if you can call it that, separated from the town by fields. But there's planning permission for a large housing development on the open land that lies between the two communities. Building work there has already begun. In fact, it will more or less join it to the town.'

'Same everywhere, I suppose,' murmured the visitor. 'Abbotsfield . . . I've heard the name. There's a guy who runs a wine import business from there. Baxter, his name is. Ever come across him?'

'Bought a couple of cases of wine off him once. He held a wine tasting at his place last year. It was a pleasant evening but one couldn't leave without buying something. What's your interest in him?'

'Oh,' murmured Turner, 'Customs and Excise officers at Dover passed his name on to us a while ago. He makes numerous short trips across the Channel and that always interests them! But they didn't catch him bringing in any-thing illegal. The paperwork was always in order, and there has never been anything but cases of wine found in the lorry. They opened a file on Baxter as a matter of routine.'

There was a pause in the conversation. Markby had no idea what Turner was thinking. But it wasn't up to him to make the running. Turner had come to him and, if he had a question, he'd ask it.

'The weapon . . .' said Turner now, meditatively.

'We believe we have the weapon. It's still with forensics, though.' Markby told his visitor about the discovery of the knife.

Turner listened in silence, nodding. Keeping the conversation hopping around from one subject to another was part of Turner's method, Markby remembered from their previous encounter. He never let the interlocutor settle. He'd throw in anything on the spur of the moment. Who could say if he was really interested in Baxter, or just muddying the water? But I'm an old hand, too, thought Markby with grim satisfaction.

'Where had Hooper been living while he was here? London is his usual stamping ground.' Turner made another of his sideways leaps.

'He was staying with his sister. Steve Kendal dealt with her. Have you met Inspector Kendal before?'

'Once,' said Turner. 'Any use my talking to this sister?'

'Kendal's opinion is the one you want on that. I didn't meet her.'

'Because,' Turner gave a diffident smile, 'you've got a corpse and a murder to investigate. I'm not here to interfere with that. Oh, I want to know who killed Hooper, too. But chiefly we're investigating the distribution of drugs in the area, and the chain of supply. My outfit is throwing its net more widely, you might say.'

'I only want to know who killed him,' Markby agreed. 'The drugs angle is your area of expertise.' That sounded like a nice harmonious agreement for two separate investigations to work together. Quite often, however, it didn't quite work out that way. 'Come and chat to Inspector Kendal,' he said. 'And you might like to meet DS Santos who is working on this with Kendal. She's recently joined us.'

Turner's expression brightened. 'Do you mean Beth Santos? Was she the officer present at the discovery of the second body?'

'Yes,' said Markby uneasily, and wishing he'd not told Turner so much about the second corpse.

Turner looked quite cheerful. 'I've met her before. She used to be married to a mate of mine.'

Now he grinned, openly displaying the chipped front tooth. And that, thought Markby crossly, is because he knows he's succeeded in wrong-footing me. But I'm entitled to my revenge. I was intending to ask him to join me in a pub lunch in the interest of cementing interdepartmental harmony. Now he can get his lunch in the canteen, like anyone else.

Chapter Ten

Steve Kendal was interested to meet Turner, but was extremely disconcerted to find out that this bruiser from the drugs enforcement agency had a prior acquaintance with DS Santos. How many other little secrets did Santos have? It got worse.

'I know how busy you are, Steve,' said Turner in a friendly voice. 'So perhaps I could borrow Beth for an hour? Perhaps she could take me to meet Hooper's sister and, after that, show me exactly where his body was found in that churchyard. That OK with you?'

'Be my guest!' replied Kendal through gritted teeth.

To be fair, when Santos was told the plan, she did not seem very enthusiastic either. However, her lack of enthusiasm was outmatched by that of Kylie Hooper. She opened the door wearing a grubby sweatshirt over leggings and cheap imitation Ugg boots, overtrodden at the heels. She greeted her visitors with little attempt to disguise outright hostility.

'Oh, it's you coppers again,' she said, on finding Santos and Turner on the doorstep. 'What d'ya want now? You've already bothered me half out of my mind with your questions about my brother. I can't answer any of 'em, because I don't know what he did, and you've searched my house.' She drew breath. 'And never found anything, I'd like to remind you!'

'Just a chat, Kylie,' said Santos soothingly. 'This is Inspector Turner. He's working with us on your brother's case.'

'Oh, yeah,' retorted Kylie, running a sharp eye over Turner's burly form. 'What's his interest, then?'

Santos hid a wry smile. Kylie might not be gracious but she was sharp. Turner represented a new element in the investigation into her brother's death. Beth guessed that Kylie had a pretty fair idea which outfit he represented.

Turner didn't beat about the bush, either. 'Distribution of controlled substances,' he said.

Kylie squinted at him. 'Swallowed a dictionary? You mean drugs.'

'Absolutely correct, Kylie. Your late brother was a pusher.'

Kylie drew herself up in readiness for a battle. 'Not outa my house he wasn't! I don't – never have – allowed anything like drugs in the house. I got kids. You can't hide anything from them. Kids'll find it, whatever it is. Natural little snoops, kids are. Aaron knew I wouldn't have drugs in the house and what's more,' she turned to Santos, 'when your lot searched, they didn't find any!'

'We haven't come to search your house,' said Turner. 'I'd just like to talk to you about your brother.'

'Perhaps indoors?' suggested Santos. 'Where we would have more privacy?'

Kylie glanced to either side. Her neighbours, who had disappeared indoors as soon as Turner and Santos got out of the car, had re-emerged. They were now either clearing snow from their parked vehicles or brushing it from their doorsteps.

'All right,' agreed Kylie and turned to shuffle back into the house. The two officers followed.

They sat down in what Kylie called her 'front room'. Santos knew this was a sign of a formal visit but guessed it wouldn't include an offer of tea. She also suspected that the 'back' room was no tidier than the one they were in. Nothing had been dusted in here for a while; and some flowers stuck haphazardly in a chipped vase were in the last stage of expiring from lack of water.

The short interval had given Kylie Hooper time to review her options and she'd decided to plump for bereavement. Seeing Beth's gaze rest on the flowers, she pointed at them and said sorrowfully, 'Me neighbour give me those. Old girl next door. On account I lost my brother.'

Before Turner could ask any questions about the late Aaron, Kylie continued, 'It's not decent, the police hounding me like you are. Not at this very sad time for my family. Aaron was my only brother. Now I got no one. My dad's long gone. Mum pushed off somewhere. My sister lives in Bethnal Green and we don't speak.'

'Did Aaron not speak to her either? Is that why he left London and came to you?' asked Santos.

'Don't be daft,' retorted Kylie, 'he couldn't go to her, my sister. Her husband couldn't stand him. He'd have murdered him if he'd turned up there!' She was apparently unaware of any irony in her last words.

'Could you give us your sister's address in London?' asked Turner.

Kylie sighed but plodded in the imitation Ugg boots to a sideboard, rummaged in a drawer, and produced a well-worn address book. 'Here,' she said, holding it out. 'Her married name is Russell. Cindy Russell. But you're wasting your time. I told you.'

'We are determined to find out who killed your brother,' Santos assured her, as Turner found the address and copied it.

'I'm not paying for any funeral,' warned Kylie. 'You needn't think that. I haven't got the money and, even if I had, I wouldn't pay.'

Turner returned the tattered address book to its sullen owner, and took up from Beth. 'Anything at all that you may remember later, just tell us. We'll decide if it's important or not. Did anyone call here, asking for him? Had he seemed more than usually worried or nervous? Did you meet any friends of his?'

'Aaron didn't go in for friends,' retorted Kylie with a sniff. 'So it's not a bit of good you lot asking me about anything. I don't know anything. All I can tell you is that he turned up here wanting to stay for a while. I didn't have to ask him why. I knew why. He'd got himself into some sort of trouble and he was trying to avoid someone who was after him. I didn't want him here. But I let him stay. He was my brother and anyway, since my partner and I split up, it's been difficult for me. A woman on her own, with kids, and no man in the house . . .' She stared at them tragically. 'It's been really hard. People try and take advantage. I don't let them, mind you! But that don't stop them trying.'

Turner knew when prolonging a visit was useless. 'All right, thank you for talking to us. If you should chance to think of anything later—'

'I'll tell you one thing!' Kylie interrupted him. She leaned forward.

'Yes?' asked Turner.

'If you lot were as keen to return my son's bike as you are to take up my time, that would be a big help to me! You still got it. He needs it to go to school. It's hard enough getting him to school, anyway, and if he has to walk there, well . . .'

'I think the bike is still with forensics,' said Santos, 'but I'll inquire.'

'Forensics!' squawked Kylie. 'What do they want with my son's bike? Ain't they got no transport of their own?'

'Well,' said Turner, when they'd left the house, 'I don't think she'll be much use.'

'She's not as dumb as she makes out,' retorted Santos.

219

'I don't think so, anyway. But it suits her to know nothing and we won't shift her.'

'Casework apart, how are you getting on here?' asked Turner. 'Like it? Rest of the team OK to work with?'

'Yes, thanks.' Santos had been ready for Turner to make one of his conversational leaps.

'Any objection to my telling Gary I've seen you?'

She'd been ready for that question too. 'None at all. He's all right, I suppose?'

'He's fine. Do I tell him you asked after him?'

'You can tell him what you like,' Santos snapped. 'But you started this conversation.'

Turner chuckled. 'You don't change, Beth!'

'Why should I? By the way, you don't change either, Inspector Turner, and I know how you like to catch people out,' she warned.

'Catching people is my job!' he retorted cheerfully.

'Well, don't try your interviewing techniques on me. Do you want to see the churchyard and where Hooper's body was found?'

'Lead on, DS Santos! The gates will be open, I suppose?'

'Sure, during the day. They only close them at night. Besides, there will be a search team at work in there around the location of the second body.'

'They will be lucky to find anything in the snow,' remarked Turner.

'That's their problem. We'll start at the new cemetery because that's where we believe the original attack took place, and the team won't be looking there. But the snow will also have covered everything in the area where we believe Hooper was attacked and died.'

Santos began her guided tour where glittering white bumps indicated the broken flowerpots still on the ground. 'This is where the meet took place, we believe. Hooper was mortally wounded but didn't realise it. He set off following the wall until he collapsed in the old churchyard. This way . . .'

She led Turner to the gravestone in the old churchyard where Callum had come across the body. With its snow decking, the whole area looked breathtakingly beautiful, a different world, untouched, unsullied, a place that had seen generations come and go, and stayed another world. Small showers of snow fell from the branches of the old trees and fluttered to the ground as if angels had passed through. Santos caught her breath.

Turner studied the area. If he thought it picturesque, he wasn't about to say so. He asked, 'Where was the knife found?'

'Over there, hidden in chippings on that grave, the one with the police tape round it.'

'And do we now know if it's the murder weapon?'

'Yes, confirmation came in last thing yesterday. The blade had traces of Hooper's blood on it. The grip appears to have been handled by more than one person. The prints are very smeared and still being worked on.'

Turner gazed thoughtfully across the snow-decked churchyard towards the maintenance hut in the distance. A group of uniforms worked methodically around it.

'That's where the second body was found?'

'Yes, but we don't think it has anything to do with the first body. Hooper had a criminal record and had been living here for just under a year. His only connection with the town seems to have been his sister. We don't know why he met his killer here. The second body is that of a local woman, elderly, lived with her brother and sister-in-law. She was on her way to a meeting of a reading group she belonged to.' Beth paused and added soberly, 'She had arthritis. She couldn't have beaten off an attacker.'

'And you fell on her, so I understand,' said Turner in a conversational way.

'No, I climbed the wall into the churchyard over there and jumped down to land beside her. It took me a couple of minutes to realise the body was there.'

'Nasty shock,' said Turner.

His voice was sympathetic but that didn't fool Santos. However, the best way to deal with Turner was to say as little as possible. Kylie Hooper had the technique down to a fine art. Beth intended to copy her.

Turner dropped the attempt at sympathy, since it wasn't working, and asked much more brusquely, 'What the hell were you doing climbing over that wall in the late evening, in the company of a suspect?'

'He's a witness!' snapped Santos unwarily and was furious with herself for walking into Turner's trap.

'He's also a suspect and you know it, Beth! He has to be. Do you really buy this story that he's in the habit of cutting across the churchyard to get to the pub?'

'Yes, as it happens, I do; and so does Superintendent Markby.'

'Does he, indeed? I wouldn't presume to know what the superintendent is thinking. OK, then, Beth! Show me this route. When Henderson found the body, he'd just climbed over that wall, about here, right?' Turner pointed to the rough stone wall. 'His original plan was to exit the churchyard over there, by that hut, climb over the second wall to drop down into the street, and make his way home across the fields. So why don't we do the same?'

'All right,' agreed Santos briskly. 'But we don't need to climb that wall by the hut to get out. Besides, we'd risk disturbing the crime scene. The main gates will be open now and we can walk through them, turn the corner, and walk through a couple of streets to reach the fields.'

A couple of the uniforms glanced up as they approached, but, recognising Santos, returned their gaze to the ground.

'That's Markby's house, is it?' asked Turner, as they passed by the Old Vicarage.

'Yes,' said Santos stonily.

'And that's where your pal Callum raised the alarm?'

'Yes!'

Turner chuckled.

Santos suppressed her fury. *Please, please,* she prayed. *Don't let us meet Callum out in the fields; and let me find the right path. Please God I don't lose us both out there! It'll be snow covered, everything will look different. Callum said I'd get lost on my own. If I do, Turner will tell everyone and Callum will hear about it. He hears about most things.*

'Snow seems to have stopped the building work,' said Turner. He indicated the area across the fields where excavations, machinery and half-built walls lay under a clean white sheet. The site certainly looked deserted.

For Santos, the building site was a marker. If she kept it to her left and struck out at an angle across the open land, she should reach Abbotsfield. She strode out as confidently as she could. It wouldn't do to let Turner see she was anything less than quite sure of her way. It seemed to be going well and her confidence was growing, when she saw an approaching figure heading straight towards them.

'Hello, who is this, then?' asked Turner.

Panic flooded Beth's mind. She repressed it, and then relaxed, because whoever this was, it wasn't Callum Henderson. The solitary walker heading so purposefully their way was a tall, thin figure in a heavy cagoule and a woollen hat. Callum wasn't one for knitted hats. As they drew nearer there was a moment of recognition on the part of the walker and of Santos. She'd seen him before. He'd had an argument with Steve Kendal about damaging the natural habitat in the churchyard.

'Hello,' said the walker cheerfully, 'Detective Sergeant Santos, isn't it?'

'Yes,' said Beth, trying not to sound relieved. 'Mr Finch, the botanist.' She indicated her companion. 'Inspector Turner.'

'Not much to be seen in the botanical line under the snow,' observed Turner, after he acknowledged the introduction with a nod.

'Oh, I'm not actually a professional botanist!' said Finch earnestly. 'DS Santos pays me a compliment. I'm strictly an amateur. It's a hobby of mine. In addition, I run a local rambling group. I'm also something of a local historian.'

'So,' asked Turner, 'what's your day job?'

'Professionally, I'm a mathematician and teach at a local school, as it happens.' Finch waved at the snowy surrounds. 'You are quite right, Inspector Turner, not a lot to see by way of plant life. I've just been over to the building site.'

'Not much going on there, either,' said Turner.

'Not a workman to be seen; it's like the *Marie Celeste*,' agreed Finch. 'But they'll be back.' He sighed. 'They have no idea what they're destroying and they don't care, that's the worst of it. Have you replaced Inspector Kendal, Mr Turner?'

'No!' chimed Turner and Beth together.

'Just visiting,' said Turner.

'Ah,' said Finch despondently, 'Kendal's finished in the churchyard I hope.'

'Inspector Kendal isn't there at the moment,' said Beth, 'But we're not finished there, I'm sorry to say. There is a new search just started. There's been a second murder, another body found there.'

A look of baffled fury crossed Finch's face. 'Merry hell!' he said. 'That's all we need. I was hoping you'd all finished in the churchyard.' He glared at them. 'Who is it this time? Do you know?'

We all have our priorities, thought Santos. Most people's first concern would be about the victim. Finch was more worried about police boots trampling his cherished nature site.

'Yes, we do, the victim is a local woman, Melissa Garret. You wouldn't happen to have known her?' Beside her, she sensed Turner watching Finch closely.

'Who'd want to kill *her*?' Finch looked genuinely bewildered. 'Was it a mistake? I mean, did the killer mean to attack someone else?'

'We don't know. But you do seem to know something of Melissa Garret. Anything you could tell us might be helpful.'

'Oh, well, I wouldn't say that I knew anything much about her.' Finch was discomfited. Perhaps he'd realised that his skewed priorities had been officially noted. 'She's – she was – pally with Celia Benton. You know, the old girl who found the knife hidden in the marble chippings on one of the graves? I didn't know Melissa except by sight, but I knew she belonged to Mrs Benton's reading group. Mrs Benton knew my grandmother, which is my bad luck. Every time she sees me, she stops to give me the third degree. But I can't tell you anything more about Melissa Garret. Oh well, I shall hear all about it when I run into Celia Benton again. She's the one you need if you want to know about the Garrets. I hope you soon find out who killed Melissa. But I wish your chaps weren't trampling all over the churchyard again. Foxes have been sighted there recently, you know.'

'It would be best not to interfere in a police operation, Mr Finch!' Santos warned him.

'Oh, I have no intention of interfering,' retorted Finch with some vigour. 'Because it wouldn't make any difference. I just hope it's all over soon. Well, good luck to you, anyway, Officers!'

He nodded and strode off.

'Now then,' murmured Turner. He had been listening with a gleam in his eyes. 'There's another one I sense knows more than he's letting on.'

'Why do you say that?' Santos asked him curiously. 'I don't think he'd heard about the second body until I told him. He lives at Abbotsfield. Why did you say "another one"? Who's the first one?'

'Your pal Henderson, of course,' said Turner with such blithe assurance that Beth was stopped from snapping back a denial.

After all, hadn't she herself been thinking along the same lines earlier? Not about Finch, but about Callum, and that he heard most things. She'd not felt uneasy about Callum before now. But she was beginning to. And she had this rugby-playing chum of her ex-husband to thank for it.

'He's not a friend,' she said firmly.

'Of course not,' agreed Turner. 'He's a witness.' The chipped front tooth came into sight as he smiled down at her. 'And they both happen to live at Abbotsfield. Well, it's not my investigation.'

'No, it's not!' snapped Santos.

★ ★ ★

Callum Henderson was aware he already carried the label of the Man Who Found The Body. Henceforth, in the popular local view, he'd be the man who wandered round at night finding dead bodies plural. Sensibly, he had made up his mind to lie low. Keep away from everyone, that was the plan. He got too many strange looks when he went to the pub, which meant the Black Dog was off limits for the time being. So was anywhere else where he was likely to meet anyone. Besides, he decided, he couldn't ignore the state of his van, inside and out, any longer. It had to be cleaned up. Gus's motorbike was missing from the yard, so he was away about one of his other mysterious bits of business, or just socialising with his cronies in the travelling community. Callum set to work. At this time of year, the light faded early. He was hunched inside the interior when a fist rapped on the side of the van and he heard his name called. He emerged, jumping down to peer through the pearl-grey atmosphere within the yard to see his visitor.

'Hello, Baz!' he greeted him on recognising the gangling figure in a cagoule standing by the rear of the van. 'Why aren't you teaching those kids their sums? Or is school out already?'

'School heating conked out,' said Basil Finch. 'We had to phone round and tell the kids not to come in. It's always a problem. Most of the parents work.'

'Gives you a chance to go hiking over the fields, I guess,' said Callum. 'I see you're wearing the gear. Want a cup of tea? Or something stronger? Beer and cider in the fridge. Go on indoors. I'll be with you as soon as I've cleaned myself up.'

A little later when he joined his visitor in the kitchen, he asked, 'Go far on your ramble?' Callum popped a can of cider and seated himself across the kitchen table from the caller. He swept a stack of catalogues aside to give himself table space. Basil, he noted, had made himself a mug of coffee. Abstemious sort of bloke, was Baz Finch. But then, he'd been out on a hike on a cold day and needed a hot drink.

Even years earlier, when they had waited together at the crossroads for the bus to school, Callum wouldn't have been surprised if told that Basil would choose teaching as a career. School had always appeared to be what Finch himself would call a natural habitat for him. Baz always had strongly held beliefs and a determination to impart them to others. Callum recalled him as a lanky fourteen-year-old, fringe of fair hair flopping over his brow as he doggedly tacked up his home-made posters around the school, on the subject of the latest bee in his bonnet.

Since then, he'd taken up the cause of rural preservation. Instead of posters, he had his bird-watching and nature-rambles; and the campaign he'd led, unsuccessfully, against the new development and the threat to the natural path of the mediaeval right of way. He'd once asked Basil why he'd chosen to teach maths. 'There's something reassuring about numbers,' had been Basil's reply. 'They make sense. People often don't.'

Which meant, Callum decided, that people didn't always agree with Basil. There were the makings of the fanatic in old Baz. Perhaps he should have gone into politics.

'I walked over to see how the house-building is progressing,' Basil said now, 'but it seems to have been called off on account of the snow. The site manager doesn't like it when I turn up. He generally tells me, fairly politely, to clear off. He gives me the lecture about a building site being a dangerous place; and the insurance wouldn't cover it if I fell into some foundations and got stuck in concrete, or some such tale. I tell him he should realise he's putting bricks across an ancient way, used by drovers for hundreds of years to get their flocks to market. He just says there are no drovers any more, the animals are all transported in trucks by road, and walkers will still be able to cut through between the houses. Then I ask him how on earth he thinks surface water will be able to drain away in the future, if he puts asphalt and concrete over the soil. That makes him pretty cross. But there was no sign of him today and his Portakabin office was locked.'

Basil sounded wistful at having missed his duel with the site manager, but – although he mourned the loss of the fields as much as his old schoolfriend did – Callum felt some sympathy for the site manager. The poor bloke was only trying to do his job; and the last thing he needed was Basil lecturing him as though he were a class of unruly teenagers.

'Why do you bother, Baz? I mean, why bother to have

the same arguments with him over and over again?'

'Because it's the only thing I can do,' returned his visitor simply. 'I can't stop it, or change anything, but perhaps I can open a window to let him see another view of it. You're going to say I'm wasting my time, as well as his. You'd be right. Of course I am. I won't get him to change his point of view, but I do believe he's slowly starting to see mine, even if he doesn't agree. After all, there are people, like you, Callum, who still walk to town from here across the fields. OK, not many of them. But I did meet a couple out there today; and that's what I came to tell you about, actually.'

'Oh, yes?' Callum wondered why he felt a sense of foreboding.

'That woman detective and another copper, big bloke, rugby player by the looks of him, and with a stare like a laser. Friendly enough, to talk to. Wouldn't like to be shut up in an interview room with him.'

'Don't place him,' muttered Callum. 'Doesn't sound like Kendal. Certainly isn't Markby.'

'Not a local man, and certainly not that officious little Napoleon, Kendal!' said Basil with unexpected vehemence. 'I gathered he'd parachuted in from somewhere else; but wasn't saying where. They told me there's been a second murder.'

'You don't have to tell me,' growled Callum. 'It was another one in the churchyard and we – I – found the body on a compost heap by the workmen's hut.'

'With the lady detective at the time, were you? *On a compost heap?*'

'Yes, and I'm ordered not to talk about it. And it was the body that was on the compost heap, not us.'

'Perish the thought! I don't want the gory details; but listen, Callum, you've got to stop finding bodies.' Finch leaned earnestly across the table. 'Kendal and his merry men have already trampled all over the old churchyard once; and now they're all set to do it again.'

'I don't go looking for bodies,' retorted Callum vigorously. 'And I don't control what the police do!'

'And finding poor old Melissa Garret, of all people, stiff as a post on the compost heap! Mind you, I say "poor old" Melissa, but that's being charitable about the departed. She was a strident old bat. She didn't like me taking groups of students around the churchyard. She said they dropped sweet wrappers. Not if I caught them, they didn't. And people leave worse things in there! She was as bad as Celia Benton.'

'Who on earth is Celia Benton?'

'Lives in that big Victorian villa on the edge of the churchyard. She's another one doesn't like the children being in there – or anyone else, come to that. She keeps telling me she knew my grandmother. It's her way of letting me know she thinks I'm letting the side down.' Basil squinted over his coffee mug at Callum. 'What were you doing in the churchyard this time, anyway? And with that DS Santos. Not that she isn't a looker, I agree. Pretty tough, though, I should think.'

'You should see her shin over a wall or chase after an intruder,' murmured Callum.

'You've seen her do both those things; I suppose?' asked Basil shrewdly.

Callum avoided giving an answer by getting up and going to the fridge to fetch another cider for himself, and one for Basil, who'd finished his coffee.

Basil accepted the cider and raised it to toast his host. 'Good luck, if you're going to play Watson to that female Holmes.'

'I don't intend to have anything to do with it, whatever is going on!' snapped Callum.

'Whatever you may intend, or have intended, you're still getting pretty tangled up in it all. No tracker dog needed to find a body. Send out Henderson! Ever thought of offering your services to Mountain Rescue?'

'Give it a rest, Baz!'

'OK, but it's all got something to do with Abbotsfield, hasn't it? That's why your girlfriend Santos and that steely-eyed prop forward are prowling around out there.'

'Just shut up, Baz. And she is not my girlfriend!'

'Sure,' said Basil.

Chapter Eleven

'I'm going to have to take her off the case,' said Markby, staring gloomily into his grapefruit chunks.

'You mean Beth Santos, I take it? Don't you like grapefruit?'

'I like it well enough. We're not on a diet, are we?'

'I'll scramble some eggs.'

'No, don't! I mean, no need. I'll have some more toast; and if I can't last out the morning, I'll send down to the canteen for one of those triangular boxes of sandwiches they specialise in.'

'I'm sorry you feel you have to take Beth off the case, but I understand,' Meredith sympathised. 'It's because of her friendship with Callum Henderson, I suppose?'

'What would you do? Henderson's a likeable chap. I don't think he's a murderer. But he's managed to find two bodies and he does behave a little strangely at times.'

'All that hanging about in churchyards?'

'Only one churchyard, to my knowledge. He doesn't

hang about in it; he just uses it as a short cut. Of course, finding Melissa Garret's body has put another complexion on that, even if finding Hooper's hadn't already done so. I gather Santos persuaded him to show her where he climbed the wall on the street side of the churchyard. Unfortunately, it was above the spot where the killer had left Melissa. That is, if I accept the account given to me by Callum himself and by DS Santos.'

'Don't you accept it?'

'Yes, I do, fantastic though it sounds. But what the devil is Santos playing at? Anyway, I just can't risk having the pair of them together stumbling across anything else, a body or any other evidence connected with either case. And that's another thing I have to make clear to Santos. She is supposed to be part of a team. The police team, not some DIY twosome she's formed with Callum. I'm impressed by her enthusiasm. But she's not supposed to go haring off on some line of investigation she hasn't first discussed with a senior officer, Kendal in this case, or me.'

'Stick to the rules, eh?' Meredith murmured over the rim of her cup.

'Always!' he told her firmly. 'Eventually, remember, we hope to have a case that will stand up in court. We need to have done everything in the right way, down to the last bit of procedure. Don't leave gaps a good defence barrister will spot.'

'Point taken.'

Markby sighed. 'It's important not to assume the two deaths are part of the same case. I don't think they are. Turner certainly doesn't. And that's another thing, having Turner arrive on my doorstep like that; and fishing for information relating to some investigation of his own. Thank goodness, he's left and I hope he doesn't return.' Markby heaved a deep sigh. 'But before I sort all that out, I have to speak to Steve Kendal, and he's a bit of an awkward sort. Very good officer, but touchy.'

'What do you have to speak to him about?' asked Meredith.

'I can hardly call in Santos; and tell her she's off the team for this one, without first warning Kendal I'm going to do it. He is, after all, the officer I put in charge of the case. Oh, well, *when troubles come, they come not single spies but in battalions,* as Shakespeare so truly wrote. Or something like that. Why are you grinning?'

'Inspector Kendal says you want to see me, Mr Markby.'

'Yes, I do, Beth. Sit down. Did Steve Kendal give you any indication as to what this might be about?'

'No, sir.' Santos sat as directed and fixed the superintendent with a truculent glare.

'Hm. Well, from the look on your face I think you may have worked it out for yourself.' Markby smiled at her.

'You're taking me off the team, aren't you?' Santos burst out. 'Is it because I was with Henderson when the body of Melissa Garret was found?'

'Partly. But to be frank, I've been concerned about your friendship with Henderson. I intended to speak to you before about it. When all this is over, and both murders solved as I hope they will be, and if Henderson isn't further involved than we're already aware of, well, you're free to make your friends where you will. But right now, it's inappropriate.'

When she didn't comment, Markby added, 'Come on, Beth, I think you must have been expecting this.'

'When I saw how smug Inspector Kendal looked,' muttered Santos, 'I knew I was for it.'

'Steve Kendal is an experienced and valued officer,' Markby told her sternly. 'Personalities can and do clash from time to time. It doesn't help any team when that happens.'

She nodded. 'Can I speak frankly, sir?'

'I'd much prefer it if you did.'

Beth leaned forward in her chair and began earnestly, 'I do know I've been pushing my luck, sir.'

'Aha!' Markby managed, just, to suppress a grin.

'It's just that I have no evidence I can put forward, only a feeling.'

'The Crown Prosecution Service likes evidence, not emotions, DS Santos. You know that. So do I. Look, speak off the record, if you like. I've been an investigating officer for a long time. I'm heading for retirement. Ask any retired officer and he'll tell you of the unexplained situations he's seen and unsatisfactory explanations he's been given in the course of a long career. But, unlike fictional sleuths, we don't act on hunches. We need to get a conviction at the end of the day. That's not simply because we want a pat on the back. It's because we owe it to the bereaved relatives and all those whose lives are ruined by an unsolved crime. If we get it wrong, an innocent person may be convicted.

'Above all, we must work as a team and not go haring off investigating our private suspicions. I think that's what you've been doing. Am I wrong?'

'No, sir.' Santos hesitated and added, 'It wasn't Callum Henderson's fault that we climbed that wall and landed near Melissa Garret's body. I talked him into it. I mean, into the whole expedition. I figured that if he climbed into the churchyard over the wall by the pub, when the gates were locked, he must have climbed into it somewhere else first. I asked him to show me.'

'Why?' asked Markby coolly. 'Just idle curiosity, or some theory you hadn't seen fit to share with the rest of us?'

'It's that place, Abbotsfield!' Beth burst out. 'It's really odd. And I'm not the only one who thinks so. Inspector Turner asked me to show him the route from the churchyard across the fields to the village, well, it's not a proper village, is it?'

'No, it's not. It's what used once to be called a hamlet. Inspector Turner told me he asked you to show him the way across the fields to it. Did he tell you why?'

'No, he didn't!' said Beth crossly. 'Nick Turner never does tell you anything unless he wants something in return.' She flushed, 'Sorry if that sounds rude about a senior officer, but he's an old rugby pal of my ex-husband. I know him fairly well.'

And you've got him summed up pretty accurately, Markby thought but didn't say aloud. He didn't tell me, either.

'Well, anyway,' Santos continued. 'It's a very strange place. There are only a few people living there but they're a real mix. I don't know anything about the ones who live in those shabby old bungalows.'

'They're mostly elderly and at least two of them are disabled,' said Markby. 'I don't think you need worry about them.'

'Oh, well . . . There are the people who run the wine business and are pretty well off, it seems. They're off skiing, Callum says. There's that high-flying solicitor who commutes up to London. You'd think he'd have chosen somewhere nearer to his office. He's got a wife who's a potter, and an unemployed son who does nothing but roar round on a motorcycle. I'm sure he's the one who nearly collided with us when we first drove out there. There's Callum, who has pretty well always lived there and has his landscaping business. Oh, and Gus Toomey who seems to live, quite irregularly I suspect, in a caravan in a field.' Santos drew a deep breath. 'And there's Basil Finch, who teaches maths, but is obsessed with protecting the countryside and is harassing the site manager where the new building is going on. He's got a thing about ancient rights of way. Inspector Turner and I met him in the fields.'

'Turner told me that, too.'

'Finch was very upset to learn of another body

being found in the churchyard, mostly because it means the police will have a search team back in there. I have a nagging feeling they all know more than they're saying.'

'Even Callum Henderson?'

'Maybe even Callum, although I think he just wants to be left alone. Nothing appears to link the Abbotsfield lot, apart from where they live. So why do I feel they all share some sort of secret?'

Markby drew a deep breath. 'Small communities often appear clannish to visitors from outside. For what it's worth, I also suspect Toomey shouldn't be living full time in that field. But that's not our problem. Let the local council tackle that one, if they feel like it.'

'Oh,' said Beth, momentarily deflated. 'Don't you think Abbotsfield is an odd place?'

'It always has been,' Markby told her calmly. 'Up until the middle of the nineteenth century it was the reputed haunt of witches. That pub isn't called the Black Dog for no reason. Oh, and local tradition has it that a gallows, long gone, once stood at the crossroads, just after you leave the village on the far side. But don't worry about it, Detective Sergeant Santos. It's not your problem any longer! We'll find you something else to do.'

'Now what?' muttered Callum.

A car he recognised had drawn up outside his home and a familiar female figure had emerged. He opened the front door as she reached it. Something's wrong, he thought as he saw the expression on her face.

Before he could ask, she told him. 'I've been taken off the team!'

Callum had read and heard the expression 'through gritted teeth' without knowing exactly how words so expressed would sound. Now he knew. She was pale with suppressed rage and her eyes gleamed.

'You'd better come in,' he told her.

'Oh,' said Beth, moments later. 'Is this your sitting room? I didn't know you had one.' She looked about her. The anger faded from her expression to be replaced by dismay.

'I don't use it,' Callum defended himself. 'I only use the kitchen and almost everyone comes to the back door. Even if it's about work, they go into the yard first and then knock on the back door.'

Beth seemed to be itemising the contents of the tiny room: its old-fashioned armchairs, dust-covered ornaments, faded photographs and an aged TV set. 'Don't you ever clean up in here?'

'No!' retorted Callum, angered not only because he didn't like being criticised but because he was embarrassed. 'Why should I? I don't use it. Come into the kitchen – my office,' he amended quickly.

'Yes, I think I'd rather. Although I'm not staying long.'

'That's a relief.' Now, that did sound rude. He added, 'I'm pleased to see you, of course. If I sounded a bit tetchy, it's because I thought you wanted to go marching around the countryside again. I've had a busy day and don't feel like it.'

'I can't go anywhere with you,' was the gloomy reply. 'I told you, I've been taken off the team. I only came out here to tell you that; and also to tell you that I've been warned that any association with you is inappropriate.'

'What! Why?' demanded Callum, annoyed. After all, it was one thing for him to want her out of his hair; and quite another for him to be declared an inappropriate person for her to befriend. That was an insult.

'Because of the investigation, of course. You found the first body and we both found the second one. And because we were climbing into the churchyard over the wall after dark. That was my fault, sorry. I badgered you into showing me the spot. And Markby has found us twice together.'

Technically, this was true. But it made him appear weak willed (as well as inappropriate). 'You didn't badger me!'

'Yes, I did.'

'All right, you did.' They had progressed to the kitchen/ office. Feeling he ought to offer his visitor some refreshment after his ungraciousness, Callum asked, 'Do you drink beer? Or I think I've got cider, or I can make tea.'

'Cider would be fine.' Minutes later, seated either side of the kitchen table, she added, 'I should be going as soon as I've drunk this. I shouldn't be here at all.'

'It's a free country, you're not on duty, and an Englishman's home is his castle,' declared Callum, and raised his can of cider in salute. 'Cheers!'

'None of that would wash with Superintendent Markby. He said our friendship was – you know . . .'

'Inappropriate? Yes, you said that. He can tell *you* that, as he's your boss. He can't tell *me* that any friendship I have is inappropriate. I'm a free man!' Callum set down the cider. 'Who was the new bloke? The one with you when Baz Finch met you, out in the fields this afternoon?'

'Oh, him, he was just visiting.'

'What was his interest in walking the old right of way?'

'He didn't tell me,' said Beth, 'he just asked to be shown the cross-country path to the churchyard. As he's an inspector and I'm a lowly sergeant, I do as he says.' She hesitated. 'Callum, there isn't something . . . well, do you know anything you ought to tell the police? You don't need to tell me, and it would be better now if you didn't, because I'm not supposed to be here. But something you ought to tell the superintendent? You respect Markby, or I think you do. You could talk to him. You don't dislike him, do you, even if he thinks our meetings are inappropriate?'

'I don't dislike anyone,' said Callum with dignity. 'It's not worth the effort.'

'But you don't tell people anything unless asked directly, I've noticed.'

'Bully for you! Such as?'

'How do I know? You won't tell me!' She paused. 'Markby told me Abbotsfield used to be known for witchcraft. And that there used to be a gallows at the crossroads.'

'If you want local history, talk to Baz Finch. He's a mine of information. Don't ask me. If there ever was a gallows, it's long gone. There used to be a bus-stop, too, and that's vanished, like the bus service. I think, like the witches, the gallows was around in the days of Good Queen Bess. Or Queen Anne, one of 'em. I'm not interested in that sort of thing. I'm not superstitious. I like a quiet life.'

And whatever happened to my quiet life? Callum asked himself.

'You see, I don't particularly want an uneventful life,' said Beth seriously. 'That's why I joined the police, I suppose.'

'And if I were to say perhaps you joined the police because you like organising people?'

'I'm going now!' she said, standing up. 'Thank you for the cider.'

'Don't get stopped and breathalysed!' Callum grinned at her.

'It's not funny! This will be a negative comment on my record, this "inappropriate" friendship business.'

'Can't help you there, I'm afraid.'

'Won't, you mean!' she snapped and stormed out.

He followed her to the car and, in a disastrous attempt to defuse the situation with humour, asked, 'Is this our first quarrel, then?'

'I'm not quarrelling with you!' she yelled. She slammed the car door and drove off.

Callum went back indoors and sat for a while in thought. Then he murmured, 'You've got a problem, old son.'

Chapter Twelve

The covering of snow barely lasted over the weekend and by Monday morning, it had all but disappeared. With it went the crisp bright sparkle and now they were back to a dull, grey, cold wintry day. Jeremy Hawkins took his usual train up to London. The heating was working again in the school where Basil Finch taught. Laura, on her way from the house to her studio, saw him drive by and waved. Rob, waking early and unable, for once, simply to go back to sleep again, sat in the kitchen with his cup of coffee and considered his options. Callum's van was in its usual spot in the street by his cottage. Rob hoped he hadn't to worry about another unwelcome call from him. But even as he thought this, he heard the slam of a car door and, moments later, heavy footsteps approaching the front door.

Not Callum, but a caller, all the same. A prickle of apprehension ran along Rob's spine. Who on earth? The postman? The doorbell rang. Rob went to answer it, after taking a quick precautionary glance through the hall window. No red van. Not the postman. A strange four-by-four with mud-splashed wheels and lower bodywork stood outside. He could only see part of the caller, enough to observe that he was male, tall, and wore a sheepskin coat. He was standing outside waiting patiently; and something about his stance told Rob that this caller wasn't going to go away. No, if Rob didn't reply to the bell, this guy, whoever he was, would head for Laura's studio in the hope of finding someone there. Rob didn't know anything about the newcomer. But instinctively, he knew he didn't want his mother troubled by him. He opened the door.

The fellow seemed even bigger now that Rob was confronted with him, topping six feet and wide enough to fill the doorway completely.

'Can I help you?' Rob croaked.

'Sorry to disturb you,' said the caller with a smile. It was the sort of smile that didn't reach his eyes. What it did was reveal a chipped tooth. Otherwise, he was a fair-haired, weather-beaten sort who, even without the sheepskin coat, must be built like the proverbial brick outhouse. 'I was wondering if you have any idea when your neighbours, in the other barn conversion, might be at home. I called about some wine, but they're out and the house looks deserted.'

'They're away, on holiday.' To his dismay, Rob's voice obstinately refused to rise above the husky croak.

'Got a cold?' asked the caller sympathetically. 'Time of year for it. You wouldn't know when they'd be back?'

'No!' In an effort not to sound like a bullfrog, Rob could hardly force the word out at all.

'Anyone else here who might know?' The caller half turned and lifted his arm to point in the general direction of Laura's studio.

That was the last thing Rob wanted, for Laura to be disturbed by this thug. The conversation so far had been minimal and, on the face of it, innocuous. The trouble was the caller himself, standing there like a stone monument, with no sign of moving – unless it was towards the studio. Rob sought desperately for the best thing to say or do. He couldn't think of anything.

Fortunately, reinforcements arrived. Callum had emerged from his yard and gone to his van. Then he'd noticed the caller at his neighbours' front door and Rob's frozen figure in the doorway. He abandoned whatever project he'd been engaged on, and ambled purposefully towards them.

'Morning, Rob!' Callum hailed him amicably. 'I was going to drop by and cadge a coffee off you. Inconvenient moment?'

'No!' Rob almost shouted in his relief. 'Come in! This – er – gentleman was inquiring about the Baxters. He wants some wine. I've told him the Baxters are away and I don't know when they're coming back.'

'Oh, they'll be gone at least another week, so I understand,' said Callum. 'Sorry, you've had a wasted journey.'

The visitor and Callum stared at one another and Rob had a strange feeling of being the only one of the three who didn't know what was really going on. Because something was going on. The atmosphere fairly crackled.

'You'll be leaving now, then?' asked Callum pleasantly enough, but it wasn't a casual question.

The caller smiled and that chipped tooth flashed in and out of sight again. 'Perhaps I could cadge a cup of coffee?' he said.

'And perhaps, Officer, you might happen to have official identification on you?'

The guy was a copper. Rob almost fainted. *How did Callum know?*

The caller silently put a hand inside the jacket and produced an identity card.

'Inspector Turner!' said Callum, sounding positively smug. 'Well, well, you are interested in our little community. A neighbour of mine told me he met you on Friday, out in the fields, in the company of another officer, a local one.'

'Just taking a walk,' said Turner smoothly. 'You, I think, might be Callum Henderson, the landscaper.'

'I am.'

'You find bodies,' continued Turner, in the same tone as he might have said Callum grew prize-winning roses. 'Specifically, I believe you found the body of Aaron Hooper. As it happens, I'd rather like to talk to you about that. So, lucky I ran into you.'

'Saved you the trouble of knocking on my door, asking about the Baxters, I suppose,' retorted Callum. 'I thought Inspector Kendal was in charge of that investigation, reporting to Superintendent Markby?'

'Oh, he is, he is. My inquiries are what you might call

parallel to Inspector Kendal's. Where might we conveniently have a chat, Mr Henderson?'

'Come over to my office,' said Callum, turning to lead the way. Over his shoulder he added, 'I might even offer you that cup of coffee.'

Turner nodded a farewell to Rob, then followed Callum.

Rob watched them go until they reached Callum's yard, then he slammed the front door, ran into the downstairs toilet and threw up into the bowl.

'That young chap seems to be the nervous type,' remarked Turner, when he'd settled in Callum's kitchen with the promised mug of coffee.

'No disrespect,' said Callum. 'But this is a small, quiet community. We notice strangers. Big bloke like you, ringing the doorbell, well, it's unsettling to anyone here. We watch out for one another, you understand.'

'You certainly dashed over there pretty quickly,' retorted his visitor, with a nod of his head in the general direction of the Hawkins's home. 'Well, I was going to seek you out, anyway.'

'Superintendent Markby know that?'

'Yes, as it happens, he does. What makes his nerves so bad?'

'I didn't know Superintendent Markby suffered with his nerves,' Callum said calmly.

'Don't disappoint me, Mr Henderson.' Turner gazed reproachfully at him. 'You're not a fool and neither am I. I'm talking about that lad back there.'

'I'm not aware of any particular reason for Rob's mental health issues. I understand, from his mother, that he suffers from depression.'

'I'd be depressed, if I had the time for it,' said Turner, shaking his head sadly. 'But in my line of work, I can't afford to take the time to brood on my misfortunes.'

'You wanted,' said Callum with a faint growl of frustration, 'to talk to me about the dead bod, Hooper. How I found him is all in your records. I know nothing about how he died.'

Turner put his elbows on Callum's kitchen table, also his desk, and ignoring the paperwork he was disturbing clasped his hands and stared down at his fists. 'You see, Mr Henderson, it isn't so much his death that concerns me. That concerns Superintendent Markby and his officers, naturally. I'm more concerned with the connections he had when he was alive. We are still hoping to find Hooper's phone. That would tell us with whom he'd been in contact recently. He must have had one; but it wasn't on the body. If he dropped it in the churchyard, where is it? A search of the scene of crime has failed to turn one up; and they are very thorough. Did his killer to take it? To do that, the killer would have had to take the time to search Hooper's pockets. Yet, you see, it seems you must have been on the scene within minutes of the wretched Hooper expiring, propped up on that gravestone. You saw nothing.'

After a pause, Callum said, 'You're from the drugs agency, or whatever they call it now, I suppose.'

Turner opened his fists, spread out his fingers and then clasped them again.

'I can't tell you anything about Hooper's phone. I never saw it. I didn't take it out of his pocket before I alerted Markby, if that's what you're thinking. I've no idea about his activities,' continued Callum vehemently. 'How the hell should I know what the guy did? I'd never heard of him before I climbed over that dratted wall and landed in front of him! Since then, I've heard about nothing else. Although, now that woman has turned up dead in the churchyard, the cops will be bending my ear about her also, I suppose.'

'You certainly appear to be unlucky,' remarked his visitor. 'But I've no interest in Melissa Garret. If you could tell us anything at all about Hooper that you've so far omitted to mention—'

'Oy!' interrupted Callum vigorously, 'are you cautioning me, or what?'

'Good grief, no, why ever would I do that, if I don't have reason to believe you've broken the law? I apologise if it sounded that way. Force of habit. I meant to ask, would you tell me, or anyone else? DS Santos, for example? If you knew any little thing – anything at all.'

'I don't! I can't tell you; and I can't tell DS Santos anything. I've been informed that any association I might have with her is inappropriate.'

'Ouch!' said Turner sympathetically.

'Save it!' snapped Callum.

'You might be in touch with her, even so. You know,

odd phone call, catch up . . . Purely social, of course.' That chipped tooth flashed into view for a split second.

It was beginning to irritate Callum. He didn't know who had inflicted the injury, but Callum applauded him, whoever he'd been. 'Well, I'm not. Nor is it any business of yours.'

'Good. I wouldn't like Beth to get a black mark against her name, career-wise.'

Callum scowled at him. 'What's it to you?'

'She used to be married to a mate of mine,' explained Turner.

'Oh? I see. And this desire to protect her career in the police force has made you very anxious to pin something on me, I suppose?'

'I'm not trying to pin anything on anyone,' Turner told him, heaving a sigh.

Like heck! thought Callan uncharitably.

'I am trying to unravel a very tangled knot that, if I can straighten it out, will lead me to some very unpleasant and dangerous people. I'd be obliged, Mr Henderson, if you'd think about that.' Turner stood up. 'Thank you for the coffee.'

If Turner's purpose had to been to unsettle Callum, he'd succeeded. Over the next half an hour, he tried to concentrate on some work and failed. He needed to talk to someone. What he really wanted desperately to do was talk to Beth Santos, but that was out of bounds. He ran through the other options but they were depressingly few. *Baz is teaching those kids how to measure the height of a tree using a stick and a bit of string, or whatever the subject is today. So I can't talk to him. It's no use trying to talk any sense into Rob. I hardly know Jerry and he'd rightly tell me to mind my own business. He's in London, anyway. Only one other person, Laura. That's going to be awkward. But it's got to be done.*

Callum pulled on his jacket and, carefully keeping his distance from the house itself to avoid observation by Rob, made his way to Laura's studio, and knocked at the door.

She called, 'Come in and just sit down a mo!'

He found her seated at a table, carefully painting a vase with a design showing wheeling gulls against a background of cliffs. Callum took a seat far enough away from her to avoid any danger of knocking against the table with disastrous results for the artist. He had done that once on a previous visit. She'd been very good about it at the time, and later presented him with the finished vase, ready for use, with the wonky pattern still on it and nicely glazed.

'You should have it, Callum,' she'd told him kindly. 'Because you had input into the design.'

Which was a nice way of saying, 'Here you are, you clumsy clot. Don't do it again!' Callum had appreciated her tact and made sure it didn't happen again.

Waiting for her to take a break, he sat and watched her work for five minutes in silence. At the end of it, he felt much calmer. Because she was working on the vase, that didn't mean she wasn't aware of him. Eventually she leaned back, wiped off the brush, then her hands on a rag, and swivelled to face him.

'We're miles from the sea here,' observed Callum, with a nod at the vase.

'I supply a couple of gift shops in Cornwall. I go online for pics of the cliffs. If I get the birds wrong, Basil will tell me. Want a coffee?'

'Just had one, thanks.'

'With Rob?' She raised her eyebrows and her voice tensed.

'No, with someone else. I wouldn't mind a drink, though,' he added.

'See that little fridge in the corner? There's some small bottles of Belgian beer in it. Want one of those? Help yourself. You can bring me one, too.'

Callum did so. They raised their opened bottles in a silent toast.

'You've told Jerry about the second body, I suppose,' said Callum.

'Yes. It's such a nuisance. I had to mention it to Jeremy but I don't like telling him any bad news because he has so many work worries. He's feeling a bit fed up, these days. He's also got family worries, his family, not mine. He's got a dotty old uncle who keeps wanting to marry women. One at a time, I mean, not all at once.'

'Fair enough, I suppose, if that's his hobby,' replied Callum after due consideration.

Carefully, Laura asked, 'Rob says you've got a girlfriend, Callum, is that right?'

'No, because I've been warned off by her boss. That's Superintendent Markby. Besides, she wasn't my girlfriend.

We just got on quite well, in a sort of way.'

'Oh, Callum, I am sorry. She's a policewoman, Rob said. If Markby is her boss . . .'

'Detective Sergeant, that's what she is.'

'Good girl! Bully for her. Look, don't despair. If it's meant to be, well, it will work out in the end.'

'Don't see it, somehow,' said Callum.

'Is that what brought you over to see me? I'm not much of an agony aunt, I'm afraid.'

'And I'm disturbing you, sorry. But I thought you ought to know, if you don't, that there's a heavyweight from the National Crime Agency hanging about.'

'*What*?' Laura froze, beer halfway to her lips.

'The part of it he represented,' explained Callum helpfully, 'is, I fancy, what you and I used to hear called the Drugs Squad.'

'What's he doing in Abbotsfield?' asked Laura. 'We're only a dozen households here and all of us are very ordinary.'

'He called at your house first. Rob opened the door. I nipped over there and got him away. Then he, Inspector Turner, came and sat in my kitchen and bent my ear. I got rid of him.'

'But what does he want?' she asked sharply.

'Perhaps you should ask Rob!' Callum suggested.

This roused her protective instincts. 'Why Rob? Why should he know?'

'Perhaps he doesn't. But if I don't know and you don't know, Rob might be able to suggest something?'

He was glad to see the indignant look fade from her eyes. It was replaced by despondency.

'Rob doesn't tell me anything,' she said sadly. 'And we used to be so close. I feel so sorry for him, because he seems so lost.'

Callum resisted the urge to say that Rob wasn't lost. Rob, thought Callum unkindly, is bone idle, that's my view.

'He's a well-meaning boy,' continued Rob's mother earnestly. 'He told me the other day he'd always look after me. But he can't look after himself, can he?'

Grandma's voice echoed in Callum's head. *The way to hell is paved with good intentions.* Too true, thought Callum, I had good intentions in coming here, so I've got to go on, now I've started. But I should have left Rob to tell his mother about Turner's visit – or not tell her, either way.

Aloud, he said in a firm voice, 'I think he's made a few wrong choices. Now he's stuck with them and he doesn't know what to do. Do you ever ask him where he goes on that motorbike? What takes him there, wherever it is. I drive around the area on my business and I've seen Rob all over the place.'

'Such as?' snapped Laura.

'Well, let me give you an example. He passed me a couple of months ago, well before Christmas. I remember it was a Sunday and I'd been to a garden centre. I can't say I recognised Rob because the rider was all dressed up like Darth Vader with his helmet on, but I reckoned it was Rob because I recognised the bike. I saw him turn into those disused industrial units. Why? I wondered. Just curious. There's nothing there but a few rough sleepers; and late in the year very few of them. So, I stopped, got out of the van and walked in, keeping by the walls, low profile, you know? There were a few kids there, fooling about with a football, very half-hearted. They'd propped up their bikes nearby. Rob's bike was parked near them. I couldn't see Rob at first and then I just caught sight of him going into one of the units. That made me wonder why. Like I said, there's nothing there. He wasn't in there more than a few minutes. I kept out of sight and waited. Sure enough, out he came, jumped on the bike, and whoosh! He was off again.'

'What's wrong with that?' she asked defiantly. 'Perhaps you were mistaken and he wasn't Rob. Even if it was, he must have had a reason.'

'You bet he did! As soon as he got on the bike and left, all the kids stopped pretending to play football and raced into the same unit. Out they came, almost at once, jumped on their bikes and pedalled away like fury. They didn't even bother to pick up the football. They'd collected something Rob had left there. I'm not suggesting what it was, Laura. But I can make a shrewd guess and so can you.'

'There will be a perfectly simple explanation!' Laura protested. 'Have you asked him about it?'

'No. I leave that to you, or Jerry.'

Alarm filled her expression. 'Have you told Jerry? Please don't! Let me deal with it, *please*!'

'Fine, I won't say anything to Jerry. I hardly ever see him, anyway, except leaving in the morning or coming back in the evening. But I've told you and – well, you sort it out. Rob can't just be left to flounder about, Laura. He's keeping the wrong company and whatever business he's mixed up in, well, it's a bad idea. I think you know it.'

White faced, Laura said tightly, 'Rob wouldn't hurt a fly!'

'I agree, and I didn't say I thought he had. But there has been a murder and the police won't let it go. Unsolved murder cases aren't just dropped. They stay open on file. Markby and his team will keep at it. So will Turner, now he's on the scene. If Rob was, oh, let's say, running errands for Hooper . . .'

She leaped to her feet, eyes blazing. 'Don't say that! You don't know it! You saw something you didn't understand: and you may have got it all wrong. Perhaps it wasn't Rob. There are plenty of bikers and if he had a helmet on . . .'

'All right, I don't know it,' he agreed. 'But Rob seems to have money. Maybe you or Jerry keep him in funds, I don't know and don't care. But he's got the cash to spend and it has to come from somewhere. If it's from Hooper, there will be enough of Hooper's customers out there who will know it; and they won't keep their mouths shut, if the police find them.'

There was silence. He began to wish he'd kept his own advice, and his mouth shut. She left her work table and came across to him. He stood up, not sure what she was going to do. He was startled when she reached out and took his hand.

'Callum, I really meant it when I said don't mention this to Jerry. He's got so much on his mind.' Her voice trembled and her eyes fixed his pleadingly.

'Sure, won't say a word,' he promised hastily. 'Nothing to do with me, after all, is it. Well, thanks for the beer. I'll leave you to your work and drag myself back to mine!'

There was a curious moment as the tension seemed to seep out of the air. Laura relaxed and gave herself a little shake, as if she'd come in from the rain.

'I know you mean well, Callum, and thanks for rescuing Rob from that plain-clothes officer. Inspector Turner, you say? What does he look like?'

'Big chap with fair hair and a chipped front tooth. Don't worry, you'll recognise him for what he is, if he comes back. But don't be scared. He's very polite; although I reckon what he really would like to do is kick in your door and turn your house upside down. I reckon he's also pretty quick on the uptake.'

'If he worried you, then perhaps we should all worry, if he comes back,' she said, with a smile that didn't reach her eyes.

'He didn't worry me,' Callum growled. 'He got my goat!'

'I'll go back to work tomorrow,' Meredith said at breakfast. 'I would like to pay another visit to the Garrets today. You've no objection to that? I'm worried about them both.

I feel very bad about turning them away when they came here.'

'You didn't turn Charles away. You brought him in and we sat and talked with him for nearly an hour.' Markby poured himself a last cup of coffee, and glanced at his watch. He'd have to go in a couple minutes.

'We might have been able to help them.'

'No, how?' he replied simply.

'I turned the women away. So did you. They were clearly in some distress, both of them.'

'It was a domestic matter.'

A domestic. That was how the police referred to so many cases of violence within the home. The pattern was familiar. The police were called. Later no one would give evidence. The victim withdrew her – sometimes his – complaint. Markby felt a chill run down his spine. More to reassure himself than his wife, he said, 'The body was found in the churchyard. It makes sense. Melissa had left the house to go to her book club meeting at Celia Benton's house, only yards from where she was found. You suggested she might have been followed . . .'

'Yes, I know I did. Poor woman, do you think some-one was watching out for her? Or was she a random target?'

'We don't know. I am determined we'll find out, though. This killing has caused a lot of concern in the town because she was a local woman and she wasn't a wrong'un, like Hooper.'

'I'd like to call at the Garrets' home, Alan. This is so

distressing for them. I can't imagine how they are coping, if they are coping.'

'Let me know how you get on,' Markby said, getting hurriedly to his feet. 'I'm running late.'

It was a few minutes before anyone answered Meredith's ring at the door. She had begun to wonder if the Garrets had gone out. Then her ear caught the sound of shuffling progress being made towards the door. It opened a crack and Felicity's pale face peered out.

'Oh!' she said. 'It's you, Mrs Markby.' She frowned. 'Charles has gone out. He hasn't gone far. We ran out of milk. He's only gone to the little shop round the corner. He'll be back any time.'

'Well, I just came to see how you both are coping. It can't be easy.'

'What?' Felicity frowned again. 'No, nothing is easy, is it?' She pulled the door open wider and stepped back.

Meredith took that as an invitation to enter and stepped into the hall. Felicity turned and led the way to the sitting room where Meredith had been before. She was wearing mule slippers, which accounted for the shuffling manner of her progress, and had an apron tied round her waist. It was the type with a large pocket in the front and patterned with sunflowers. The bright yellows and oranges of the design struck an incongruously cheerful note. Felicity kept one hand in the pocket and, with the other, indicated a chair in a gracious gesture. Meredith sat down.

'I can't make tea until Charles comes back,' she apologised. 'We've run right out of milk, you see. It's because we made cocoa last night, before we went to bed. A hot milky drink is very settling, isn't it? We used the little bit left at breakfast. But Charles won't be long.' She pulled the sleeve of her cardigan down to cover the long scratch on her arm.

Jasper! Meredith was reminded. She looked around for the cat but couldn't see him. 'Have you put something on that scratch, like TCP or Germolene?' she asked.

'It isn't the first time he's scratched me, you know,' said Felicity. 'He doesn't like me. Melissa didn't like me, either. I did try, when Charles and I first married, to make a friend of her. But Melissa would have none of it.' She leaned forward as if to impart a further confidence, and spoke in a whisper, as if her departed sister-in-law were still in the house and might overhear her. 'Melissa was not a nice person.'

'I can believe she was very difficult,' said Meredith warily.

'You can have no idea,' Felicity told her sadly. 'She broke my little china pillbox during the night. It was on that little table over there. When I came in here this morning, it was on the floor in pieces.'

'Perhaps the cat . . .' ventured Meredith.

'No, I'm sure it was Melissa. She's still here. People don't just leave a house because they die. They wait, watching. I thought I'd be free of her now. But I won't, never will be. She's taking her revenge. That was always

Melissa's way and she won't have changed, just because she's dead.'

Damn! This is all wrong, thought Meredith. I should have asked James Holland to come with me.

'Where has Charles got to with that milk, I wonder?' asked Felicity, gazing absently round the room.

'It's quite all right, please don't worry about tea,' Meredith urged. Her hostess turned her gaze towards the window, giving a view of the tiny gravelled area where once a front garden had been, and the street beyond. Meredith took the opportunity to study Felicity more closely. She looked very tired and her gaze, fixed on the window, presumably to watch for her husband's return, was at the same time curiously unfocused.

'Felicity, dear,' asked Meredith, 'have you seen a doctor?'

The wavering gaze turned back to the speaker. 'Oh, no,' said Felicity with unexpected firmness. 'It's far too late for a doctor. He'd be no good at all. She's quite dead.'

Then she withdrew her hand from the apron pocket and it held a knife, a small, sharp vegetable knife. 'It was this one!' said Felicity, more brightly. She held up the knife. 'It was this one I stabbed her with.'

'Oh, I see,' said Meredith as calmly as she could. 'Perhaps you should put it down, Felicity. You might cut yourself.'

But Felicity's grip on the knife was tight. 'I didn't mean to do it, but she ran at me. I thought she was going to hit me! She was a horrid woman.' She leaned forward. 'And she had a horrid cat!'

'Where is Jasper now?' asked Meredith. She had to keep this conversation going. Charles, if he really had only gone to the shop nearby, must be back soon.

'He's gone. Charles took him away with him when he went out. He put him in the little travelling cage Melissa used to take him to the vet. He didn't like that. He scratched Charles, too!'

Felicity contemplated the long red scar, visible again now that she'd moved her arm and the sleeve of the cardigan had ridden up. 'And he was a thief. He stole the fish! Right off the kitchen table. Just jumped up, grabbed it, and ran for the cat-flap in the kitchen door. He knew, if he could get through the flap and outside, I couldn't catch him.'

A smug look crossed Felicity's face. 'But I moved pretty quickly, too! And he had a problem with manoeuvring a whole piece of fish as well as himself through the flap. So I got to him, and even though he scratched me, I grabbed him by the scruff of the neck. I didn't release my grip. I opened the kitchen door with my free hand and just threw him outside. He dropped the fish. I picked it up. I don't know whether we could have eaten it.' Felicity considered this problem. 'It might have been all right, if I'd washed it off. But when I turned round, there was Melissa.

'Oh, if you could have seen her face, Mrs Markby! Such fury! She hated me, really hated. She'd often told me I'd taken Charles away from her. Taken *her home* away from her, although we'd assured her she could always live here with us. The house belongs to Charles, you see. She had been his housekeeper and got very possessive about it. She was born in this house, too. Upstairs, in the front bedroom. It was later turned into her needlework room because it has good light. She started shouting it all at me again, accusing me of taking her whole life.

'I told her why I put Jasper outside. It didn't make any difference. "You've never liked him!" she shouted.

'I don't usually bother to argue with her. I just let her grumble on. But this time, I showed her the fresh scratch on my arm. This one.' Felicity turned her arm so that Meredith could see the scar again. 'He's vicious! I told her, "He's got a thoroughly nasty disposition, just like you!" At that, she started forward. Her face was bright red and her eyes were blazing. She was going to attack me. I could see it.' Felicity leaned forward and a triumphant glow suffused her pale face. The contrast to her previous pallor was shocking.

Meredith stared at her in horror. Alan had been right to focus on that cat, she thought, even if he didn't realise why at the time. It wasn't being robbed of the fish, or the dislike of being put out in the snow, that made the cat so aggressive when Alan arrived at the house. Jasper could still scent Melissa's blood. The Garrets had cleaned the kitchen; but not well enough to deceive an animal's keen sense of smell. That is what his aggressive attitude was all about. He saw Alan as another attacker.

'Felicity,' she said quietly, 'what did you do?'

'I snatched up the vegetable knife, this knife, to ward her off. But she kept coming, so I stabbed her. I'm not sorry. I can't be sorry. She deserved to die.'

'And Charles?' asked Meredith. 'She was his sister. What of Charles?'

Felicity frowned uncomprehendingly. Then her expression cleared. 'Charles is so much better off without her.' She smiled. 'You can see that, can't you? She was such a burden, all his life. She clung to him like a sort of limpet. He couldn't free himself. I had to do it. To do it for both of us.'

'Felicity, if you tell the police exactly what happened, you might be able to plead self-defence, so don't do anything to make matters worse.'

Her hostess was a small woman and didn't look strong, but she'd admitted to being capable of violence. Meredith calculated how quickly she could get to the door of the room, down the hall, open the front door and escape. Probably not quickly enough. It was impossible to take her gaze from the knife. It was important not to do so. If Felicity made a move . . . The little figure in the bright apron leaned forward. Meredith tensed, got ready.

'When you think about it,' Felicity said confidingly, 'Melissa was right, after all. I did take her life, didn't I?' An odd little smile crossed her face. 'But I couldn't do anything else.'

'It was a dreadful experience for you, Felicity, and I do understand,' Meredith told her. She managed, just, to control the tremble in her voice. 'But you don't need the knife now. Why don't you put it down?'

Felicity studied the knife in her grip thoughtfully. 'No,' she decided, 'I don't think I will.'

* ★ *

'Good morning, sir!' said Steve Kendal. 'The pathologist's report is in on Melissa Garret. It confirms that the body was moved before DS Santos and Henderson found it. She'd been stabbed in another location and probably up to an hour earlier. Rigor was setting in well, and there would have been considerable blood loss at the time of the attack. The amount of blood where she was found just doesn't account for it, not nearly enough. She was moved, all right. I think this might turn out to have been a domestic, sir. We need to get a forensic team out to that house.'

Markby jumped to his feet. 'Get a car, Steve. Meredith has gone to visit the Garrets this morning!'

Charles Garret had returned home. Markby found him sitting with his wife and Meredith in the neat little room. There was no sign of any disturbance. Charles held his wife's hand. Meredith held an object loosely wrapped in a crocheted doily. It was a long, thin object. The murder weapon, thought Markby. Kendal thought the same and moved calmly towards Meredith and held out his hand. She put the crochet-swathed item in his palm. Steve pulled an evidence bag from his pocket and dropped the whole lot in it.

'All right?' Markby asked his wife tersely.

'Absolutely fine. Charles had gone to a corner shop when I arrived. But he came back in time.'

'She didn't attack your wife!' said Charles firmly. 'She was only showing her the knife.' He patted Felicity's hand.

'All right, dear. It's all going to be all right.'

'You did get the milk, didn't you, Charles?' asked Felicity anxiously.

'Yes, dear. I bought two pints.'

'Oh, good,' said Felicity, 'because if we're going to make tea for all these visitors, we'll need quite a lot.'

Chapter Thirteen

'I put Melissa in the churchyard,' said Charles. 'I thought, if she – her body – was found somewhere else, no one would think she'd died at home. Everyone would think she'd been attacked on her way to the book club.'

'Postmortem examination established that the body had been moved,' pointed out Steve Kendal. 'We knew fairly soon that she'd been killed elsewhere.'

Charles shook his head sadly. 'It was still a good idea.'

Funny, thought Kendal, how people stick to a story when it obviously doesn't hold up. You'd think they'd realise no one believes it. But they don't. They're so pleased with themselves, they pretty well come to believe their fantasy.

Charles leaned forward confidingly. 'I didn't have much time but I thought it all out. She would have walked, as usual, to Celia Benton's house and that's right by the churchyard, where that fellow, Hooper, was stabbed. One reads about serial killers. Why shouldn't people assume there was one loose around the churchyard, some maniac? I got the car out, and put Melissa in it. I drove to the road by the church wall and dragged her out, pushed her over . . . I came home.' He fixed Kendal with a defiant look. 'It really was a very good idea,' he repeated.

'Mr Garret,' said Steve Kendal firmly, 'I do not believe you could have managed to do that unaided.'

'Oh, but I did!' insisted Charles. 'I don't say it wasn't very difficult; because she was very heavy. She was only a small woman but her body weighed far more than I could have imagined.'

'So, did you have help?'

'Oh, no,' said Charles immediately. 'Nobody helped me. Felicity couldn't. She was in such a state. And she isn't strong. I left her to clean up the kitchen, the blood . . . I just moved the body. It's surprising what you can do when the matter is urgent.'

The montage of photographs on the computer screen in Markby's office all showed the scenes relating to the death of Melissa Garret: the kitchen in which the attack had taken place and the body sprawled in the churchyard where it was found. Meredith would say it should include Melissa standing at the door of the Old Vicarage, before being turned away, as had Felicity Garret earlier. But neither Meredith nor I suspected it could turn to murder, he told himself. Even when Charles Garret came and we let him in, sat him before our fire, listened to his story, sympathised with him in his troubles; at no point did we think it might turn to violence like this. But should we have thought it might? More to the point, *should I*? Meredith feels guilty and I tell her she shouldn't. But if I'm honest, I've known similar cases before, over the years, dozens of cases of domestic disputes or difficult situations, ending in death. It can happen in 'the best-regulated families', as the phrase goes. Why didn't I even consider this was how it would end this time?

Perhaps because it was Charles we listened to; and neither of the women, whom we turned away. Charles, deeply worried, cut such a neat and tidy figure, sitting there telling us his tale, and deeply regretting he had let it get to such a state. But not in a panic, not distraught . . . Charles, who was now proving such a problem, refusing to tell them how he managed to move the body. Yes, he had transport, his car. Traces of blood had already been detected on the back seat. But no, definitely no way, could he have done it alone. Might he have had Felicity's help? Come on, really? The help of his wife who was such a wisp of a woman and traumatised by what she had just done? She'd have been useless when it came to moving the victim.

He was distracted from these thoughts by a tap at his office door. It was a very apprehensive tap, and that generally meant someone was bringing unwelcome news. Markby looked away from the scenes on the screen. He called, 'Come!'

The door opened and DS Santos entered. 'May I have a word, sir?'

Now what? thought Markby, trying to control his

irritation. She's not been hanging around with Henderson again, has she? I thought I'd made myself clear about that.

He opened his mouth to ask what brought her, but she was quicker and spoke before he could.

'Sorry to disturb you, sir.' She didn't look apologetic. She looked, if anything, resolute. 'But I need to tell you something. It might not be important,' she added hastily, seeing his expression. 'But well, I thought you'd like to know. It's to do with that.' She pointed at the screen. 'Melissa Garret's body being found where it was.'

'Santos,' he said as calmly as he could. 'You are off that investigation, as well as the other concerning the first death in the churchyard. I should not have to remind you of that.'

'I know!' she said hastily. 'And I'm not interfering. It's just, well, I had an idea . . .'

'Then share it with Inspector Kendal! He is heading up the investigation.'

'He wouldn't listen,' said Santos bluntly.

'Are you surprised? All right, Steve Kendal, who is still leading the team, won't listen to you, who are off the team. So, you go over his head and come to me! Is that it?'

She frowned and seemed to be thinking about that. 'Yes,' she said at last. 'Sorry if it seems sneaky,' she added.

'Sneaky?' Markby was not often bereft of speech but for a moment he almost was now. 'DS Santos, it's completely out of order! You can't go behind Steve's back and come to me. How would it be if everyone did that? The whole system of investigation would collapse!'

She abandoned the argument she couldn't win for one she knew she could, or had a good chance of winning. 'I think I may know how Melissa's body came to be in the churchyard.'

She's a good tactician, thought Markby with reluctance. Now she knows I'll listen. 'Well?' he asked aloud tersely.

'We know she wasn't killed where Callum and I found her. Dr Hutton is certain the body had been moved; and probably had only been where we found her for a very short time. But we don't know how her body was moved there. Even a small, elderly woman like Melissa is pretty heavy as a dead weight. Charles Garret and his wife are both old and his wife, in particular, is frail. He's saying he moved it alone but he couldn't have done.'

Frail, maybe, thought Markby, but strong enough to stab her sister-in-law. Aloud he said, 'This is not new thinking, DS Santos. The investigating team has managed to work that one out. I was thinking it myself, only a few minutes ago.'

She pressed on, rolling over his objection. 'It would take someone very strong to heave a body over that stone wall, right?'

'Yes, if that's how the body came to be there. Are you saying you can prove that is what happened? If so, who managed to do it? We know Charles couldn't have done it unaided.'

'I might have a suggestion,' she said happily. 'Who do we know locally who is very strong and could lift Melissa over, no problem?' She paused, but when Markby didn't answer, only sat waiting, she added, 'Gus Toomey.' She stopped speaking and waited.

'Why?' asked Markby simply. 'What's Toomey's connection with the Garrets? Toomey lives in a field, in a parked caravan, without the necessary permission for long-term residence, out at Abbotsfield. He does labouring work for Henderson. When he isn't doing that, he's knocking seven bells out of an opponent in unregulated bare-knuckle boxing matches. Granted he's got the build and the strength. He grew up working with a travelling fairground, according to Henderson. Roustabout, probably, and that takes strength. But how on earth could he even know the Garrets, let alone well enough to do them a favour that could land him in gaol?'

'I thought,' she explained, 'that Gus probably has a record of some sort, even if it was long ago, because he does seem to like fighting. There was a good chance he got into some trouble in his teens, before he took up the bare-knuckle matches, possibly faced one or two charges of grievous bodily harm.'

'He's probably harmed a few opponents in the bare-knuckle bouts. They, of course, are unregulated but they aren't actually illegal. But if he did the same thing in a pub brawl, or following a football match, yes, he'd be in trouble. Good thinking, DS Santos.'

'Thank you, sir!' Santos beamed at him.

'And has he got a record?'

'Yes, sir, for disturbing the peace, affray, smashing up pubs and waylaying visiting supporters of rival teams – all the usual stuff, and ages ago, not for years. The last time he was arrested and charged, he wasn't working as a roust-about. He gave as occupation a job in an abattoir. Can't you see him carrying all those sides of meat around on his shoulder? He could have helped deliver them to butcher's shops around the area. Garret had a butcher's shop. He might have known Gus from then. Toomey's not the sort of person you forget, is he? And Toomey might have been willing to help the Garrets just because they are old, and needed help. Gus's background is very traditional. Look after the elderly, that sort of thing. Also, I don't think Gus is terribly bright, been punched in the head too many times, probably. He might not have thought about the consequences of his good deed, as regards himself, I mean. Gus is probably proud of his strength. Charles Garret was giving him the opportunity to show off.'

If this turns out to be the case, thought Markby, I am going to have to work very hard to calm down Steve Kendal!

'I really am very sorry,' said Charles Garret mournfully. He was a man whose fantasy castle had come tumbling down. 'I just thought, if I could move the body away from the house, Felicity might not be suspected. After all, she isn't a murderess, you know. It was all entirely unintended. Melissa had been particularly difficult since she suspected Felicity had gone to talk to the vicar. Only she didn't find the vicar because he's moved, and Superintendent Markby and his wife live in the former vicarage.

'The situation had become intolerable and that evening there was the stupid quarrel over Jasper and the fish. Melissa was in a hurry because she wanted to set out to her book club meeting, and our evening meal wasn't ready. So she was very irritable. Celia Benton likes everyone to be on time. Felicity was doing the cooking and trying to hurry it along to keep Melissa happy. Then Jasper stole the fish. He's – he was – my sister's pet. She was the only person who even liked him. I have nothing at all against cats; but Jasper is a very surly animal. He only liked Melissa. We couldn't let him remain with us, not now, after what happened. I took him to one of those animal rescue centres yesterday. He's been put up for rehoming.'

Blimey! thought Kendal, who was conducting the interview.

'Anyway, Felicity, who is normally the sweetest-tempered of women, lost her temper when he jumped up on the table and snatched the fish from a plate. It was just for a moment. She grabbed Jasper by the loose skin at the back of his neck, like mother cats do with kittens. It didn't hurt him. Normally, she'd have been too worried about being scratched to touch him. But, this one time, she grabbed him, opened the kitchen door and threw him outside. He still managed to scratch her. Melissa came in, just at that moment . . .'

Charles stopped speaking and fumbled with his handkerchief, wiping his eyes. 'I knew something had happened because I heard the back door slam. Then I heard Melissa shouting, in the kitchen. She seemed to have been interrupted, because she stopped the shouting and made an odd noise, like . . . *ouf*! I hurried out there and saw my sister lying on the floor and Felicity standing there with the vegetable knife in her hand. I knelt over Melissa to see how badly she was hurt. There was a lot of blood. Blood doesn't worry me, of course, because I was a butcher. But also, having been around carcasses most of my life – animal carcasses of course – I know what dead creatures look like. Melissa's eyes were open but she wasn't seeing anything. She wasn't breathing. I knew immediately that she was dead. Well, now you know the rest.'

'No, Mr Garret,' said Steve Kendal, 'I don't know the rest. I hope you're going to tell me. We can't believe your wife helped you to move the body. We believe you may have asked Gus Toomey for his help. You do know Toomey?'

'Oh, yes, I know Gus, have known him for years,' agreed Charles. 'Since I had the shop. I used to select the carcasses I wanted at the abattoir; and Gus worked there at the time. That's how I met him. He also drove the delivery truck to the shop and unloaded them, carried them into my cold store. I used to talk to him. He's a very interesting person, you know.'

'How did you know how to contact Toomey, when you needed his help to move the body?' Kendal was trying to rid his mind of the image of little Mr Garret in his butcher's apron, chatting with huge Gus Toomey as the latter lifted carcasses with the greatest of ease, and left them hanging from hooks in the cold store. It was almost too grotesque. Like something out of a horror film, thought Steve.

'Well, as you seem to know all about it . . . I'd seen him in the town from time to time and he always stopped to say hello. I knew he lived at Abbotsfield in a caravan. So I drove out there and he was at home. I asked for his help. He agreed without any objection, and came along with me. He had no trouble lifting Melissa. He slung her over his shoulder just like he used to do with the meat. It upset me, rather. I didn't intend to get Gus into trouble. I shouldn't have asked him to do it. I wouldn't have asked him, if I hadn't been in a blind panic myself! Will he be charged with something?'

'I'm afraid so, Mr Garret,' said Steve. 'So will you. Acting with the intention to pervert the course of justice is very serious. So is failure to report a crime.'

'Oh, dear, oh, dear,' whispered Charles. 'Poor Gus. He is such an innocent, you know. Really, no harm in him.' He saw the expression on Kendal's face. 'Oh, I know about the bare-knuckle fights. Gus told me about them one day when he brought a delivery. His hands were cut and his face bruised. He had a shiner of a black eye. I thought he'd been in some awful accident. But he wasn't worried at all and told me he'd been in a fight, an organised one, and he'd won a lot of prize money. It sounded horrible and I'd have hated to see it. But Gus was in very good spirits because he'd won.'

Kendal said, 'For some, it's entertainment. We'll get the statement printed out, and you'll have to sign it. So, think hard and make sure there is nothing you'd like to add to, or change in, your story.'

Charles nodded and heaved a deep sigh. 'To think this is all over a piece of smoked haddock,' he said.

It was the evening the platform lights failed at Bamford station. The train drew in and the passengers looked out on a weird, dystopian scene of darkness, in which figures armed with torches patrolling both the up and down sides of the line made wild gestures. Meredith, one of the passengers descending, was directed to safe landing by a young woman whose features were too shadowy to discern and who directed the torch beam at her feet.

It really had been her intention to take more of the leave due to her, but somehow, returning to the familiarity of the workplace had seemed very attractive. She would not have to spend the whole day thinking about Felicity Garret. It had meant, of course, fending off Ben Owusu's questions. But, after dealing with the problems back home, that had been a doddle.

The London train came in on the far platform from the station building exit and car park. To get across meant going up a flight of steps, over a footbridge, and down a flight of steps to *terra firma* again. The lifts, of course, were out of action. The train had been crowded and a lot of people had reached their destination here. The figures with torches herded them towards the overhead bridge, torch beams flashing to right and left.

'Mind how you go!' she was advised by a voice in

the gloom. Fellow passengers stumbled past her, jostling one another. Even with the staff assisting, it wasn't easy to make a path safely to the overhead bridge across the lines.

Meredith, encumbered with her briefcase, managed to keep a grip on the handrail and make the bridge crossing. She began the descent to safety on the platform below, where more staff with torches urged them to take care. Suddenly, from the gloom and the throng, she spotted a dimly perceived but somehow familiar form. It came towards her and shone a beam into her face.

'Good evening, Mrs Markby!'

'Callum? What are you doing here?' She shielded her eyes from the direct glare and Callum, with a muttered apology, directed it away from her face.

'I'm looking for Jerry Hawkins, the solicitor who lives out at Abbotsfield. Did you see him on the train? I really need to find him.' Callum's voice was anxious.

'Sorry, I may have done, but I wouldn't know because I've never actually met him, not to know his name. Callum, what's happened?'

'They've arrested Gus!' Callum sounded more upset than she could remember. Even when he'd found Hooper's body, he hadn't been this distraught.

'Who's Gus?'

'He works for me. And your husband's ruddy well arrested him! Well, not Mr Markby himself, in person. It was that chap Kendal, the one who looks like a hungry ferret. There he is! Jerry! Jerry Hawkins!'

Callum darted forward and was roundly cursed by the last travellers descending the stairs.

'Oy!' yelled a station employee with a torch. 'What are you trying to do? You can't go up! Wait until everyone's come down!' As Callum took no notice, she added, 'If you're hoping to catch that train, you're too late. It's pulling out now!'

But Callum had his quarry in his grip, a tall man in a dark overcoat, whom Meredith recognised as a fellow passenger on this route.

'For crying out loud, Callum!' protested the tall man. 'You'll cause a pile-up! Let go of me. I'm coming, what's wrong?'

The girl armed with a torch had summoned reinforcements in the shape of a burly male colleague in a hi-vis yellow vest.

'Mind out there!' bellowed this newcomer. 'You're going to cause an accident!'

Somehow, Callum, Hawkins and Meredith, who was determined not to be excluded, were all bundled out of the station exit into the car park, where lights had also failed and more chaos reigned. This whole area of the town seemed to be suffering from a power cut. Cars inched forward, horns blaring. Callum now had a grip on both Hawkins and Meredith, and dragged them towards his parked van.

'Calm down, man!' ordered Hawkins. 'What's all this about? No, I'm not getting into your van! I have my own car parked over there and, anyway, it would be better to wait until the rest of the traffic has cleared and we can leave more easily.' He looked at Meredith. 'I know you from the train,' he said. 'Jeremy Hawkins.' He put out his hand formally.

'Meredith Markby, Superintendent Alan Markby's wife.' They shook hands.

Callum was by now bouncing up and down in frustration. 'There's no time for that! This isn't a ruddy cocktail party! I told you, they've arrested Gus!'

'What has Gus been charged with?' asked Jeremy in a practical tone.

'He put the old girl's body in the churchyard!'

'*Melissa!*' exclaimed Meredith.

'Is Gus being charged in connection with her death?' asked Jeremy.

'He didn't kill her, if that's what you mean!' snapped Callum. 'The other old woman did that.'

'We should have listened to both of them when they came to the house,' said Meredith despairingly.

This comment being incomprehensible the other two, they decided to ignore her; and turned back to their own discussion.

'Why did Gus put the body in the churchyard, if he had nothing to do with her death?' asked Jeremy. 'Has he been charged with anything?'

'He put her in the churchyard to do old Charlie Garret a favour. They're talking something to do with perverting the course of justice.'

'Sounds as though that's what Gus did, if it's true. Why

have you waylaid me here in this scrum to tell me?' asked Jeremy.

'Because Gus needs a solicitor, a good one! You're a solicitor, aren't you? You seem to have made a decent living out of it, so you must be good at it.'

'Yes, but I deal mostly with wills and property trans-actions, private prosecutions and all that sort of thing. I don't deal with people moving murder victims round at night!'

'Then it's time you tried your hand at something new,' Callum told him crisply. 'Look, Gus is illiterate, or as good as. He won't know what to say or how to say it. He's probably making things twenty times worse for himself, even as we stand here, wasting time discussing it.'

'Gus is certainly entitled to have a solicitor advise him and there is always a duty solicitor—'

Callum interrupted him. 'If you're worried about getting your fee, I'll pay you. Mrs Markby is witness to my saying that. It's no use expecting Gus to confide in a duty solicitor. Gus won't say anything to someone he doesn't personally know.'

'He doesn't know me,' objected Jeremy.

'He knows who you are! He knows your missus and Rob. He knows you live at Abbotsfield. Abbotsfield people,' Callum concluded his argument, 'look after one another.'

Meredith, standing by in the gloom and momentarily forgotten, frowned at these last words. She didn't know exactly what had happened, but the chances were, Alan was still at work. If she made her way home, she'd have to sit there and wait until he turned up to find out anything more. She'd do better to stick to the other two, if she could and they didn't notice it.

Hawkins had given in. 'All right, I'll come to police headquarters and talk to Inspector Kendal. But I'm not getting in that van! I've got my own car. I'll follow you.'

That's me cut out of the loop, thought Meredith crossly. But she had underestimated Jeremy Hawkins.

'Do you have your car, Mrs Markby?' he asked, turning to her. 'I believe I've passed you before, walking out of the station.'

'Oh, yes, I usually walk. I live in town, in the Old Vicarage by the churchyard gates.'

'But you can't possibly make your way home on foot without street lighting, and the pavement being so slippery. I'll give you a lift. We can drop you off on the way.'

'We can't waste any more time!' objected Callum, before realising this sounded ungallant, and adding, 'If we all go directly to police HQ and Jerry can tell them he's Gus's solicitor, then I'll take you home, Mrs Markby.'

'Fair enough,' agreed Meredith. She wondered what Alan was going to make of all this.

It was not too long before she found out. At least the Police HQ, a new-build on the edge of town, had lighting. The three of them, herself, Callum and Hawkins, had left the power-cut behind them, but soon found themselves in a mini-version of the chaos at the station as Jeremy explained that he'd come to advise Mr Toomey, and no, Mr Toomey didn't yet know that. But he'd been given to understand by Mr Henderson that Mr Toomey was under arrest on quite a serious matter.

'It's not that serious!' interrupted Callum at this point. 'He was only trying to help.'

'And I am a neighbour of Mr Toomey and of Mr Henderson here, so they believe that Mr Toomey would feel happier with me giving him advice than the duty solicitor. No disrespect towards the duty solicitor, of course. But Mr Toomey is unused to official procedures and, I understand, only semi-literate.' Jeremy glanced towards Callum with raised eyebrows.

'He can just about write his name and that's it!' declared Callum. 'And he's no good dealing with any kind of officialdom.'

'Mr Toomey has been advised of his rights, including the right to legal advice from a solicitor. He hasn't so far requested that,' said Kendal, who had been attracted to the front desk by the sound of raised voices, and stepped in to deal with it as soon as he recognised Callum.

He had still been in the building. Another ten minutes and he would have left and avoided all this. Wasn't that always how it went? It was that blooming landscaper again! Kendal glared morosely at Callum.

The reply did nothing to reassure Callum. 'That's because he doesn't like strangers knowing his business. He won't mind being advised by Mr Hawkins because he knows who Jerry – Mr Hawkins – is. Go and tell him Jerry Hawkins is here to help.'

'Mr Henderson!' said Steve, who had had enough of this. 'If you don't leave the building immediately and go home, I'll charge you with causing a disturbance!'

'Leave it to me, now, Callum,' Jeremy told him. He said it with authority and Callum's protests were stopped.

'OK,' he mumbled and left the others, reappearing shortly afterwards in the waiting area where he sat down opposite Meredith, stretched out his legs and studied the toes of his boots in glum resignation.

'Callum, you've done your best,' Meredith consoled him. 'If Mr Hawkins takes on the case, Gus will be very well advised.'

'Doesn't mean the cops won't fit him up with something,' mumbled Callum to the floor.

'Alan wouldn't allow that!' Meredith said sharply.

'Sorry. Shouldn't have said it. It's just that if they give Gus a lot of grief, he might just lose his temper and hit one of them. It's not that he hits people normally, except when it's a prize fight. But there's not much space back there and Gus is a big guy. He must feel trapped. It's like an animal when it's trapped. It strikes out.'

'Jeremy Hawkins is there to make sure no one pushes him that far.'

Callum looked up and at Meredith. 'What's probbono? Jerry says he might advise Gus probbono.'

'Probbono? Oh, *pro bono*! It means he won't charge a fee.'

'I can pay him!' said Callum indignantly. 'I want him to do a proper job.'

'I'm sure he'll give Gus excellent advice.' Meredith paused. 'Perhaps it would be best if you went home now, Callum, and let Jerry do whatever he has to do. I'd be grateful if you'd drop me off at the Old Vicarage. I'd rather my husband didn't see me here . . .'

Too late!

'Meredith?' asked Alan, appearing in the doorway, 'what on earth are you doing here? And my, my, Mr Henderson. We meet again!'

'I'm not causing any disturbance!' said Callum truculently. 'I'm waiting for Gus.'

Markby looked surprised. 'I'm afraid Mr Toomey is going to be our guest tonight.'

'Why?' Callum demanded, standing up. 'He's got Jerry Hawkins to advise him. He's told you he moved the body; and he'll do his best to sign a statement, and you can witness it. He can make his mark, if he can't sign it legibly, and it can still be witnessed, can't it? He won't go anywhere but home!'

'Well, that's the problem, Callum. We can't know that. Technically, too, Gus hasn't a regular home. That is to say, he has no recognised address.'

'Of course he has! He lives in his caravan at Abbotsfield, you know that, Mr Markby.'

'He lives there quite illegally. The owner of the land might know he's there. We can't even be sure of that at the moment. But the council has certainly been unaware he's been living there. The land, the field in question, has no planning permission on it for a permanent residence. Or not a caravan, anyway. What's more there is a semi-permanent structure in the shape of a little wooden earth closet, constructed by Gus. Very ingenious, actually.'

'I know. I helped him build it.' Callum thought about it. 'OK, he can stay with me, at my place, until this is sorted out. And I've got main drainage.'

'Callum,' said Markby firmly, 'could you, in all good faith, give me your word that he wouldn't just take off and disappear into the travelling community?'

'No,' said Callum dejectedly. 'He's in a lot of trouble, isn't he?'

'Yes, I think you can safely assume that.'

'If planning permission can't be got for his caravan, and Gus ends up in prison and can't take care of it himself, will it be confiscated by some council order or other?'

'It's a possibility,' admitted Markby.

'So poor old Gus loses his home. How about if I move it? You know, hitch it to my van and tow it. I can park it in my yard. It's not that big a caravan. I think there would be room. I could store it there until Gus is able to collect it.'

'That's generous of you, Callum, but Toomey might not be able to collect it for some time.'

'Abbotsfield people,' said Callum stubbornly, for the second time that evening in Meredith's hearing, 'look after one another.'

Chapter Fourteen

'What will happen to Felicity now?' Meredith asked.

It was later in the evening. She and Alan had finished supper and cleared away. They now sat before the fire, at first in silence, each waiting for the other to broach the subject on both their minds.

'Honestly, Alan, I believe she's what used to be called "away with the fairies". Before you came, and before Charles walked in with the milk, I was talking to her for a while. She'd really lost it. I don't mean she wasn't dangerous. I realised that! She was almost – pleased – with what she'd done.'

'Who took the knife off her? You or Charles?' asked Alan.

'He did. He saw at once what the situation was. He must have known for a long time that she was at the onset of some form of dementia. He just held out his hand and said, "Oh, you don't need a knife to make tea, dear!" And she handed it over to him, as meek as a lamb.

'I put out my hand and he passed to me, with such a sad look in his eyes. It was heart-breaking. He really loves her. I wrapped it in one of Melissa's crocheted efforts, to protect any prints or blood traces on it. Best I could do.' She paused.

Alan took her hand. 'I came close to losing you then,' he said soberly. 'She would have killed again without hesitation.'

The long-case clock in the corner ticked softly. It had been included in the sale of the house because James Holland had no place for it in his new vicarage; nor did anyone else seem to know what to do with it. In the end, as it had always stood there from the day it was moved in new by the first Victorian parson, it remained.

'Successive vicars inherited it,' James told them. 'You'll need to have it looked at, if you want it to keep good time. For some reason, it's been twenty-six minutes slow for years; all the time I lived there, certainly.'

Meredith wondered how many sad secrets the old clock had been a party to. When Felicity had come to the front door that evening, she had been doing what so many other townspeople had done before her, when faced with a difficult situation. It's no good, thought Meredith. Turning her away will be for ever on my conscience, no matter what Alan says.

Replying to her earlier question, Alan said now, 'My understanding is that she will be assessed by a psychiatrist. Depending on the outcome of that, well, who knows? She may be declared unfit to plead. If that happens, she'll be spared a trial, but a place in a psychiatric unit will have to be found for her, and that's not easy. There are nowhere near enough places to fill the demand. Or a doctor might diagnose early-stage dementia, meaning she is unable to look after herself, and she could be placed in a suitable secure hospital. Charles might not be there to look after her, even if he could.

'On the other hand, if there is a trial and she goes into the dock, I suspect the charge will be manslaughter. She didn't plot to kill her sister-in-law. But there again, who knows? Perhaps she had been fantasising about killing Melissa and that was why she came here to the Old Vicarage. She feared she was about to commit a terrible sin.'

'Don't, Alan!'

'Well, the jury – and I suspect the judge – will be sympathetic. Extenuating circumstances . . . Her brief will no doubt claim Felicity truly believed Melissa was about to attack her.'

'I think it very likely that Melissa was going to at the very least hit her sister-in-law,' said Meredith.

'There you are, then. You believe it. The jury will probably believe it. The history of being bullied by Melissa and inadequately protected by her husband, that will all be put forward in her defence. I wonder whether Charles wasn't a little afraid of his sister, too. Then there's Felicity's age, that's a factor, and her general state of health.'

'When she came here that evening, wanting the vicar, it

was the last throw of the dice, wasn't it?' Meredith stared at the fire. 'A bad situation, allowed to go on unchecked, or without any outside help being sought – until that evening. And then Felicity didn't get it, not here, anyway.'

'Look here!' Alan said vigorously. 'Neither you nor I are mind-readers. No policeman is, that's for sure. Of course, some factors in the case are familiar. But the situation in that house was no different from the situation in a thousand other homes, lived in by families who don't get along. They don't all end in murder . . . and they certainly don't all end with the victim's body being hoisted over the wall of the local churchyard and being left there to be found by the first person to come along!'

'So, what happens to Charles? And to poor Gus?'

'Charles? Perverting the course of justice and failure to report a serious crime, those are serious charges. Poor Gus, as you call him, was his willing assistant. No doubt his defence brief will argue he was motivated by a misplaced loyalty.'

Markby paused for a moment. 'I tried to talk to Toomey myself. It was a frustrating interview. The impression I got was that he sees little difference between moving Melissa's corpse to another location, and delivering beef and pork carcasses to Garret's cold room in the days when he worked at the slaughterhouse. Jeremy Hawkins has tried to explain to him how serious it is. It still doesn't appear to trouble him. Undoubtedly, he is of limited intelligence. If he's worried about anything, Toomey is anxious about his caravan. Callum plans to relocate it in his back yard, by the way, to keep it from being confiscated by the council.'

'To whom does the land belong?'

'What land?'

'The field where Gus kept his caravan?'

'I understand it's part of the Beckenham estate. Old Sir Andrew Beckenham originally gave Gus permission to park it there, or so Gus claims. He may well have done so. Sir Andrew was a well-known local eccentric. He'd travelled a lot in North Africa, among the nomadic peoples of the desert. Perhaps he saw in Gus a version of that kind of independent life?'

'So it's all right for Gus to be there. He has the owner's permission.'

Meredith spoke firmly, but her husband still looked unconvinced.

'That doesn't mean Sir Andrew's heir – I understand it's a nephew – will see things the same way. The old fellow died five years ago. He left his affairs, I've been told, in something of a mess. Sorting it out is taking time, and Gus's caravan – even if those concerned know about it – is at the bottom of the things-to-do list.'

'If the nephew hasn't done anything about it, and it wasn't parked illegally in the first place, the council should mind its own business!' insisted Meredith.

'Well, at any rate, it's none of our business. Let Callum fight Gus's battle over the caravan. He seems to be doing so, anyway. Perhaps, if he's occupied with that, he'll stop wandering around burial grounds, with or without DS Santos.'

'Poor Callum! Do you think he's missing Beth Santos?'

'Perhaps,' her husband suggested, 'you might do well to think about how he'll feel if – or when – he learns that it was Beth's research that turned up the fact that Charles Garret knew Gus and turned to him for help.' Alan paused. 'That was bright of her. She's a bright officer. Whether Callum will see it that way, if he finds out, is something else.'

'Thanks again for your help, Baz,' said Callum.

Between them, and using Basil Finch's four-by-four to tow the caravan, they had successfully relocated Gus's dwelling in Callum's yard, where it took up much of the available space. They were now celebrating the achievement with a beer in Callum's kitchen/office.

'You're welcome!' said Finch, raising his can of lager. 'But it doesn't leave you much room out there for all your stuff.'

'I'll manage.'

'What will you do for help? If Gus goes inside, even for a short time, you'll be stuck, won't you, without a labourer?'

'I'll find someone.'

'Oh, well,' Basil observed thoughtfully. 'That's one murder solved. At least that wretched Kendal bloke won't be coming back with his horde of minions, trampling all over the churchyard again in their police boots.'

'I think they are still hoping to find the first victim's

mobile phone. I'm talking about Aaron Hooper, that horrible little drug-pusher I nearly fell on, when I climbed over the wall.' Callum took a swig of beer.

'Oh, that phone,' said Basil enigmatically. 'They won't find that, I mean, not now, I shouldn't think.'

'Baz?' asked Callum suspiciously, setting down the can of beer.

'Look here!' said Basil in a sudden burst of energy. 'I'm a teacher, right? And I teach teenagers, some of whom – possibly even several of whom – are likely to be targeted at some point by that creep Hooper, or someone like him.' He leaned across the table to emphasise his argument. 'As far as I'm concerned, whoever killed him did society a favour.'

'Please don't tell me it was you who did for him, Baz!' Callum pleaded.

'Of course it wasn't me! Do you think I go round murdering people – even people like the odious Hooper?'

'Thank heaven for that! But why did you say they won't find the phone, Baz? Come on, we've known each other all our lives.'

'And one of us,' Basil reminded him, 'has grown up to get himself a copper for a girlfriend.'

'For a start, she's not my girlfriend. I'm not even allowed to associate with her. Her boss has told her so. It compromises the investigation or something like that. Well, not until both murders are solved, not just Melissa's. I might see her again then, although I'm not sure about it, because she seems pretty mad at me for some reason. I don't know why.'

Callum stared gloomily across the room towards, though he also didn't know why, his parents' wedding photograph. 'Runs in the family, perhaps. Any girl I've ever had even the slightest chance with has disappeared over the horizon after a bit. It's the mud, I reckon. Anyway, speaking of unsuccessful relationships, what happened to that art teacher you were hanging out with for a while?'

'She lost interest in me as a subject,' said Basil with a rueful grin. 'That, and she met a merchant banker with a Porsche.'

'And a front garden full of bird-feeders couldn't compete?'

'Something like that.'

'Sorry about that. But listen, Baz. You won't sidetrack me. You know something about that missing phone.'

'Oh, all right, cross your heart and hope to die?'

'Oh, don't talk so daft. Of course, I won't tell anyone else.'

'Oh, well, then . . . You remember the morning following your discovery of Hooper expired on a grave? A police search team was out in force in the churchyard. I heard they were there, and I rushed down to buttonhole them before school. I realised they probably wouldn't appreciate how much damage they could do, clumping around and knocking the vegetation for six with sticks. I had a bit of a barney with Inspector Kendal. Well, he's the sort of chap who'd make you want to argue with him, whatever the circumstances! I tried to explain to him, but, of course, I got nowhere, and I had to get to school. So I had no choice but to leave him and his marauding band to do their worst. Only, I did hear them talking, and I gathered one of the things they were looking for in particular was the victim's missing mobile phone.'

Basil paused and looked a little shame faced.

'Have another beer!' urged Callum.

'Oh, thanks. Well, I was on my way out of the new cemetery through that gap in the hedge – where there used to be a stile, remember? I'd parked my car on the other side.'

Callum nodded.

'I was upset, pretty angry, in fact. I happened to look down, and blow me, there it was!'

'*The phone?*' asked Callum incredulously.

'The very same. Or I suppose it was the very same. It was a mobile phone, anyway. It had dropped into a little gap by a headstone. You know those headstones in the new cemetery? All the same, lined up like soldiers on parade? It was only a tiny space, but the phone had fallen in edgeways. Narrow object into narrow gap, see? All I could really see was a strip of plastic, but it had to be the phone they were all after. It was wedged in there. So I bent down, and managed to hook it out. It obviously hadn't been there long. It was clean and shiny. I started back towards Kendal, to hand it over to him, good citizen-like. But when he saw me coming back towards him, he yelled at me to go away. Threatened to arrest me for obstructing the search. I thought, please yourself, mate! And I left. I thought I'd hand it over to one of the search team later, when Kendal would be out of the way. I went to my car and drove off to the school, with the phone still in my pocket.'

Basil looked shame faced again for an instant. 'Shouldn't have done that, should I? But I did. Of course, I didn't then know it could be Hooper's phone, because I didn't know, even the cops didn't know then, the body was Hooper. I drove on to school and sort of forgot about it. It was a busy day, followed by a staff meeting, and the phone went right out of my mind.'

'So, have you still got it?' Callum demanded impatiently.

Basil looked like one of his own pupils, caught out cheating in a maths test. 'Um, no, I haven't.'

'Well, where is it? Have you lost it?'

'Sort of lost it. On purpose.' Basil straightened up and stared defiantly across the kitchen table at Callum. 'They identified the victim and it was that tyke, Hooper, and he was a known contact in the town if anyone wanted to buy drugs. Then I remembered the phone, and I was worried because I didn't know whether one or more of my senior pupils might have their contact number stored on it. So I decided to get rid of it.'

'Where?' asked Callum. 'I mean, I do understand how you felt, but perhaps you should retrieve it, if you can.'

'Well, no, nobody can. Or it would be pretty difficult and even if they got it, it wouldn't be much use to them now, I shouldn't think.'

'*Baz! What did you do?*'

'I walked over to the new building site. I thought a stroll

in the fields might clear my brain. It usually does. They were working there that day, all sorts of machinery and vehicles clunking and rattling. The chap in charge does his nut if he sees me. But the brickies and others don't mind. They know who I am, and just say "Hi!" when they see me. I put my hand in my jacket pocket and my fingers closed on the phone. I took it out, didn't really think what I was doing. Sort of instinctive action, you know? There was a concrete-mixer going nearby, churning round all the grey stuff, and I chucked the phone into it.'

Basil paused. 'It was quite satisfying, to tell you the truth. I just glimpsed it for a moment, as it went round, before it was lost from sight. They will have poured out the mix soon afterwards. It will be in the foundation of one of the new houses, don't even know which one. There will be a load of brick walls, floors, rafters and roofing et cetera, all in place on top of it by now.'

'Oh, right,' said Callum after a moment. 'I suppose that's it, then. It's gone for good.'

'With any luck!' said Basil.

When Finch had left, Callum walked out into the yard and checked on Gus's caravan. It seemed pretty stable on the blocks he and Basil had put under it. He gave it a pat, as he might have done to a horse, and turned to go back to the kitchen. But there was someone standing behind him, the yellow light streaming through the open back door outlining a blacker shape in the dusk.

At first, he thought Basil had come back; and opened his mouth to ask him why. But almost as he thought this, he realised the shadowy figure couldn't be Basil, because it was too slightly built.

She said, 'Good evening, Callum.'

'Oh,' he said. 'It's you.'

Chapter Fifteen

Laura said, 'Jerry's not home yet, so I came over to see if you were back. I know he's at the police station with Gus. He phoned me about that.'

'It's good of him to advise Gus,' Callum told her, a little embarrassed. 'I do appreciate it. I'm sorry I grabbed him moments after he'd got off the train. In the dark, too. Did he tell you all the lights were out in that part of town?'

'Yes, he told me, but I hear they're on again now. It was on the local radio station.' She leaned to one side and peered past him towards the bulky form of the caravan. 'You and Basil brought Gus's caravan over here. I saw you both manhandling it into your yard. Isn't it going to be rather inconvenient there?'

'Gus is worried the council will tow it away. I'll just have to get used to it being there.'

'I'm glad the snow has almost gone. I didn't like the snow.' She shivered as she spoke and thrust her hands into the pockets of the long wool cardigan she wore, hunching her shoulders. 'Is Basil still here?'

'No, he's gone home. It is pretty nippy out here in the yard. Would you like to come in for a cup of tea, or a drink of some sort? Not that I've got much of a selection. There is a bottle of wine somewhere. Harry Baxter gave me a case of the stuff the last time they came back from France. But I'm not a great wine drinker.'

'Thanks, but no. I have to get a casserole into the oven, ready for Jerry's dinner. Callum?'

'Yes?'

'When you and that police detective girlfriend you have—'

'No such luck!' interrupted Callum. 'Any romantic developments there have come to an abrupt halt.'

'Oh? I'm sorry to hear that. You did say something about that when you came to talk to me in my studio, after Turner was here. I thought you might have made up any quarrel by now.' Laura paused. Getting no reply, she continued. 'But anyway, you and she were in the churchyard that night when Rob was there. You saw him, didn't you? She shouted at him to stop, but he ran.'

'Ah,' said Callum, 'he's told you about that. Actually, I didn't get a good look at him, so I couldn't be sure who it was. It was the way he moved, when he ran off, that put me in mind of Rob. I didn't tell Beth I thought I knew who it might be, by the way. After all, I only had a glimpse, not to see his face.'

'Rob said she – your friend – chased after him, but you

didn't. Was that because you thought it might be Rob? Or because you had realised Rob and Hooper . . . that they'd had some business link?'

Business link! thought Callum. I don't think I called it that when I was at her studio.

'You're smart, Callum,' she said sadly.

'Listen, Laura!' he said energetically, 'I didn't chase after Rob in the churchyard, because it wasn't my business. I was a bit surprised when Beth dashed off like she did. I wasn't expecting her to do that, and she left me standing there, flat footed. But then she fell over, so I went to see if she was all right. Whoever it had been she was chasing had disappeared into the darkness by then. It's a good thing Rob scarpered as he did, because Superintendent Markby turned up shortly after that. He and his missus live in what used to be the vicarage, that big Gothic-style house by the main gates. They had heard the disturbance; and Beth shouting.'

She didn't reply, but didn't move away, only shivered again as she had at the studio. Perhaps it was only because of the cold.

'Laura?' said Callum gently. 'If you don't want to come into the house, there are a couple of chairs over there by the wall. It's where Gus and I take a coffee break. They aren't wet, there's sheet of plastic over them. You'll know when Jerry gets back to Abbotsfield. You'll be able to see the headlights of his car.'

She followed him meekly to the chairs. He pulled off the plastic sheet and they sat down.

'I didn't know,' she said, 'that Markby lived so close by the churchyard. If I had known I'd have chosen somewhere else to meet Hooper.'

Damn! Callum thought. I was afraid of this!

He was in a tricky situation here. If he could keep her talking long enough, Jerry should arrive home before things got worse. They were going to get worse; he was sure of that. Rob was her child and she was determined to protect him. But to what extent would she go?

He cast a cautious sideways glance at her. She sat, looking down at the ground in a dejected attitude. Her fair hair fluttered around her face in the evening breeze. Her whole appearance made her appear vulnerable; but he knew she wasn't.

'Hooper was a nasty little beast, vermin, you know? And he was greedy, too. It's not wrong to kill vermin, especially when it's doing damage.' Laura heaved a sigh. 'You've always lived in Abbotsfield, haven't you, Callum? This cottage was your grandmother's, you told me.'

'Yes, that's right.'

'My grandmother was a countrywoman, too. She lived in the Vale of Evesham. They grow a lot of fruit in that part of the world. The fruit attracts wasps. Wasps like sweet stuff. My grandmother had a way of dealing with them. She used to make lots of jam. I remember rows and rows of pots in her kitchen store cupboard, all with labels. Whenever a pot was finished, she wouldn't wash it out. She kept it, with just a little bit of jam left in it, no more than a smear round the inside of the glass. She put a little water in it so that it was, oh, about a third full. Then she put a piece of brown paper over the top, with an elastic band round it, and made a slit in the paper. Only a little slit, just enough for a wasp to wriggle through. And they did wriggle through. You wouldn't have thought they could smell the jam, but they could. They'd squeeze in, but they couldn't get out. Eventually they fell in the water and drowned. It sounds cruel, but Granny said, "It's better than using chemicals! It's their own greed that kills them."'

'Fair enough!' said Callum.

'Well, it was his own greed that killed Hooper, not the knife. That was just the means. He was a small creature in his own world, I suppose. Just like a wasp. But he had a sting and he could do a lot of damage. And he was damaging my family, my son!'

'That motorbike of Rob's, I suppose,' said Callum. 'He had independent transport and Hooper could make use of that.'

'Yes, Rob's not a bad person. But he's young and he's lost. Somehow Hooper got a hold on him and then, of course, he became Hooper's runner. He didn't want to do it. I'm sure the first time he agreed to run an errand for Hooper, he had no idea how deeply he would become involved. Rob longed to be free of him, but he didn't know how to shake him off.'

'Did Rob tell you this?'

'Not at first. I realised something really bad was troubling Rob, so I played detective. I know Rob thinks I snoop on him. He's right. That's exactly what I did. I was in town one day, shopping, and I saw Rob with Hooper. Rob's body language told me how frightened he was of that man. At first, I couldn't think why. Hooper was such an insignificant, scruffy little fellow. I eventually got Rob to own up. But we couldn't tell Jerry and we couldn't go to the police. Rob would be in trouble and besides, as Rob said, behind Hooper were some really violent people. He couldn't "grass". That's the word, isn't it?'

'That's the word, I believe,' Callum agreed.

'The only thing to do,' said Laura thoughtfully, 'was to eradicate Hooper, like the wasps.'

Callum peered into the unforgiving evening gloom. No sign of help out there. 'Are you sure you don't want to go indoors, Laura? It's freezing out here.'

She ignored him. She probably hadn't even heard him.

'Anyway, I decided to tackle Hooper myself and I got the opportunity sooner than I expected. I was in town again, and as I walked past one of the pubs, Hooper walked out, all on his own. I took my chance. I stopped him and said I needed to speak to him. He was pretty startled. But he replied, "Not here!" He thought, you see, that I was a potential client. He arranged to meet me in fifteen minutes in the churchyard. "Quiet there, if you want to do a bit of business," he said. So I went to the churchyard and told him I knew he was using my son as a courier, you'd call it, I suppose. That gave Hooper a bit of a shock. Unfortunately, I misjudged how he'd react, because I wasn't used to dealing with people like him, crooks! I thought I could frighten him away from Rob. But Hooper, slimy little beast, saw an opportunity for himself, for blackmail.'

'Makes sense,' said Callum. 'Hooper had done his homework, a background check on Rob. Family with a bit of money. Father a top-notch London solicitor. A son riding a motorbike around with little packages of illegal substances . . . Oh, the scandal would never do.'

'Exactly, that's it!' Laura sounded pleased. 'I knew you'd understand, Callum! But I realised immediately what I was dealing with. A wasp! Hooper didn't know about the jam jars. I had to tempt Hooper with a promise of a large payment. I would pay him off and he would leave Rob alone in the future. That was the deal I proposed. He was obviously used to doing business in the churchyard. I said I would meet him there when I had the money together. It had to be at a time when there was no one about, and my husband wouldn't find out.'

Laura sighed. 'I thought that would be my biggest problem. I couldn't meet Hooper by day, or someone might walk through the churchyard and see what I did. It is a quiet spot but people do visit graves or just cut through. The meeting would have to be after dark, and that was a bigger problem. Jerry's always at home in the evening and at night. But then I had a bit of luck. He's got a dotty old godfather, Uncle Philip, who lives in the Lake District. The old chap had taken it into his head he wanted to get married again. His family was very worried. He is extremely wealthy, you see. They rang Jerry and asked him to go up there for the weekend and talk sense into Uncle Phil. It meant I had a whole weekend to meet Hooper and – get rid of him.'

Laura's tone changed. 'It was all going so well, Callum, and you had to mess it up!' she said crossly.

'Sorry!' Callum apologised because he felt she expected it.

'I arranged to meet Hooper in the new cemetery. There's a gap in the hedge and space to park my car just outside. He came, just as arranged. I had an envelope ready. It really did have money in it. I knew he'd want to count it. I handed it to him, and he couldn't grab it fast enough. He was concentrating on opening it and I do believe, even though the light was poor, that his hands were shaking with excitement. He was paying no attention at all to me. I slipped behind him and I stabbed him.'

Callum closed his eyes. He felt sick. But not surprised. Asked to choose between Rob and his mother, he knew which one was capable of resolute action.

'I'd thought a lot about which knife to bring along, and I chose one I use for carving bits off the clay, really sharp and pointed. It went in beautifully.'

Callum didn't want to hear any more. She needed to talk to the police, not to him. If only Beth were here! Beth would know exactly what to do. But Beth wasn't here. Nor was she in any way likely to arrive. He had to handle it himself somehow.

'Laura,' he said, as calmly as possible. 'You're telling the wrong person. You should be talking to Jerry. You should tell him exactly what happened. He'll know what to do. I make gardens, that's what I do. I'm not the person you need.'

Had she even heard him? Probably not. She'd reached that point at which the need to confess had become overwhelming. She couldn't stop and he couldn't stop her. It was now a question of what she would do when she'd finished her sad, desperate tale. She shifted her position slightly and he tensed. But she only twisted her head to look sideways and up at him. A look of puzzlement briefly entered her eyes.

'I thought he'd just drop down and expire at my feet. But I hadn't ever stabbed anyone before, so I was wrong there.'

Callum nodded his understanding but dared not speak.

'He staggered, turned, looked at me and saw I still had the knife in my hand. He swore at me, so I lunged at him again. He tried to escape, making off towards the old graves in the churchyard. He might have been able to hide there. But I couldn't leave him alive. I followed, hoping for another chance. He had begun to stumble, putting out his hand to support himself against the wall. We were in the old churchyard now. He wobbled about a bit, turned in a half-circle, and looked back at me. His expression was so surprised. Then he just sank down on one of the graves, propped against the headstone, and didn't move again. He was dead. I'd done it. I was really pleased! I took his phone from his pocket and put it into mine. I thought that if anyone – the police – checked the call history, then Rob's contact with him would be on record.

'Before I left, I looked at him again, and he seemed so peaceful. That was wrong! It really made me angry. I thought, he's helped to ruin so many lives! He's got blood on his hands, not physically, but metaphorically. I decided to cut his palms as a symbol. I made a very neat job of it. But, of course, it took a couple of minutes. I would have been OK if I'd left at once. But I'd just finished, and stood up to leave, when I heard a scrabbling noise on the other side of the wall and a man appeared on top of it. Honestly, Callum, you gave me the fright of my life!'

'Sorry!' croaked Callum, thinking, *Where the hell is Jerry?*

'I ran off and hid among the graves as you were looking at the body. I knew I had to get rid of the knife in case you, or anyone else, stopped me and wanted to know what I was doing there at that time of night. There was a grave nearby with a stone surround and marble chips filling in the oblong shape. I pushed the knife down among all the little bits of marble and smoothed the top over. I thought no one would find it there; but that old woman did! Really, it was as though no matter how well I thought everything out, someone who had nothing whatsoever to do with it came along and messed up my plans.

'After that, you stood up and went running off through the cemetery. I didn't know you were going to Markby's house, of course, but you were going, that was enough! Time for me to slip away. I went back to my car and drove home. It was when I got home I realised that somewhere I'd lost the phone. It must have been joggled out of my pocket while I was running.'

'And Rob guessed what you'd done?' Callum asked gently.

'Yes. He's got his problems but he's a clever boy. I told him about the lost phone. I'd dropped it in the churchyard, I thought. He went back that night you saw him, to look for it.'

'I thought,' said Callum, 'he might be looking for the knife.'

'No, I wasn't worried about the knife. I thought I'd hidden that safely. But both of us, Rob and I, were desperate to find the phone. I know the police have been looking for the phone, too. But they haven't found it, or, if they have, they've not said so.'

'They won't,' he told her. 'They won't find it.'

'Callum! Have you got it?' she asked eagerly.

'No. Never had it. Never even seen it. But I have it on good authority it's lost for good. No one is going to find it. Don't ask me how I know that. Just trust me on it.'

After a pause, Laura said sadly, 'I do trust you, Callum. That's not the problem. The problem is that, just as the jam attracts the wasps, you seem to attract the interest of the police. First Markby came out here to talk to you, with that sergeant. Then she came back on her own one evening. I saw her car parked out front here. Then, to top it all, that frightening man came.'

'Turner? He wasn't here about the murder.'

'No, he was here about the drugs, wasn't he? Rob was so scared. I saw Turner arrive and go to our house. I was in my studio, and just happened to glance out of the window. I was about to go over there and deal with it when you appeared and took Turner away with you. He was here with you quite a while.'

'I got rid of him and, with luck, he won't come back.'

'Luck?' asked Laura sadly. 'That's just what I've been missing in all this. Things have gone wrong that should have gone right. People like your girlfriend and Turner have been hanging round. You even managed to find another body, Callum!'

'It wasn't my intention!' snapped Callum, finding his voice in his determination to defend himself. 'I'm pretty sick and tired of the way everyone seems to assume I go round looking for corpses. I don't want to attract the interest of the cops. I just get it!'

'That's what I said, more or less. You attract the interest of the police – and you talk to them a lot, especially to that woman officer. You might not mean to say something you shouldn't, but it could happen. And the simple truth is you know too much now. That's why I have to kill you, too. I'm really sorry about this.'

As she said the last words, she stabbed him.

Chapter Sixteen

He'd been waiting for her to strike, keeping an eye on the hand she kept hidden in the woollen cardigan pocket. He had not wanted to believe she could have been involved in it all, much less that she could be a killer. But he recognised that there had been a corner of his mind where he'd hidden the growing realisation that she was. That was very stupid of him. As soon as she'd appeared in the gloom like that, a vengeful Fury in disguise, he'd realised she come for one purpose only.

But Callum still didn't move quite quickly enough. That was probably because he was trying to do two things at once: twist aside to avoid the wicked point of the knife, and simultaneously grab at her arm. They ended up in an ungainly wrestling match. Callum felt the sudden searing pain across his ribs, as if he'd been branded with a hot iron, but he knew it was the blade of the knife, slicing into his flesh.

This was not the time to be gentlemanly. He gave her

wrist a vicious twist. She squealed in pain but the knife, thank goodness, dropped from her hand and clattered to the ground. He suspected it had bounced or rolled away into the darkness. He hadn't time to investigate because she kicked his shin hard.

'Ow!' yelled Callum. 'Stop this nonsense, Laura! You haven't got the knife now and I'm stronger than you are!'

Her response came in language that surprised him.

'I said, stop it!' he ordered. 'It won't do you any good.' Something tickled his ribs. It was warm blood running down. He didn't know how badly he was hurt and hoped it was superficial.

'But I've got to kill you!' she protested. She sounded almost in tears, but they were not the tears of regret. Rather, she sounded like a thwarted child in a tantrum.

A child needs to be treated like a child. 'Laura!' said Callum as sternly as he could in the circumstances. 'You are not allowed to kill people.'

'I killed that horrid man Hooper,' she argued.

'And look at the trouble that's caused!' he snapped. 'Don't make it any worse, Laura. Think of Jerry! Think of Rob!'

She was crying now. 'I've got to protect Rob! I've got to protect my child!' With that, she began to claw at his face.

He was obliged to use both hands to push her away and knock aside her flailing nails. If I were fighting off a man, he thought, I could wrench one arm free and take a swing at his jaw; knock him cold with a bit of luck. Or try to. But this is Laura and I can't do that.

'Pack it in, Laura!' he shouted. 'This isn't going to do either of us any good. It isn't going to do Rob any good, either.'

As if his name had conjured him up, suddenly Rob himself was there. Neither Callum nor Laura had heard the motorbike, so intent were they on their desperate struggle.

'Mum!' Rob cried out. He ran forward and threw his arms around her, dragging her away from Callum, and pushing himself physically between the contestants. 'Whatever do you think you're doing? Callum! Let her go!'

'Tell her to calm down!' snarled Callum. 'She's gone off her head! I can't control her. It's not a question of me letting her go. She's trying to kill me!'

'Mum?' Rob succeeded in dragging her away from her target. 'What's going on?'

'Help me, Rob!' she pleaded. 'You've got to understand. Callum *knows*! He knows everything! He'll tell that policewoman girlfriend of his. He's bound to tell her, sooner or later, don't you understand?'

'She's just stabbed me,' explained Callum hoarsely. His shirt was soaked in blood now and the injury was really beginning to hurt.

'*My mother stabbed you?*'

'I had to!' protested Laura, and burst into tears of frustrated rage. 'I have to keep you safe, Rob!'

'Well, this isn't going to do it!' Rob shouted at her. 'For crying out loud, suppose you'd killed him, what would you have done with his body?'

'Put it in my car, driven it into the country somewhere, left it there . . .' she muttered sullenly. She had given up the struggle, at least temporarily until she got her breath.

'Whatever you do, Rob, don't let go of her!' gasped Callum. 'She'll go for me again!'

'Where is the knife?' demanded Rob.

'She dropped it. I made her drop it. It's around somewhere. *Don't let go of her!*'

'Put him in your car?' Rob turned his attention back to his mother as he struggled to understand and to catch up on events. 'You mean, you thought you could manhandle a big, solid chap like Callum, a dead weight?'

'If you have to, you can do anything,' argued his mother. 'I didn't think I could ever kill anyone. But I killed that horrid man Hooper, didn't I?'

Callum propped himself against the wall behind him. 'I think,' he gasped, 'if you two can stop arguing for a minute, I think I need some first aid.'

'You're badly wounded?' cried Rob in distress.

'I told you, didn't I? I don't know how badly, but yes, I'm wounded; and I'm losing a lot of blood. So, if you don't mind?'

At that moment a beam of headlights swept over them. A car door slammed and footsteps crunched towards them.

'What the deuce is going on here?' demanded Jeremy Hawkins.

'Mum stabbed Callum!' cried Rob. 'And she's told him she stabbed Hooper!'

All three members of the Hawkins family were talking at

once by then. But Callum didn't take in any of it; because that was when he passed out and crumpled at their feet.

'It's only me. I brought a four-pack of beer.' Basil's gangling form appeared in the kitchen/office. 'As you can't easily get to the Black Dog at the moment. But if you miss the old drinking haunt, I'll happily drive you over there. I take it you couldn't make the walk across country in your condition, even if I came along to pick you up, if you fell down?' He set the pack of beer on the table and seated himself opposite Callum, subjecting him to a critical look.

'Appreciate the offer, Baz. But I'm staying away from the pub right now. It was bad enough when I was only the ghoul who wandered about finding bodies. Since then, I've been the target of a potentially murderous attack, and my notoriety will have increased. The last thing I want is an audience of gawping regulars, to say nothing of Mick, behind the bar.'

At the hospital they'd given him a blood transfusion, stitched the wound, bandaged him up, and told him how lucky he was. He hadn't then, and didn't now, feel very lucky. He didn't like being shut up indoors. He didn't like not being able to bend or twist. He didn't like having someone else's blood running through his veins, although grateful to the donor, of course. They'd kept him for forty-eight hours, after which he'd insisted on going home.

Once there, unable to do any physical work for the time being, he had been tackling the office side of the business, trying to sort everything out and tidy it up. It needed doing, but it made him think of Beth and that was a real downer. He wanted to be able to say 'Look! I've tidied! I've got organised!' Well, semi-organised. He couldn't talk to her but he did talk. He'd spent a lot of time 'thinking aloud' while he'd been sitting in the office. Mostly he addressed his remarks to his parents' wedding photograph. But, just occasionally, he addressed his thoughts aloud to the absent Beth.

'How's it going?' asked Basil, indicating the paper-work.

'OK. I'm pretty well sorted out. But it's grindingly dull work.' Callum waved a hand at the general surface of his table.

'What news of Gus?'

'He's been ordered to stay in approved accommo-dation – what used to be called a bail hostel – until his case comes up.'

'And you're stuck with the caravan in your yard?' Basil raised a quizzical eyebrow.

'It's no problem,' said Callum obstinately.

'If you say so. Have you eaten? Only, if you haven't, I can rustle up something. But it will have to be vegetarian, of course.'

'Appreciate the offer. But I like my fry-ups and I'm able to manage those. I'm not an invalid. I'm just slow and awkward.' Callum sighed. 'Perhaps I was always slow and awkward in a different sort of way.'

'Of course you weren't, aren't! You're just down in the

mouth because you can't get out there doing the gardens thing. Still, I'm glad you're not going to croak.'

'Thanks!'

'Listen!' said Basil. 'I've got a bit of news.'

'Is it bad? I'm fed up with bad news.'

'Either way, you'll hear this sooner or later, anyway, if you haven't already.'

'Go on, then.'

'The Baxters flew back from their hols in the snow yesterday, and were both arrested on landing in England. Seems the wine business was just a front. Perfectly legal, of course. It just hid their main source of income.' Basil sat back and beamed at Callum. 'Go on, make a guess!'

'They're a pair of wine-loving drug smugglers, I suppose?'

'That's it, on the nose! Customs and Excise kept stopping their wine lorries, which were perfectly legit, and found nothing. Meanwhile, I'm told, the drugs were coming across the Channel by boat and being landed quietly at night along the coast. Quite a traditional sort of smuggling, really. *Jamaica Inn* and all that.'

'That bloke Turner will be a happy chappie, then,' said Callum, after a minute's thought. 'It will keep him out of my hair, I hope.' He frowned. 'Think about it, Baz. Abbotsfield is such a small place and, I thought, a really quiet spot. It's turning out to be a breeding ground for crime! It wasn't like that when we were kids, was it?'

'Not to my knowledge.'

'Nor mine,' said Callum. He frowned. 'Although my

old grandma was always going on about the devil standing at everyone's shoulder. Perhaps she knew a bit more than I thought.'

'Oh, well,' said Basil, getting to his feet. 'I'll leave you to fry up those disgusting sausages you live on. I won't suggest you try the meat-free sort.' He ambled out.

Alone again, Callum stared towards the wedding photograph and observed aloud, 'You lot heard all that, I suppose?' He stood up and made his way to the cooker and began to unwrap the sausages that caused Basil such distress. 'Nothing wrong with these!' he said firmly.

Another figure loomed up out of the twilight and entered the kitchen behind him.

'May I come in?' it asked politely in a female voice.

'Bearing up, Jerry?' asked Marcus down the line to his cousin.

'Just about. Oh, I'm all right, Marcus. I feel a bloody fool. I was a fool, but, even worse, I was a coward. I knew Rob had some sort of problem. But I left it to Laura to sort it out, and I shouldn't be surprised that she did decide to sort it out, drastically so. I have no excuse.'

'And I was bending your ear about Dad and our problems here,' Marcus replied. 'I'm really sorry about that. It seems so trivial in comparison.'

'Don't apologise. You didn't know what was going on here at the time, any more than I did.' Jeremy paused. 'How is Uncle Phil, by the way?'

'Oh, well, Dad's got married.'

'*What*? Not to the doctor's receptionist? Or is it to one of the church ladies?'

'None of them. The cunning old devil got himself a special licence on the sly and married his housekeeper, Hester Wills.'

'Good grief!'

'Could be worse,' returned Marcus philosophically. 'She won't spend all his money and, at least, he'll eat well.'

It occurred to Jeremy that Marcus might still be worrying about his father's will and any possible changes to it. Tough, he thought. He can bother someone else about that! If I hadn't traipsed all the way up to the Lake District and spent an entire weekend trying to sort that out, and calm Marcus, Laura would not have been left alone and might not have been able to put her desperate plan into action.

Aloud he said: 'If he does want to review his will, Marcus, I've got rather a lot on my hands. One of the partners will be happy to advise him.'

'Good heavens! I'm not calling you to ask for that kind of help. Not just now! I wouldn't dream of troubling you with it, Jerry. You've got more important things on your mind. How is that fellow doing, the second one Laura stabbed?'

'He's back at home and I have called round to see him. I felt I should; though it was a bit of an awkward conversation. Surreal, really. I apologised for the action of my wife in stabbing him. He's being very decent about it. Fortunately, he's pretty fit and a tough nut to crack.'

'Is he going to sue?' asked Marcus, ever practical when it came to money, thought Jeremy.

'Not to my knowledge, and I've got enough on my plate with Laura and Rob both in trouble. At least Laura hasn't become a double murderer, as she could easily have been. She – she doesn't seem to realise how wrong it was for her to act that way! She believes it was justified. She wanted to protect Rob. Rob's blaming himself, of course. But it's my fault, isn't it? When you think it through?'

'Nonsense!' argued Marcus. 'How can it be? Don't you go to pieces now. They both need you.'

'I should have got a grip on the situation at home long before now. It's the trouble with commuting up and down to London all week. For years I haven't really lived at Abbotsfield. I've been a visitor, a sort of lodger in my own house. Everything was left to Laura to sort out. Poor love, all she had was her pottery and Rob. No proper neighbours, just a chap who designs gardens, another one who's a wildlife fanatic, a pair who have turned out to be drug dealers, a prizefighter, the bare-knuckle sort, and a bunch of old folks who leave their homes once a week, by volunteer taxi service, on a visit to the shops.'

'What about the prizefighter, is he the chap who moved a dead body?'

'That's right, Gus. They've let him out for now. He'll be recalled to court later. It's a serious charge he's facing. My understanding is that he's currently on bail and ordered to live in approved accommodation. That way they can keep an eye on him. His caravan had to be moved and is still parked in Henderson's yard. He's the garden chap. It gives Henderson a reason to leave his wretched van in the street overnight. He would do that, anyway.

'As for Laura,' Jeremy hesitated. 'I'm sorry to tell you that she's rather lost the plot at the moment. She's in a psychiatric unit, on suicide watch.'

There was silence on the line, then Marcus said, 'My dear fellow. You must be devastated. I only wish there were some way I could help. This – er – breakdown, it's a temporary thing?'

'We are told she should make a good recovery. But then, of course, if she's deemed fit enough to face trial for murder, well, that's the next problem.'

'I see,' said Marcus. 'Have you found a good barrister to defend her, if and when the case does eventually come to court?'

'Yes, Sir Montague Ling. He's a little long in the tooth now, but his mind's still sharp and he knows Laura. He's itching to get into court and defend her, when the time comes.'

'How about Rob?'

'Monty Ling will take care of him, too, if it comes to that. Rob didn't kill Hooper, nor did he conspire in the murder. I mean to make sure no one suggests he did. Yes, he was delivering drugs round the neighbourhood. But he was desperate to get away from Hooper's grip. He didn't reckon on Laura doing what she did. True, once he'd realised what Laura had done, he went back to the scene of the crime to try to find the victim's phone, which Laura had confessed to him she'd taken off the body, but then lost. But he couldn't find it. It's still not been found. It seems somehow to have disappeared. Any kid might have picked it up, I suppose.'

'I'm truly sorry about all this, Jerry.'

'I know you are and I appreciate it, Marcus. I'm sorry you're landed with Hester Mills for a stepmother.'

'Oh, well,' returned Marcus with an audible sigh, 'we should've seen it coming, I suppose.'

'Yes,' said Jeremy, 'I should have seen it coming, too. Or something like it. Well, wish me luck, Marcus.'

'Of course. God bless, Jerry, old fellow!'

Chapter Seventeen

For one wild moment Callum feared that Jerry had persuaded the cops to release Laura; and she was back to finish off the interrupted attempt on his life. He turned suddenly towards the door in an unwise movement that tugged at all the stitches, and dropped the sausages. They fell to the floor, fortunately still wrapped. He first exclaimed, 'Ow!' and then, 'Damn!'

'Sorry, didn't mean to startle you. If you prefer, I'll go away again,' said Beth Santos.

'No, I didn't mean you startled me! It's just the packet of bangers has dropped on the floor and I have a bit of trouble bending to pick things up. Um – don't go away. Of course, come in.'

'Let me?' She came forward to join him at the cooker, stooped, and scooped up the packet. 'Ever thought of varying your menu?' she asked.

'Don't you start, too! Basil was here trying to convert me to the meat-free wonders of his preferred diet.' He removed the packet from her grip and clasped it protectively against his gilet.

'I'm not going to snatch it away from you.' She essayed a smile.

Oh, lord . . . thought Callum. He felt unexpectedly at a loss. His mind wouldn't function at all. It was because of the stitches, of course.

They stared at one another. 'I thought,' Beth said, 'you might not want to see me.'

'Oh, yes? Why is that?' Callum avoided her gaze as he spoke because, if he had continued to look at her, he wouldn't have been able to say a word.

'Well, we did have a bit of a spat the last time I came.' She paused. 'And I did suggest to Markby that Gus might have helped Garret move his sister's body. It had to be someone big and strong and poor little Mr Garret didn't fit the description.'

'Oh, it was you fingered Gus, was it?' snapped Callum, recovering his presence of mind in the face of this revelation. 'I might have known you'd have some bright idea on the subject. And now, as you'll have seen, I have Gus's caravan parked indefinitely in my yard.'

'Yes, I really am very sorry about that, Callum. But I am a police officer. It's my job. You'll miss Gus's help, I know. It's question of priorities.'

'Never let it be said I hindered our police force in its work. Well, make yourself at home.' He turned back towards the stove, adding, in a contrived careless tone, 'Markby know you're here?'

'Not that I'm here at this minute,' Beth confessed. 'But he did say that if I wanted to check on you – as a victim of an attack – that would be in order.'

Callum uttered a sort of growl. 'So, do I take it I am no longer inappropriate company for you?'

'Don't be awkward, Callum. You must have realised our – association – was causing a problem in the investigation.'

'And that would never do!'

'You're being childish, Callum.'

That was more like it. The out-of-character uncertain Beth, anxious to placate him, he couldn't cope with. Beth the combative? Ah, yes!

Callum pushed the frying pan away from the hob and turned to face her. 'Oh, am I? Listen up, DS Santos! During the last three weeks, I've twice stumbled across a murder victim. I've become an object of general morbid curiosity, so that I can't now go to my favourite drinking spot, because of the attention I'd get. I've had a visit from a heavy from the drug enforcement agency. My labourer has been charged with perverting the course of justice; and I've got his caravan parked for an indefinite length of time in my yard. Oh, let's not forget I've been attacked with a knife. As a result, I am just a little annoyed!'

He paused. 'And let's not leave out that I've been declared by your boss to be inappropriate company for one of his women officers! If that's not an insult, what is?' Callum snorted. 'Markby chose the right house to live in, that Victorian pile. It suits his personality!'

'Come on, be fair. Our – association – was a bit tricky for a while, because of the investigation, you must see that. But it's not now.'

'Markby's said so? Given it his seal of approval?'

'Yes, in a tactful sort of way.'

'Glad he's tactful. Nobody else has worried about my feelings in all this.'

'I have, Callum! I've been worried about you. I wanted to drive out here and see you. But, well, I couldn't, could I?'

'Kind of you; but give it a miss. I am perfectly all right.'

Callum's words sounded, to his own ears, pompous, not to say ungrateful. He didn't want to sound either. He wanted to tell her how pleased he was to see her again, for her to be here in his untidy kitchen-cum-office. But he had his pride. On the other hand, if she had been worrying about him, that was nice to know. Well, she should worry. Look at the trouble she caused, insisting he take her across country in the dark, climb that wall into the churchyard – and then she had to jump down and land by another body!

If she'd noticed any frostiness in his tone, his visitor was unabashed. But critical, oh yes, he couldn't stop her being critical.

'No, you're not all right. You're limping round the place. You can't work at your landscaping and you can't even bend down and pick up a pack of sausages from the floor.' She paused. 'It's awful that you were hurt. When I heard about it I, well, I was very upset.'

There was a pause. 'How many of these damn sausages am I cooking?' he asked.

'Oh, give them to me! Go and lay the table and sit down. It won't take long.' The old Beth was back.

'I do not,' said Callum with dignity, 'lay tables. I am not a perishing waiter. I clear a space, put the salt and sauce bottle to hand, and a knife and fork. That's it!'

'Well, do that, then! But if you are going to grouch all evening, I'm not staying. Look, I know you are in considerable discomfort from your injury . . .'

'Yes, I am. It hurts like hell!'

'*Then sit down.* You're your own worst enemy, Callum. You knew something was going on out here at Abbotsfield. But did you say anything to me, or any other police officer? No, because "Abbotsfield people look out for one another!" That's it, isn't it?'

'Thought it wouldn't be long before it was all my fault! Look here, I didn't suspect Laura. I thought it possible Rob might have got himself into a fix, but I had no evidence. I didn't know Gus knew old Charlie Garret. Oh, and I didn't know Harry Baxter was Mr Big in the drugs business.'

'I wouldn't describe Harry Baxter like that. He was part of a bigger organisation run by others; but definitely not one of the top men. Clearly he's been doing all right out of it.'

'Silly sod,' said Callum moodily. 'Why couldn't he stick to importing the wine?'

'Because,' said Beth, 'like most crooks, he was greedy.

Also, like a good many crooks, he was just a bit stupid. He thought he could hide indefinitely behind the wine business. He couldn't.'

'Pity, though. I quite liked him. Not so sure about his wife. She was always all warpaint and bling.'

She didn't reply, busy dishing out the sausages. Callum realised he hadn't put out the cutlery as requested and hastened to do so. The stitches in his side really were hurting. He must have pulled at them, getting so worked up. Well, that wasn't his fault. It was hers, turning up unexpectedly like this.

Beth brought the plates to the table, where she paused, a plate in either hand, and looked around her. 'You've tidied up in here,' she said approvingly.

Secretly, he was delighted she'd noticed, but at the same time he was unwilling to abandon his position. 'Glad I've got something right,' he muttered.

'Callum, do stop being so awkward! It's unworthy of you. I didn't come here to quarrel. I came because – I was concerned for your welfare. I thought you might be trying to carry on as if you didn't have those stitches in your side. And you might not be cooking proper meals.'

'I can fry sausages, thanks, without any difficulty.'

'I know you can fry sausages.' She didn't add to that, but unspoken criticism of his diet hung in the air.

'You came here to organise me!' growled Callum.

'Rot! Of course I haven't. I wanted to see for myself what sort of state of health you're in; and if you need any help. By help, I don't mean bossing you around. You'd

rightly resent that. In your shoes, I wouldn't like it. I cam
as a friend.'

'OK, well,' mumbled Callum. 'It's nice to see you.
Appreciate the thought, and all that.'

Beth turned to give him a bright smile, which had the
curious effect of lessening the pain from the stitches. She
set one plate in front of him, and the other opposite him.
Then she sat down.

They ate in silence for some minutes during which
Callum watched her surreptitiously. The wedding group in
the photograph watched them both. He felt calmer, really,
quite happy. He was glad she'd come back. He wouldn't
like to think he'd never see her again. With her sitting
across the table from him, sharing his supper, the cottage
seemed suddenly more comfortable, more a home.

I suppose, he thought, it would be nice if you were here
much more often.

'Really, Callum?' She looked up from her plate, her
expression surprised and – could it be – pleased?

With dismay, Callum realised he'd been 'thinking
aloud' again. He hadn't meant to speak the words aloud,
but he had.

'We could give it a try,' said Beth cautiously. 'No long-
term commitment. Just a trial run. I know my last
partnership hit the rocks and you've not had much luck.
But that's not a reason never to try again, is it?' She
hesitated. 'What do you think?'

'Sounds fair enough to me. All right,' said Callum.
'Just a trial run.' He drew a deep breath. 'When you first

Markby, you remember that day?'

 ̖ ̖ ̖e I do. Something about me seemed to worry

'̖ ̖ ̖ wasn't worried!' he denied. 'I was – surprised because you were, well, very attractive. I hadn't expected that.' He cleared his throat. 'I wished you'd come out to see me on your own, and we could talk without Markby there – and later Gus came to join us and that was that. I also wished the place looked less of a shambles.' Callum grinned.

'Oh?' She smiled before adding earnestly, 'Sorry if I looked as if I was finding fault, either with you, or with your home. I was there with the superintendent on police business and if I was taking any notes – and I'm not saying I was! But if so, it was as background to the investigation. Before you make anything out of that,' she added firmly, 'I wasn't looking at you as a possible suspect. I was thinking you were really interesting and I'd like to know you better, away from the investigation, just as a person.'

'That's all right, then.' Callum glanced at the wedding photograph. It was only his imagination, of course, but his grandmother looked slightly less disapproving than she had. *I knew you'd like her*, he told his grandmother, taking care this time not to say it aloud.

Beth pushed aside her plate. 'Stitches still hurting?'

'I hardly know they're there . . .'

'DS Santos,' said Alan, 'has moved in with Callum Henderson.'

It was a month later. The snow was completely gone,

334

replaced by wind and rain. Still, the days were getting longer and the season was edging itself cautiously towards spring. The Markbys had just finished their supper and settled on the sofa. Meredith twisted to look at her husband in astonishment.

'Into that cottage he has at Abbotsfield? No offence, but you've got that right, have you? Both of them? Living there together?'

'Yes. I meant to tell you earlier that they were planning it. But I thought I'd better wait until the move actually took place. Like you, I was pretty startled. Either one of them might have cried off the idea. But it's really happened and they are settling down to domestic bliss. Well, with a bit of luck.'

He gained an unworthy satisfaction from seeing the expression on Meredith's face. It didn't last long. You couldn't rattle her that easily. But, just for the moment, she'd looked satisfyingly stupefied.

'Will it last, do you think?' she asked. 'It's a big step to take and well, considering what's happened and both cases yet to come to court . . .'

'Three cases. Gus Toomey's as well,' he reminded her. 'It's no use asking me if it will last. Who am I to say? I can't see into the future. With a bit of luck, it might. But I wouldn't put any money on it, if I were you. Callum is an independent sort of chap and Santos likes to get her own way – or so I imagine. She's – ah – strong minded.' He paused and gazed into his whisky. 'On the other hand, Callum was brought up by a strong-minded old

335

grandmother, or so I gather. He might accept having a woman of high principles about the place.'

'She'll organise him,' said Meredith. 'She'll make him tidy up that office-cum-kitchen. You told me it was a terrible tip. She won't let him keep his computer on that home-made desk of his. The one with four odd legs that you described.'

'Two of the legs do match, but don't come originally from a regular table, I fancy!' mused Alan. 'They curve outwards, like a pair of bow-legs.'

'From a dressing table in a bedroom, perhaps?'

'Probably. With luck his new domestic arrangements will keep him from wandering around tombstones after dark.'

Any further discussion about Callum's lifestyle and future domestic prospects was interrupted by the shrill call of the doorbell. Alan and Meredith looked at one another. Apprehension was in both their faces.

'It can't be someone who's found another body,' whispered Meredith. 'The odds are against it.'

'The odds were against Callum finding the first one. Even more against Santos and he finding a second one!'

'I hope it's not Celia Benton. She's threatened to call.'

'I wouldn't put it past her to leave her card first. Stay there, I'll go and look out of the window.' He went to the nearest window to the front door and peered into the ill-lit outside world. 'Not a woman. Definitely a man. Hold on, I'll go and see who it is.'

There was a murmur of male voices in the hall. Not Mrs

Benton, at least. When Alan returned a few minutes later, he had the subject of their earlier conversation, Callum, padding along behind him in his socks. There had been a small delay, Meredith gathered, while Callum took off his muddy boots in the hallway.

'Sorry to disturb you, Mrs Markby,' apologised the visitor.

'Not at all, Callum. How are you? How's the injury?'

'Oh, that,' said Callum. 'It's healed very well, thanks. I've been advised not to lift heavy objects yet, but I've got a lad working for me now, while Gus is unavailable, as I suppose he will be for quite a while. They've set up a date for the hearing of the case against him, moving that body.'

'You'll miss him,' said Meredith. 'Who is the young man you've hired to work for you?'

'His grandfather lives in Abbotsfield, in the cottage next door to Basil Finch. The old chap isn't too steady on his pins now. He really needs someone there, not every minute of the day, but keeping a check on him. It suits the family to have Tom – that's the grandson – live with his grandad and work for me.'

'And Abbotsfield people look out for one another,' said Meredith with a smile.

Callum grinned back at her. 'That's right!'

'A pity Rob couldn't have worked for you, and not for Hooper,' mused Meredith.

'Never on the cards!' said Callum firmly. 'He'd have been a downright liability. If I'd asked him to carry a paving slab, he'd have dropped it on his foot – or my foot. Well, he's on probation and poor Laura is still in the psychiatric hospital. Jerry's aged ten years. I'm keeping away from that family.'

Alan was giving her a warning look, Meredith noticed. No chatting about the case! Time to change the subject and there was another subject of interest.

'My husband has told me that you and Beth have – um – that you're a couple now.'

Callum's complexion turned redder than the warmth in the room could cause. 'Mm . . .' he mumbled.

'Would you like a drink?' she asked. 'A toast to the new arrangement.'

'Better not, I'm driving,' replied Callum virtuously.

'You haven't cut across the churchyard this time?' Markby asked. 'Given that up?'

'I've gone off doing that for the time being,' said Callum. 'Beth says other people think it weird. I don't say I'll never ever cut through again, once I'm fit enough to climb over the wall. But things are different now. Beth says, if we want to go to the Black Dog, we should either walk the longer way round, or, if the weather's bad, take one of the cars. I mean, either my van or her car. Then one of us will have to be the designated driver, that's the problem. So, I think we'll have to walk the longer way round.'

Callum's brow wrinkled in thought as he sought a possible alternative. His audience waited. He muttered, perhaps thinking aloud. 'We could take Baz Finch with us, of course. He doesn't drink much. He could be the designated one, although it hardly seems fair, and it would be making use of him.'

Callum paused again, this time for longer, and appeared to be contemplating all the changes that would be taking place in his life. Probably still without realising he was speaking aloud, he added quietly, 'I don't mind vegetables but I don't care for carrots.'

His hosts were staring at him. He realised it and flushed. 'Sorry, it's a bad habit I got into when I was living alone. Talking aloud to myself, you know. I'm not off my rocker.'

'We understand perfectly,' said Markby. 'I do it myself.'

'Beth changing your diet, Callum?' asked Meredith.

'She says I eat too much fried stuff. But when you're working out of doors, as I do, you need a decent fry-up. It's not anything Beth has said that's changed my mind about cutting through the churchyard. And I'm not superstitious or anything! But, well, memories, you know.'

He glanced towards the window. 'Plus, it's started to rain, so I brought the van.' He turned to Alan. 'I've come about your garden, Superintendent,' he said. 'Do you still want me to design it for you and get it planted up?'

'Yes, of course I do,' said Markby.

Callum looked embarrassed. 'There's just one question I'd like to ask.'

'Go ahead!'

'Your back garden, it kind of fits into a rectangle cut into the churchyard. It's got that really old door in the end wall, leading directly into the burial area. Do you happen to know if, by any chance, it was previously ever part of the churchyard? Ever used for burials? Only when I start digging, I'd rather not find any bones.'

'It's in a neglected state now,' Markby said, after thought. 'But when this house was the Victorian vicarage, and even later, there must have been a gardener, and probably a gardener's boy. They would have had a vegetable area, and a shrubbery, a greenhouse, and a lawn . . . It must have been dug over repeatedly during a hundred and fifty years or so. There are no reports that I've ever seen of anyone finding bones. I can't swear that nobody has ever buried a pet there, you know, a cat or a dog. But I think I can assure you, Callum, that you won't find human remains.'

'Good!' said Callum, smiling happily. 'Only I've found enough of those already, thanks!'